Harriet stood with her for a few minutes, neither of them speaking. She hoped it was helping in some small way. She was staring into her own coffee cup, lost in thought, when Aiden came striding up to them.

"I need to talk to you," he said in a cold tone, his jaw so tense she could see the muscle jump. He grasped her arm in a rough grip and pulled her toward the door.

As soon as they were out in the hall, he whirled around to face her.

"Is it true?" he demanded. "Are you involved in not one but *two* murders? Again?"

"So what if I am? What business of yours is it? You've made it very clear—we're through. I get it. I don't like it, and it took me a few tries to hear the message, but I finally did. Aiden and Harriet are no more. So, again, what business is it of yours if I'm involved in two murders or twenty murders or anything else, even?"

"Just because I said I can't be with you doesn't mean I don't care about you. I don't want to see you get hurt, by me or anyone else. That's the whole point of all this."

"All what?" Harriet said in a louder voice than she'd intended.

"Don't change the subject. What about the dead guys? Why are you involved?"

"I'm not involved, not that it's any of your business."

"You *are* involved. I came here to take care of a dog and a cat that got into a fight. The two owners were talking about the people who had arrived from the homeless camp. They mentioned you by name. They said you were there when they found both bodies."

"That's not exactly true, but again—not your business." Harriet whipped around, pulling her arm from his grip, and went back inside the gymnasium.

ALSO BY ARLENE SACHITANO

THE QUILT BEFORE THE STORM

A Harriet Truman/Loose Threads Mystery

To Helen,
Make a cup of tea and
settle in for the storm.
Arlene.
Sachitano

ARLENE SACHITANO

ZUMAYA ENIGMA

AUSTIN TX

2012

THE QUILT BEFORE THE STORM
© 2012 by Arlene Sachitano
ISBN 978-1-936144-40-2
Cover art and design © April Martinez

"Zumaya Enigma" and the raven logo are trademarks of Zumaya Publications LLC, Austin TX. Look for us online.

http://www.zumayapublications.com/enigma.php

Library of Congress Cataloging-in-Publication Data

Sachitano, Arlene, 1951-
   The quilt before the storm : a Harriet Truman/Loose Threads mystery / Arlene Sachitano.
      pages cm
   ISBN 978-1-936144-40-2 (trade pbk.) -- ISBN 978-1-936144-41-9 (electronic/multiple format) (print) -- ISBN 978-1-934841-48-8 (electronic/epub) (print)
   1. Quiltmakers--Fiction. 2. Homeless persons--Crimes against--Fiction. 3. Storms--Fiction. I. Title.
   PS3619.A277Q8535 2012
   813'.6--dc23
                              2011050971

ACKNOWLEDGMENTS

Writing my stories is a long arduous process that would not be possible without the support of friends, family and a host of others. To those who listen, comfort, badger, buy hot chocolate, and all the other activities that make my writing possible—Thank you all.

I'd like to say a special thanks to my family: Jack, Karen, Annie and Alex, David, Ken and Nikki. I am inspired on a daily basis by my grandchildren, Malakai, Amelia and Claire, as well as Kellen and Lucas. I learn things about innovative thinking every time I talk to them. Also, thanks to my sister Donna, a major influence on my early creativity.

Thanks to my sister-in-law Beth and her family for her unending support of my marketing endeavors and her persistent encouragement to write every day. Thanks also to Kay and Sally.

I'd like to acknowledge Susan and Susan for all the things they do, large and small, that make life flow more smoothly.

Special gratitude goes to Betty and Vern Swearingen of StoryQuilts for their help, support, encouragement and the great dinner adventures at Quilt Market.

Thanks also to Ruth Derksen for the fun times during the Northwest quilt shows.

Lastly, thanks to Liz at Zumaya Publications for making all this possible.

Chapter 1

The wind threw rain laced with pine needles at the bow window, gusting and swirling before it moved on down her tree-lined driveway. Harriet Truman glanced out at the gathering storm.

"You know, I could just cook something for us to eat here so we don't have to go out in the weather," she said.

"About dinner." Aiden Jalbert tipped his head downward and glanced up at her with his catlike white-blue eyes, a crooked half-smile on his lips. He was sitting in one of the two wing-backed chairs in the reception area of her long-arm quilting studio. Harriet sat opposite him in the other.

She hated the term "boyfriend"—it sounded so high school—but she had yet to find a better word to describe the relationship status of a woman twenty years *past* high school and a man not long out of veterinary school. If the truth were to be told, *boyfriend* is exactly how she thought of Aiden, and she was okay with that.

He reached out and took her hand, pulling her toward him. She stood and shifted over onto his lap.

"Please don't tell me you have to work," she said, studying his face. As the new guy at the clinic, he often got stuck with after-hour duties when problems arose.

"No, it's not work." He sighed.

"But you're ditching me," she prompted as she stroked a stray strand of silky black hair from his eyes.

"I'm not ditching you," he protested. "Well, I am, I guess. But not because I want to. Believe me, I'd much rather be eating dinner with you than talking to my sister." He wrapped his arms around her and pulled her against him. She leaned her head on his shoulder.

"Your sister? You're ditching me for your sister?" she moaned into his fleece-covered shoulder. "You don't even like your sister. She tried to sell your house out from under you, for crying out loud."

"I know." He leaned his head back and stared at the ceiling. "She said it was important."

"And you believed her?" Harriet sat up straight. "How can you believe anything that comes out of that woman's mouth?"

"I can't. I don't. But she's my sister. I have to at least hear what she has to say."

"You can't do that over a quick cup of coffee? She has to ruin our dinner plans?"

Harriet knew she sounded like a spoiled child, but Michelle had made a bad situation much worse for Aiden when their mother was murdered earlier in the year. She had tried to steal his inheritance, and standing up to her, while necessary, had been very hard on Aiden.

He pulled her back to his chest.

"I think this is one of those times when being an only child has limited your perspective. No matter what Michelle has done in the past, or what else she'll try in the future, she's still my sister. I won't let her get close enough to do any harm, but I at least have to hear her out."

"I might not know anything about siblings, but I know greed when I see it, and your sister has 'what's in it for me' written all over her face."

"She can't touch my money or property. The lawyers have made sure of that."

"It's not your things I'm worried about. It's you," she said, and poked her finger into his chest.

He leaned his face down and kissed her gently on her mouth.

"If it makes you feel any better, I told her to meet me at Jorge's place," he said referring to Tico's Tacos, a Mexican restaurant run by Jorge Perez. Jorge was the father of Aiden's best friend Julio, and he had stepped in to fill the role when Aiden's own father passed away while the boys were still in grade school. "That way, she can't even start the discussion about what's in the house and how Mom meant for her to have it."

"She's done that in the past, I take it?"

Aiden sighed. "Once or twice."

"Did you give her stuff?" Harriet asked, her voice louder than she'd intended.

His pained silence answered her question.

"What did you give her?" she pressed.

"Not much. A necklace. A couple of teacups. Nothing I couldn't spare. My mom had a lot of stuff, you know."

"That's not the point."

"I know—you're not the only one I've had this discussion with. Jorge told me the same thing. He says she's toxic. And he said she's probably selling whatever I give her online as soon as she gets home."

Harriet brushed at the errant lock of hair again. He took her hand in his when she'd finished and brought it to his lips before setting it back in her lap.

"It's just complicated," he said in a quiet voice.

"I know. Just be careful," she said and pressed her lips gently to his. He tightened his arms around her and deepened the kiss.

A loud whoosh of wind rattled the bow window again, causing them to separate as tree debris pinged against the window.

"Hard to believe this isn't the worst part of the storm yet," Harriet said as rain fell in sheets outside.

"I've got go," Aiden said with a glance at his watch. "Michelle's supposed to be here in an hour, and I have to go by the clinic to check on a dog."

"I have fabric to cut anyway. Mavis says we need six more charity quilts for the homeless camp, and she wants them done before the storm hits."

She stood up and waited while Aiden stood and put on his outer jacket and a baseball cap with the Main Street Veterinary Clinic logo on the front.

"Call me?" she said and gave him one last kiss.

"If it's not too late," he said. "Michelle tends to drag our discussions out. She likes to bring up sentimental stories from when we were young to try to soften me up."

"Do they work?"

"Unfortunately, yes," he said. "No one knows your life like the people who've lived it with you. Plus, there's a part of me that really doesn't care if she has all the stuff. I know it's not what my mother wanted, and I know it only encourages her when I give in, but still—it's just stuff."

"Okay, go." She pushed him toward the door.

She watched out the window until his car disappeared into the rainy gloom then turned back to her cutting table. She had cut four different colors of flannel before Aiden's arrival and stacked them in piles; her gray cat Fred was batting at the stacks, trying out a new design.

"I don't think this is what Mavis has in mind," she scolded him as she organized the squares by color again.

"What didn't Mavis have in mind?" the woman herself asked as she swept into the studio, her coat flapping in the breeze.

"I was just talking to Fred—he decided to rearrange our fabric. I've got one more color to cut if you have time to wait. Aiden came by for a few minutes, so I'm a little behind schedule."

"I've got a few minutes," Mavis said as she shrugged out of her coat. "I'm not due at Connie's for another hour, so take your time. Did your aunt call you? And I could use a cup of tea.

"No, was she going to?"

"Well, after I give Connie her pieces, we'll have three quilts left to go. Beth was thinking we could meet here, if it was okay with you."

"Of course it's okay—it's her studio."

"*Was* her studio," Mavis corrected. "She gave it to you, and she's trying to respect that."

"It's not like she gave it to me and I turned it into a beauty parlor or moved to Mars or something. I am part of the Loose Threads. At least, I was last time I checked."

"Like I say, she's trying to respect your autonomy."

"Okay, whatever. The studio is free, and so am I. Aiden's having dinner with his sister."

"That sounds like a recipe for disaster."

"Everyone's told him that, but he can't say no to her. He says I'd understand if I wasn't an only child."

"Well, sister or not, that girl's poison, if you ask me."

"You're preaching to the choir," Harriet said as she folded a piece of brown plaid flannel and spread it carefully on her cutting mat.

Mavis unplugged the electric kettle and carried it toward the kitchen.

"I'm going to get some fresh water, if you don't mind," she said as she went through the connecting door to Harriet's kitchen. She returned a few minutes later and plugged in the now-full kettle. "Connie has another idea for us." She pulled a stool to the opposite side of the cutting table and eased herself carefully onto it.

"You seem to be moving a little slow," Harriet observed as she ran her rotary cutter along the long edge of her Plexiglas quilting ruler, slicing the edge off the piece of fabric.

"It's nothing. I banged my hip on the square edge at the top of my bedpost yesterday. Curly was running around while I was making my bed, and I was afraid I was going to step on him. I was looking at my feet instead of where I was going, and now I'm sporting a big purple bruise."

"You need to be careful. That little dog isn't worth you breaking your hip."

"Easy for you to say," Mavis said with a laugh. "You don't look at his sweet little face staring up at you every morning when you wake up. If he could talk, I know he'd be saying how happy he is that Aiden rescued him and brought him to live at my house."

"Cute or not, he's not worth breaking your hip, or worse, over."

Mavis sighed and rolled her eyes skyward.

"You just wait until you get Scooter home," she said, referring to the small, mostly hairless dog who was still living at the Main Street Veterinary Clinic, recovering from a series of skin grafts he'd needed after spending his short life living in squalor in the bottom cage of a tall stack in a dog-hoarding home.

The Loose Threads had all participated in a socialization program, holding the neglected dogs and getting them used to human contact so they could become eligible for adoption. So far, as each dog had graduated from the program, it had been adopted by the Loose Thread who had socialized it. They were now working on a second group of animals, hoping to release them to the public when they were ready.

"Who's saying Scooter's coming to live here?"

"Don't even go there. We all see how you look at that little fellow."

"Well, he's still weeks away from being released medically. That urine burn on his back was so deep it has to heal more before they can get a permanent skin graft to take."

"So, back to the quilts," Mavis said. "Connie came up with an idea to solve our problem."

"Our problem?" Harriet asked, looking up at her friend as she did.

"It's not *our* problem, exactly, but Connie and I have been talking about how we're making all these warm quilts for the people at the homeless camp, but we're not addressing the wetness issue. We're getting tons of rain, and the ground is so saturated that even if they've got a tarp or tent overhead, their quilt is going to get wet and we've accomplished nothing."

"And the solution is?"

"Connie saw an article in the Seattle paper about a young University of Oregon college student who did a workshop project that involved making portable shelters from discarded materials. She won the competition with her tarp made from plastic grocery bags, which she then sent to Haiti after the earthquake there.

"They call them quilts because they look like patchwork when they're finished. A group of quilters added some of that thin plastic drop cloth material, ironing it over the whole thing so they could layer in flowers or letters or other decorations cut from dark-colored plastic bags.

"In both cases, you lay a piece of tracing paper or parchment over the layers and iron the whole thing. According to the people who've made them, it sticks together. The college students even slept outside using theirs to field test them, and they say they were quite comfortable."

"That's amazing."

"Well, let's not be too amazed until we try it. Connie's been col-lecting grocery bags from everyone she knows since she read the article, so she's got enough for a couple of tarps, and if it works, we can probably get more. She said it takes about four hundred bags after you cut off the handles and bottoms to make a ten-by-twelve tarp."

"Why don't you see if she wants to come here tonight? We can try the tarp idea, give her the flannel squares, and some of us can work on sewing quilt squares at the same time."

"I'll call," Mavis started to get up, but was interrupted when the door blew open and a cluster of wet brown leaves sailed in on a cold blast of wind, landing in a soggy mess on the reception area rug. She went to the door and shut it, locking it this time.

✂- - - ✂- - - ✂

An hour and a half later, Connie Escorcia, Mavis Willis, Harriet and Beth, Harriet's aunt, were assembled in the quilt studio looking down at an array of plastic bags spread out on the large table and covered with thin clear plastic. Connie had cut three large daisy shapes from a green-and-yellow bag and now arranged them art-fully between the bags and the plastic. She laid a large sheet of white tracing paper over the corner of the plastic sandwich and pressed a hot iron to the surface. The smell of melting plastic filled the air.

Harriet found a box fan and set it up on a stool so it was at table level, facing away from the project.

"I hate to open a window the way it's storming out there, but I'm afraid it can't be helped." She went to one of the small windows to one side of the bow window and opened it about an inch. The wind whistled, and cold air shot into the room.

Aunt Beth pulled her sweater closed across her ample midriff.

"I hope this is as bad as this storm is going to get," she said and turned her back to the window.

"The weatherman says this is nothing compared to what it will be," Connie said and, after receiving a nod from Harriet, pressed the iron down on the next section.

"What are you guys doing?" Lauren Sawyer said as she came in from the driveway, pushing the door closed with a bang. "I knocked, but nobody even looked up, so I let myself in with that key you gave me."

"Come on in and make yourself some tea," Aunt Beth invited. "It's so noisy in here with the trees scratching on the windows, we didn't hear you."

"What are you doing with that iron? It smells horrible."

"We're making tarps out of plastic grocery bags," Harriet told her. "Want to help?"

"Don't you still have some quilts that need to be sewn?" she asked. "That's why I came by. I turned in a design to a client, and I can't do anything more until they test the first part, so I have a little free time."

"How nice of you to think of the project," Connie said.

"You say that like I don't do my share," Lauren shot back.

"Now, honey, I meant nothing of the kind. Harriet, don't you have some fabric that still needs cutting?"

Harriet got Lauren set up at the cutting table with a ruler, rotary cutter and several yards of brown plaid flannel.

"Where did you get so much of the brown flannel?" Lauren asked. "Didn't we put this in every quilt, front and back?"

"Marjory got a special deal from her distributor," Mavis said. "There was a defect in the print. If you look at the plaid in the whole piece, there's a swath through the center that doesn't have its yellow stripes."

Lauren leaned closer to the fabric, carefully examining the pattern.

"You're right. I can see it now that you point it out. It hardly seems like a reason to reject the fabric."

"Yeah, but if you were making a quilt for a show, you wouldn't want fabric that wasn't the same on part of it. In any case, it was all the better for us. Marjory got it for two dollars a yard and is giving it to us at the same price."

"I guess you can't argue with that," Lauren said and set about cutting the squares of flannel that would be sewn into rag quilts.

Rag quilts are so named because of the ragged edges that result when you sew two or more squares of fabric wrong sides together then sew the resulting layered squares to each other with the seams on the top of the quilt. These seams are snipped to the stitching line every quarter inch or so, and when the fabric used is a flannel or other loosely woven material, these snipped margins fray when washed. This produces a thick fuzzy seam that adds to the warmth of the resulting quilt and eliminates the need for batting or additional quilting. This also makes them quick and easy to produce in mass quantities.

"What are these big squares for?" Lauren asked Harriet. "I don't remember us using anything that big in the quilts we've already made."

"Those aren't going *in* the quilts," Harriet said. "I thought we could sew two big squares, right sides together, then turn them and topstitch them down on three sides at one edge of the top of the quilt to make a pocket."

"Why didn't you just say we're going to make quillow's?" Lauren asked, cutting off anything else Harriet was going to say on the subject.

Quillow was the term used to describe a quilt with a pillow pouch attached. The quilt could be folded up into the pocket to form a pillow or unfolded to use as a cover.

"I wasn't sure—" Harriet started, but the look Lauren made her stop. "I'll leave you to it."

She turned back to the tarp makers.

✂- - -✂- - -✂

9

"Is anyone getting hungry?" Aunt Beth asked when the group had been at work for more than an hour. "I was thinking I could call for pizza."

"Sounds good to me," Harriet said. "Anything to avoid going out in this weather."

The rest of the group agreed, and after a brief debate about which toppings they all wanted, Aunt Beth placed the order.

"They said thirty minutes," she reported when she'd hung up the phone. "I'm surprised they aren't busier than that."

"I'm glad," Connie said. "I'm getting hungry. Rod and I spent the afternoon putting our patio furniture in the garage and securing the potted plants. We ate cheese and crackers instead of a proper lunch, to take advantage of the lull between storms. He's off getting gas for our generator while I'm here."

"Hopefully, it won't come to that," Lauren said and shuddered, pulling her zip-front sweatshirt closer around her. "My new apartment has that big front window overlooking the cove and no fireplace or wood stove."

"I brought extra wood into the garage to dry," Harriet said. "You can come here if things get really bad. I've got two fireplaces, and my stove top is gas, so I can still cook if the power goes off."

"The downstairs water heater is gas, too," Beth added. "When I had the propane tank installed for the stove, I figured it might be useful to have a gas water heater, too, just in case."

"We may all be over here," Mavis said. "I've got a wood stove, but hot water and a stove top would be real nice."

"You're all welcome to come," Harriet said. "But I'm with Lauren—I'm hoping the weatherman is crying wolf."

"I heard the Methodist church is setting up a shelter for the homeless people and anyone else who needs warming," Mavis said. "They don't usually go that far unless it's pretty certain."

Rain pelted the windows, and the wind howled as a prolonged gust forced its way up the driveway and through the trees surrounding Harriet's house. The women went back to their stations, cutting bags and ironing sections of tarp together.

"Someone call for pizza?" Robin McLeod called as she came into the studio twenty minutes later, her arms laden with flat white boxes. The door slammed behind her.

"Did you get a new job we don't know about?" Harriet asked, knowing that since Robin was a mother and part-time lawyer as well as a quilter, this was unlikely.

Robin laughed. "No, I called Connie's house, and Rod said you were all over here, so I decided to join you. I stopped on my way to order pizza for *my* gang, and I heard them putting your order together. I told Theresa I was on my way here and could save them the trip, so here I am. I took the liberty of adding cheesy bread sticks and marinara sauce to the order."

"Let's go to the kitchen so we don't have to move our projects to make table space," Aunt Beth suggested.

"I've got diet and fully leaded soda in both light and dark varieties as well as fizzy water," Harriet announced as she and the rest of the group followed Robin to the kitchen. She took drink orders then prepared the requests as the group settled around the table in the sunny yellow kitchen.

"Has anyone talked to DeAnn?" Mavis asked. "I called her last week, and she had a house full of sick kids."

"Baby Kissa and one of the boys are better, but her younger son is still having ear problems," Robin reported. "I talked to her this morning, and she said they're thinking about packing up and heading south to her mother-in-law's until the storm is over. They haven't taken Kissa to meet that part of the family yet anyway, so now is as good a time as any. DeAnn hasn't wanted to travel out of state until they had some sort of custody papers in hand, and given that Kissa had no history or documents, it's been a slow process."

DeAnn Gault and her husband had adopted the baby whose parentage had been a mystery the Loose Threads had unraveled several months earlier.

"Jenny's out of town, too," Beth said. "She left this morning to visit her son in Texas for two weeks."

"The rats are all leaving the sinking ship," Lauren said and took a bite of her pepperoni pizza slice.

"Jenny planned her trip months ago," Beth said sharply. "And I don't blame DeAnn for not wanting to deal with a house full of sick kids with the power possibly going out."

"Who wants to come to the homeless camp and deliver quilts and tarps tomorrow?" Connie asked.

"I can't commit until I hear from my client," Lauren said.

"I can come," Harriet said. "I'd like to see how muddy it is at the camp. Our tarps may not help if the ground is too mushy."

"Beth and I are going to be at the church helping to put together hygiene kits," Mavis said.

"I assume that's soap and toothbrushes," Harriet said.

"Yes, and deodorant, hand lotion, aspirin packs..." Mavis looked at Beth.

"Playing cards, and a hand towel and washcloth," Aunt Beth added.

"Wow," Lauren said and reached for another piece of pizza. "Who paid for all that?"

"Most of it was donations, and what they had to buy was covered by a grant of some sort," Robin reached for a breadstick. "Mmm, these are so good," she said through her bite of cheesy goodness. "I can come if it's not too early. I have to get the kids to school."

"How about ten?" Connie looked first to Harriet then Robin and Lauren for agreement. "Ten, it is," she said when no one disagreed. "Let's meet in the west parking lot at Fogg Park. We can walk in from there."

"I talked to Marjory when I picked up the last batch of flannel," Harriet said. "She's worried about the river flooding downtown."

"Well, it wouldn't be the first time," Mavis observed. "It's been probably forty years ago, but the Muckleshoot jumped its banks and ran three feet deep down Main Street."

"I told her I'd help her put fabric up if things get to that point," Harriet said.

"She better do it sooner rather than later if she wants your help," Lauren warned. "The bridge between here and there will wash out long before the water reaches Main Street."

"Let's hope the city has done some work in the last forty years to prevent that eventuality," Robin said.

"That was supposed to be a hundred-year flood when it happened, so we shouldn't be due yet." Mavis said.

"Every time there's severe weather people claim it's a 'hundred-year event' no matter what frequency it really happens with," Lauren observed and reached for a bread stick. "You know, I never ate this sort of junk before I met you ladies."

Harriet looked at Aunt Beth, who looked back and shook her head with a small smile.

Chapter 2

A fine mist was falling from a gray sky when Harriet pulled her car into the parking lot of Fogg Park the next morning. People always assumed the park was named for the prevailing weather but in fact, the park, along with a lot of other local features including the town itself, was named for Cornelius Fogg, a Victorian pirate who had retired and settled the area more than a hundred years ago.

Harriet had stopped by the veterinary clinic to socialize with Scooter and take him a new chew toy. He wasn't mobile enough to really play yet, but he loved a good chew toy. As much as she protested to the Loose Threads, in her heart she knew Scooter would be coming home to live with her and Fred when he was able to leave the hospital. Fred would probably find some way to make her pay, but she was pretty sure he would be a good "brother."

She had hoped to talk to Aiden and see how things had gone with his sister, but after a brief hello, he said he was needed in the back and disappeared. She waited as long as she could before leaving for the park, but he didn't return. She reminded herself he was at work, and undoubtedly, an animal had needed his care; but in her heart she knew this wasn't true.

✂ - - - ✂ - - - ✂

Lauren was waiting in her car when Harriet arrived.

"My client wasn't ready yet," she said by way of greeting as she climbed into the passenger seat of Harriet's car. "Hard to believe people live outside in this weather." She shivered. "Can you turn up the heat?"

"It's all the way up," Harriet told her. "I've got a couple of flannel quilts I'm going to deliver with the tarps. You want one?"

"No, it's okay," Lauren looked out the window as the rain picked up in intensity. "I heard the next storm is supposed to come in this afternoon."

"It's hard to believe it's going to get even worse by the weekend."

"I'm just glad I'm not going to be the one with just a quilt and a tarp for shelter," Lauren said. "Here's Connie."

"Looks like Robin's with her." Harriet turned her engine off.

The four women met at the now-open back door of Harriet's car; each took an armload and followed Connie to the restroom building.

"The path to the camp starts behind the building," she told them as she stepped onto a gravel path. The trail quickly changed from gravel to wood chips and then to mud.

"You weren't kidding about it being muddy back here," Harriet said.

"Joyce tries to cover the mud with leaves and tree debris from the forest, but I think this last group of storms has been too much to keep up with."

The mud sucked at their boots as they made their way through the woods and finally came into a clearing.

"Did I hear you complaining about my trail?" a small white-haired woman said when they'd stopped. A hint of the British Isles was apparent in her speech. "You're welcome to make any improvements you want to." She added that with a smile.

"If I could think of anything that would help, I would," Harriet said.

"Nothing works against this ol' mud. Some volunteer group put down gravel two inches thick all the way from the restrooms to this clearing last spring, and you can't even find a single rock now. I'm Joyce, by the way." She held her hand out to Harriet, who took it

"I'm Harriet, and this is Lauren and…"

"We know Robin," Joyce said. "She helped us work out the arrangement that allows us to have our camp in these woods."

"We made those plastic bag tarps I was telling you about," Connie said and held one out.

Joyce took the tarp and unfolded it.

"Well, aren't you ladies clever? I'll be the first to admit, I was skeptical when Connie told me about these."

Harriet was surprised by Joyce's clear soft voice. She wasn't sure what she'd expected, but it hadn't been the tidy woman in faded blue jeans and flannel who stood in front of her. She realized her image of homeless people was largely based on television and involved dirty people who were either drunks or mentally ill. Joyce didn't seem to be either.

"I wasn't sure how you were going to use these," Harriet said, "so I brought some clothesline rope and heavy-duty clamps."

"The boat shop I live over donated a bag of bungee cords, too," Lauren added.

"Now, wasn't that nice," Joyce said as she refolded the tarp. "Let's take this to my place and see how it works."

She stopped in the middle of the clearing. A wooden table with mismatched legs stood to her right. A bench that consisted of a wide board resting on two tree stumps that were about six feet apart was on the opposite side of the area.

"This is our 'living room,' if you will. We have our group meetings here and our community meals as well. Each member of the camp has a private space separated by trees and brush. No one goes into anyone's camp without an invitation." She turned and led them down a less-defined trail to a smaller clearing. "Welcome to my home sweet home," she said with a sweeping bow.

Again, it was not what Harriet had expected. She had never really thought about the day-to-day details of how the individuals in a homeless camp might create privacy, share spaces or secure their possessions. If she had, she wouldn't have imagined what Joyce had created.

Joyce had formed a bed from tree boughs stacked in layers at the back of her area. Closer examination showed a layer of tattered plastic sheeting sticking out between the layers of greenery—a vapor barrier, of sorts. Wooden birdhouses adorned the tree branches at the head of the bed, and an empty wooden window frame dangled whimsically from a limb to the left side. There was a mirror on a tree trunk opposite the window. Two blue plastic storage bins were stacked under the mirror, a chipped china pitcher and bowl on top of the stack.

A large piece of torn plastic lay over a bush at the front of the area.

"I was just doing home repairs," Joyce said with a smile and held her arm up. A roll of silver duct tape encircled her wrist.

"Maybe this will make that unnecessary," Connie said.

"How many do you have?"

"Three so far."

Joyce looked longingly at the brightly colored sheet folded over Connie's arm.

"As much as I would love to replace my top cover, there are other people in camp who need them more," she said with a sigh. "We had a new fellow move in this past summer, and this is his first winter outside. Let's go get him set up first."

She led the group out of her space and down the trail. She stopped after about fifty feet.

"Duane?" she called. "Are you in there?"

"Come on in," a deep male voice answered.

Harriet had expected a much-larger man based on his voice, but Duane was of medium height and build. His balding head had a few long thin strands of light-brown hair mingled with gray. He was clearly letting his beard grow, but it didn't cover his face and chin uniformly, leaving him with clumps sticking out in random patches.

"If I'd known I was going to have company, I'd have cleaned house," he said with a chuckle. "I'm Duane, by the way."

Connie, Harriet and Lauren introduced themselves and explained why they were there.

"I can use all the help I can get," Duane said. "I'm sure Joyce told you I'm sort of new to the outdoor lifestyle."

"Let's see what we can do for you," Connie said.

Duane's space wasn't as organized as Joyce's; he slept in a sleeping bag on the ground. Unlike Joyce, who had on a puffy down jacket and knitted wool fingerless gloves, Duane wore a purple-and-gold University of Washington sweatshirt. The edges of a light sweater and a plaid button-down cotton shirt showed at the neck and sleeve edges. The ensemble was topped with a Harris-tweed blazer—none of it was intended for outdoor living. It looked like it might be his whole wardrobe.

"Let's start with an overhead cover," Connie said. She looked around the small clearing. "Over here." She pointed, indicating an area between two tall Douglas firs.

"Isn't it sort of thorny?" Duane asked. A low berry bush filled the space.

"You're going to pile brush up over those bushes. They're going to keep you off the cold ground," Joyce explained.

Lauren and Harriet strung a length of clothesline between the two trees, anchoring it around the trunks. When they had it pulled tight, Duane helped Connie fold the tarp over the line, securing it with large clamps at the top and tying the corners to smaller tree branches with smaller lengths of clothesline. Joyce directed Robin in the gathering and placement of large fir boughs under the tarp. She folded a second tarp on the boughs then reopened it, covering the bottom layer with more branches.

"Get your sleeping bag," Joyce directed. When Duane complied, she laid the bag over the last layer of branches and flapped the tarp over it.

"This will be a lot more comfortable and dry," she proclaimed when Duane's things had been arranged to her satisfaction.

"This is wonderful," Duane said in his sonorous voice. "How can I ever thank you?"

"We're happy to help," Connie said.

The mist that had continued to fall turned into a steady rain.

"Do you want a quilt?" Lauren asked without preamble.

"I feel as though I've already taken my share," Duane said politely. "Let's see that the others' needs are met before I take anything else."

"I think we have plenty," Lauren protested.

"We'll check with the others," Harriet said and led her back to the trail.

"I'm just doing our job," Lauren hissed. "Isn't that why we're here? To give out quilts?"

"Yes, that's why we're here, but let's allow the man his dignity. When we're finished with the rest of the camp, we can give him one, or if we run out, we can bring one back later."

"Whatever."

Connie and Joyce came out of Duane's area, and Joyce took them to a fork in the trail then down the right-hand pathway.

"Brandy lives here," she said as she held a branch aside, pointing them into the smallest clear area yet.

The brush was thicker here, letting in little light; it took a moment for Harriet's eyes to adjust. She finally saw Brandy, asleep or unconscious on a muddy sleeping bag, a moth-eaten gray wool blanket draped over her shoulders. Her dark hair would probably have been shoulder-length if it hadn't been so tangled and matted.

"Now, *she* looks like a homeless person," Lauren whispered to Harriet as they stepped aside to let Connie and Robin in.

"I'm not sure how much help Brandy will accept," Joyce said. "She's one of the more troubled members of our community."

"Maybe we could string up a tarp over her spot while she sleeps," Connie suggested.

Lauren tapped Harriet's foot with hers. When Harriet glanced her way, she was staring at the base of a small fir tree to Harriet's left. Harriet casually looked where Lauren indicated and saw a pile of empty whiskey bottles.

"I don't think she's waking up anytime soon," Lauren said in a stage whisper audible to all.

"We generally don't let people stay here if they use drugs or alcohol," Joyce said, "but Brandy has mental problems, and so far no one has been able to convince her to go to the clinic and get help. The rest of us agreed it was in our best interest to let her go on self-medicating for the near term. We're hoping we can get through to her, but I'm not sure how that's going to happen."

"Is she from around here?" Robin asked.

"She doesn't communicate well. We're not even sure Brandy is her name. Another woman and I found her passed out in the park bathroom this summer. All she would say for the first few weeks was 'brandy.' We couldn't tell if she was identifying herself or asking for her favorite drink, but she answers to it, so that's what we call her."

"That's great," Lauren said. "Can we get going with her shelter? It's wet out here."

"Please pardon our friend's lack of sensitivity," Connie said.

"She's right." Joyce gave a wry smile. "It *is* wet out here."

Harriet uncoiled another package of clothesline and handed one end to Lauren. She pushed through the brush to the trunk of one of the taller trees, tying the other end securely. Lauren did the same and Robin and Connie quickly draped the last tarp over the line.

"Let's tie the back closer to the ground," Joyce directed. "I think a lean-to would serve her best."

Harriet and Lauren did as instructed, and within a few minutes had fashioned a secure shelter that would go a long way toward keeping the rain off Brandy. Connie and Robin put two flannel quilts over the sleeping woman.

"I wish we could do more." Connie sighed then turned and went back onto the main trail. "We have a few more quilts in the car," she said when they were all together again.

"We have a new man who might like a quilt," Joyce told them. "He has a small tent he brought with him. He said he managed to sneak it out of his house and hide it in the park the week before he was evicted."

"Is he from here?" Connie asked. Harriet knew she was probably thinking about the programs the local churches had to provide transitional housing for people in that type of situation.

"We don't ask those sorts of questions when people join our community. If a person wants to share they do. If not, then we leave it at that."

"And did he?" Lauren asked.

Joyce gave her a long look before speaking.

"He didn't, other than what I've just told you. He was evicted, and he was able to hide some stuff in the park. He didn't say if the park was near his home or miles away."

"So, let me get this straight," Lauren said. "You just let any old person live here?"

"Well, we call the park ranger if someone camps here and is doing drugs or drinking to the point of being disruptive to others. Beyond that, it's federal property that backs up to a city park. No one person has any more right to it than another."

"Sounds dangerous, if you ask me." Lauren said.

"Well, the world is a dangerous place," Joyce replied.

"Let's go get those last quilts, shall we?" Harriet said and steered Lauren back toward the parking lot.

"I can't believe they don't have any vetting process to check people out before they let them move in," Lauren said when she and Harriet were out of earshot of the others.

"What, exactly, would you have them do? Plug their laptop into a currant bush?"

"Ha. Ha. You're such a wit. But really, this new guy could be anybody. Haven't you been reading the news about the serial killer who has been dumping bodies along the interstate?"

"I have seen an article or two," Harriet said. "But the ones I read said they think the killer is a truck driver, not a newly evicted homeless man."

"Well, the killer isn't going to go around with a sign saying 'I'm a truck-driving killer.' He probably masquerades as something completely different—like maybe a homeless guy."

"So, he has a truck parked somewhere nearby and goes on periodic road trips?"

"I don't know. Do I have to think of everything? I'm just saying you can't be too careful these days."

"I suppose. I have to say, what we've seen of the homeless camp so far is nothing like what I was expecting."

They reached Harriet's car, and Lauren flipped the hood to her jacket down, shaking her long blonde hair.

"I hate hoods," she muttered.

"You picked the wrong place to live if that's your problem," Harriet said and handed her two folded quilts.

"Who said I had a choice?" Lauren shot back.

A black Ford Explorer pulled up beside Harriet's car and parked, ending the discussion before she could grill Lauren about what she meant. The passenger side window slid down.

"Hey," called a male voice.

Harriet bent to look into the car.

"Tom!" she said as she recognized Tom Bainbridge, who she'd met the previous spring when she and the other Loose Threads had attended a folk art school in Angel Harbor owned by his mother. "What brings you to town?"

"And here, of all places," Lauren added.

"I'm working," he said with a smile. "What are you two doing out here in the rain? It's not really picnic weather."

"We're being do-gooders," Lauren said.

"What Lauren means is we're delivering some quilts and water-proof tarps we made to the homeless people who live in the forest behind Fogg Park."

"Well, what a coincidence," Tom said and got out of his car. "I'm here to interview the homeless residents for my new project. If everything works out, some if not all of them will be living in new housing by this time next year."

"Where?" Harriet asked and picked up an armload of quilts.

"Who's paying for it?" Lauren asked at the same time.

"A redevelopment group wants to build some multi-use apartments a couple of blocks from the docks. They're still looking at sites, but the city has stipulated that some of the apartments be set aside for qualifying homeless people."

"Qualifying?" Harriet said.

"Believe it or not, there are people of means who live without a permanent residence. Sometimes it's just a minimal pension, but it's enough that they could rent a room in low-income housing if they wanted to. Turns out they'd rather live outside in the park than in a room with cardboard walls and gun-toting, drug-using neighbors."

"I can't say I blame them," Harriet said.

"Me, either," Tom agreed. "Towns like Foggy Point are trying to provide another alternative. This proposed project will have space for homeless vets, very-low-income homeless and then lower-income and so on, up to and including luxury penthouse suites."

"Sounds like some kind of utopian sci-fi mumbo-jumbo," Lauren said. "I suppose they're solar powered and reuse gray water, too."

"Yes, they'll be green buildings, if that's what you're trying to say." Tom smiled at Harriet.

"Let's get these back to the camp," she said and turned back toward the park with her armload of quilts.

"Can I carry anything?" Tom asked.

Lauren paused as if she were going to hand off her quilts but then looked at Harriet and changed her mind.

"No, we're good," she said.

✂- - - ✂- - - ✂

Robin and Connie were standing in the main clearing beside Joyce and a man who had to be the new resident she'd told them about. He was older, maybe mid-sixties, and was dressed in foul-weather hiking clothes, Danner boots, brand-name Gore-Tex jacket, and moleskin cargo pants. His tan was more Club Med than Fogg Park.

"Hi," Joyce said when the trio reached them. "This is Ronald, the gentleman I was telling you about—the one with a tent. I think he could use one of your blankets."

Lauren glared and clutched her quilts a little tighter. Harriet handed one to him.

"Nice to meet you," Harriet said. "Enjoy your quilt."

"I'm Tom Bainbridge," Tom said and held his hand out to Joyce then Ronald. "I'm the architect hired to design a proposed housing project designed to provide alternatives to living in the park."

"I like the sound of that," Ronald said. "How can we help you?"

"I'd like to talk about space requirements. For instance, would people prefer studio-style apartments or small but separate rooms? And how about kitchen size? Is an under-counter refrigerator adequate, or do people need full-size? I guess I'm asking how much

23

cooking do you envision doing? Will people live alone or with roommates?"

"Being indoors with a roof over our heads will be such a big step up I'm not sure the rest matters," Joyce said.

"I'm sure that's true initially," Tom said, "but I'd like to build apartments people will stay in. I'd like people to be comfortable once they get beyond being warm and dry."

Joyce looked him up and down without saying anything.

Duane came into the clearing from the trail and introduced himself.

"I heard you say you wanted to talk to people about the housing you're going to design."

"That's right," Tom said.

"A number of our group are at the Methodist church warming room waiting for lunch, and a couple more are at Annie's, the coffee shop downtown. You can probably still catch them there if you hurry," Duane said.

"You might be a bit more comfortable, too," Joyce added. Rain dripped off her nose, chin and eyelashes.

Tom looked around.

"Okay, maybe you're right," he said. He looked at Harriet. "Want to meet for coffee later?"

"Sure, when?"

They agreed to give him an hour to talk to the people at the church and another half-hour to talk to the coffee shop crowd. Harriet suggested they meet at The Steaming Cup, Foggy Point's other popular coffee shop, and he agreed.

"Well, aren't you two just cozy," Lauren said when Tom was out of earshot.

"We're friends, Lauren. Don't you have any male friends?"

"Yes, and they don't look at me the way he looks at you." She held her hands up in front of her. "Okay, fine. None of my business."

"Can we leave quilts here for the people who are in town?" Connie asked.

"That would be nice, and we'd take an extra one, if you can spare it," Joyce said, looking at the full armloads of quilts. "We like to keep a few extra supplies on hand for new people. There is no typical situation when someone becomes homeless, but not many are able to bring as much from their old life as Ronald here did."

"I've always been a planner," Ronald said. Harriet couldn't tell if he was blushing, his face was so red from the cold, wet rain, but he looked embarrassed. "This was my fallback to the fallback plan." He shook his head. "I just never imagined my family would turn me away when I lost my house."

"I'll bet you didn't tell them you'd be homeless, did you?" Joyce said. She turned to the Loose Threads. "People who end up here often are turned away by family who don't realize how dire the circumstances are, and people like Ronald here are too proud to tell them the real situation."

"I won't beg," Ronald said. "My daughter was right—they have a full house with two kids and another on the way, and her husband's mother is already staying with them. She said I was always too busy with work to spend the time with her and her brother when they needed me, so how can I expect to come crying to them now that I'm the one who needs help.

"You know what? She's right. I wasn't father of the year. I can't go back and change that, but I can avoid causing them any more pain."

"Hopefully, that bed will be a bit more comfortable now that you have one of our nice warm quilts," Connie said.

"And I do thank you for that," Ronald said with a theatrical bow. "I see this as a temporary setback. I just need to find a job and start over." His eyes filled with tears.

"We all appreciate the quilts and tarps," Joyce said. "Let's get the rest of them in something waterproof before they're soaked through."

Lauren and Harriet handed off the quilts after showing Joyce the quillow feature. Connie helped her load them into two wrinkled black plastic garbage bags she'd pulled from under the large table.

The wind lashed the Loose Threads as they walked back to the parking lot.

"Anyone want to join Tom and me for coffee in an hour?" Harriet asked.

"Connie and I were going to swing by the church and see how Mavis and your aunt are doing. If we have time after that, maybe," Robin said and looked at Connie for agreement.

"We'll see after we check in at the church," Connie said.

"As much as I'd love to ruin your date with Tom, I've got to go see if anything's up with my client," Lauren said with a wicked smile.

Harriet could feel her face redden.

"Ciao," Lauren said and headed for her car before Harriet could think of an appropriate comeback.

Inside her car, Harriet looked at the clock then drove out of Fogg Park. She could go home and start sewing another rag quilt, but she drove past her turn and headed into downtown instead.

Chapter 3

$\mathcal{T}$here were no customers in Pins and Needles, Foggy Point's best—and only—quilt store when Harriet came through the door.

"How's it going?" she called as she spotted Marjory replacing a bolt of green holly print fabric to a shelf in the middle of the store. A wire stretched the length of the store with placemats, table runners, Christmas tree skirts and other small quilting projects in Christmas colors attached to it with clothespins.

"It's rough," Marjory said. "Customers aren't coming in because of the storm. Meanwhile, the same storm is not stopping my family from paying me an unplanned and, I might add, uninvited visit."

"Why are they coming?" Harriet asked. "I can't believe anyone would go out in this storm unless there was no choice."

"I tried to tell them. I told my sister Pat they could get stuck here if we have a slide or if a tree goes down in the wrong place. They're supposed to get here tomorrow."

"That's hard to believe."

"Not if you know my sister and her money-grubbing husband. Can you stay for a cup of tea?"

"Sure," Harriet said.

Clearly there was more to this story, and she wouldn't miss it for anything.

Marjory led her to the store kitchen adjacent to the classrooms at the back of the building. She filled the electric teakettle and plugged it in. Harriet pulled two mugs from a shelf and put tea bags in them.

"Remember how my mom died a couple of months ago?" Marjory asked.

"Of course." Harriet knew Marjory had been close to her mother.

"Well, my sister and her family were nowhere to be found while my mom was sick. There was always some excuse why she and her husband and daughter couldn't come. Meanwhile, my bunch came every week and did chores, read to her, listened to her stories and held her hand to the end."

"And now?" Harriet prompted.

"Mom made me executor of her estate. She didn't want to leave Pat anything. Years ago, Mom paid the down payment on a house they couldn't have afforded otherwise, and they didn't even say a simple thank-you.

"I convinced Mom that if she left them nothing, it would be miserable for me, so she agreed to leave them a little. My parents weren't rich or anything, but they both had worked all their lives. They owned their house and a couple of rentals. Their cars were paid off. They had some retirement money saved."

"I'm guessing your sister wasn't happy with what your mom decided."

"You could say that," Marjorie said. "They figured they should get the whole estate, because they need it and I don't."

"Your sister said that to your face?"

"Yes, she did. She said I was doing fine with my shop, as near as she could tell, so why did I need more money? She said they had debts and had to have the money."

"You didn't tell her you'd give it to her, did you?"

"Of course not. I told her I was sorry she had money troubles, but I was going to follow our mother's instructions."

"So, why is she coming here?"

"I'm not really sure. I guess she's hoping if she comes in person, she can convince me to change my mind."

"Sounds like Aiden's sister. She's back in town working *him* over."

"It's hard to imagine how Avanell could have had such different children," Marjory said. "That Michelle was a problem right from the start. Aiden and his brother were always well-behaved and hard workers. Avanell and her husband made the kids work for their allowance, so the boys ran a lawn-mowing service. Aiden worked for his brother then took over when Marcel went off to college. To my knowledge, Avanell never got a lick of work out of Michelle."

"Was it like that with *your* sister?"

"No, Pat was never a go-getter, but she did babysit to make money for school clothes and spending money. She started changing after she married Richard. They had to have a big house they could barely afford, and then Richard started making money and they were too good for the rest of us."

"So, what happened?"

"I'm not sure. One minute they were going to the country club, and the next thing I know she's calling and wanting all of Mom's estate and claiming all their money is gone."

"Did she say anything else?"

"No, that's what so weird. I'm hoping she's coming here to tell me in person whatever it is that's so horrible it justifies her getting all of Mom's money. Frankly I can't imagine what she could say that would change my mind." She paused a moment. "I suppose if one of them is deathly ill and needs an expensive transplant of some sort I might be swayed. I don't think she'd keep that a secret, though."

"Well, I don't envy you the upcoming confrontation." Harriet reached across the table to pat Marjory's hand. She'd noticed that Mavis did a lot of hand patting when people were troubled and it seemed to bring comfort, so she was trying it out. "Is there anything I can do to help?" she asked. "Do you need a neutral witness or anything?"

"That's sweet of you to offer. You've been a great help already, just by listening. I've been dealing with my sister my whole life. This is just one more round in an ongoing battle. Besides, if Michelle is in town, Aiden's going to need your help."

"Well, the offer stands. If you think of anything, let me know, and I'll come running."

"Thank you, honey. Your aunt raised you right. Now, how about we forget family troubles for a while and look at fabric. If you're not tired of the charity quilts, I got some more flannel donated by a distributor, and if you are, some late additions to one of the Christmas collections is in the back waiting to be unwrapped. You can have the first chance at it."

"That sounds good. I do have a few last-minute Christmas gifts to make."

Harriet managed to use up most of her remaining time choosing fabric and a pattern to make three holiday table runners.

"I've got a few more minutes, if you want to cut me some of the charity fabric," she said to Marjory when she finished paying for her purchase.

"Let's just load the bolts into your car. I've got to drive my mom's car to Seattle tomorrow to be serviced and detailed so I can sell it. If all goes well, I'll be leaving it at a dealership."

"How will you get home?"

"I can do a one-way car rental—I checked."

"Do you want me to drive you?" Harriet asked, mentally reviewing her next day's schedule.

"That's sweet of you, honey, but you've got quilting to do, and frankly, I could use the time alone to ponder this situation with my sister."

"If you change your mind, just call."

"Let's get this new flannel into your car," Marjory said, ending the discussion.

Chapter 4

Hail began to fall as Harriet pulled into the parking lot of The Steaming Cup and turned her car off. She sat for a moment, hoping the icy precipitation would pass, but realized the parking lot was only going to be more treacherous to walk on as the hail accumulated, so she got out and dashed for the door.

"Boy, it's nasty out there," Tom said as he joined her in line at the coffee counter. He shuddered, and little ice balls fell to the floor from the shoulders of his jacket.

"I'm glad I'm not going to be weathering this storm in the homeless camp."

"You and me both. It's becoming clear our local homeless people are a pretty diverse bunch. The group at the church was different yet from the ones you met. They'd obviously been living outside for a long time and are skilled in acquiring hot meals and services."

"I'd like to know Joyce's story." Harriet paused while she ordered her latte and waited while Tom ordered a mocha. "I mean, she doesn't seem like a typical homeless camp resident by anyone's measure."

"That was my thought, too. I asked the group at the church, but they're a close-mouthed bunch. One guy told me that if Joyce wanted her story known, she'd tell us."

"Well, all right, then." Harriet was quiet for a moment; then, she and Tom both laughed.

"So, how have you been since I last saw you?" he asked, watching her carefully.

"Good," she said. "Things have been good."

"And Aiden?"

"What about Aiden?"

"Are things good with Aiden?"

She paused to consider her answer.

"That's all I need to know," Tom said.

"Things are fine with Aiden," she said in a rush.

"Protest all you want, but your hesitation said it all. That and the fact that it's been more than half a year since we met and you and Aiden have progressed to...what? Dating?"

Harriet turned to leave, but he put his hand on her arm, stopping her.

"I'm sorry. I know it's none of my business, but back when we first met, I told Aiden I wouldn't interfere with your relationship. I also told him that my largess came with an expiration date."

"I'm not some kind of prize in your juvenile competition." Harriet's eyes stung with angry tears. Her drink was called, followed by Tom's, and she grabbed them both.

He led the way to a table away from the other coffee shop patrons, pulled out a chair for her and, when she was seated, sat opposite her.

"I'm making a mess of this," he said. He put his head in his hands and looked down at the table for a moment. "What I'm trying to say is this. If you and Aiden are progressing toward a lasting relationship, say the word, and while I hope we can be friends, I'll back off. On the other hand, I'm checking in. If things are merely convenient and *not* moving toward a more meaningful relationship, I'd like to offer an alternative."

Harriet sat back in her chair.

"I can see I've taken you by surprise," Tom continued. "And, hey, I'm not proposing marriage or anything. But we connected. I know you felt it, too. I'd like to take you out to dinner. Just dinner."

"Wow," Harriet finally said. "I wasn't expecting this." She looked into his clear hazel eyes.

"I know, and it's probably not fair for me to spring it on you. I see some of your Loose Threads at the Folk Art School, and I'll admit—I ask them about you. I came here knowing a little about where things stood with you and Aiden. At least as far as your fellow stitchers know."

"You've been spying on me?" Harriet asked, outraged.

"No, I'm not spying. Your fellow quilters are full of stories about the recent murders in Foggy Point and your part in solving them. They invariably mention that handsome young vet you're seeing. But always in those terms—'that young vet she's seeing.' Not your lover or fiancé or anything else that would indicate a deepening of the relationship."

Harriet's face had gone from pink to red.

"If our relationship had advanced to that point, the Loose Threads would be the last people I'd tell."

"So you admit things aren't progressing?" Tom said with a smile.

Harriet groaned, but she couldn't suppress a smile.

"How about this," he said. "Let's put dinner on hold for now. Let's just have simple coffee between two friends. How did your visit to the homeless camp go?"

"Okay," Harriet said and paused. "My tour of the camp was eye-opening, to say the least. I'm not sure what I was expecting, but it wasn't Joyce and company."

"I hear you. I wasn't sure what the homeless camp would be like, but I was thinking more along the lines of the drunks you see sleeping in doorways in Seattle."

"How many do you think will be helped by the project you're working on?"

"I'm rethinking my whole plan after talking to all three groups of people. There appear to be several subsets within the population, and I think my design needs to reflect that."

"What do you mean?"

"Our group has one person with obvious substance-abuse problems. For her, a simple, indestructible cell-like structure is probably appropriate. She has little capacity to take care of an apartment.

33

"On the other end of the spectrum are Joyce, Ronald and probably Duane. They're organized, capable of taking care of themselves and their surroundings and probably permanently located in our community. The group I met at the church are similar except for the permanency. They describe themselves as nomadic. They have no ties to the community and highly prize their lack of possessions and ability to move on without notice."

"Wow, you've already thought a lot about this."

"I wasn't sure what to expect, but I did read up on homelessness in America before I accepted the project."

"Can you design something that will meet such diverse needs?"

"I know we started badly, but there's no need to be insulting."

Harriet blushed again.

"Hey, I'm kidding." He reached across the table and took her hand. He was a touch person, and she was surprised to discover she didn't mind.

"I'll have to think about it some, but I'm sure I can come up with a solution that will work. In the meantime, I'm sure Joyce and company are going to appreciate the quilts and tarps your group made them."

Harriet looked out the window at the rain, which was again sheeting down from dark clouds.

"If this coming storm is as bad as everyone's predicting, our blankets and tarps aren't going to help much."

"I heard Pastor Hafer telling the people at the church they were setting up cots and would welcome all comers, so hopefully, they'll take advantage."

"I think I heard my aunt and her friend Mavis saying something about using the church bus to pick people up, too."

Tom joined her in watching out the window.

"I better get going. I don't like to drive after dark when there's some likelihood of encountering slides on the road between here and Angel Harbor."

"I don't blame you. Thanks for coffee," Harriet said. "I think," she added with a smile.

"Maybe we can do it again. I'll be back and forth on this project for a while."

"I'd like that," she said, and was pretty sure she meant it.

Chapter 5

Harriet drove past the vet clinic on her way home, and when she saw Connie's car alongside Lauren's in the parking lot, she turned around and pulled in. The rain beat a steady rhythm on her car's roof as she parked, pulled her jacket's hood up and made the run for the door.

"You here to see Scooter?" the receptionist asked.

Harriet nodded and went through the door to the back recesses of the clinic. Aiden had set up a socialization area in an unused storeroom with rocking chairs, a CD player and a coffee and tea setup for the volunteers. Most of the canine victims had spent their entire life in cramped cages stacked one on top of the other.

"Hey," Lauren said as Harriet entered the room. "How'd the date go?"

"It wasn't a date."

"Aiden was here all day," Connie said. "Wasn't he?"

"As you both know," Harriet said pointedly, "I had coffee with Tom Bainbridge. Just coffee. He wanted to compare our impressions of the homeless camp, if you must know. He has some interesting ideas for the new housing project he's working on."

"That Tom Bainbridge wants more than a coffee date with you. You mark my words," Connie told her.

"What if he does?" Lauren said, apparently for the sake of argument.

"I don't want to talk about it," Harriet said. "With either of you. Before I went to coffee, I stopped by Pins and Needles and talked to Marjory. Things sound kind of crazy—her sister and brother-in-law are coming to visit even though Marjory told them not to."

"In this weather?" Connie asked.

"Clearly they want something," Lauren said. She adjusted the position of the small dog in her lap. "Ouch. This one's got sharp little feet."

"For once, I agree with Lauren," Harriet said. "It sounds like her sister is trying to talk Marjory out of their mother's estate."

"Sounds familiar," said Aiden.

Harriet hadn't noticed him enter the room while she was talking. He reached over her shoulder and set Scooter in her lap. The little dog stood up and licked her face.

"I have to go," Connie said. She looked at her watch. "My goodness, I've been here almost an hour."

Aiden started to take the black dog she was holding.

"I can take her back," she said. "Lauren, don't you want to take yours back, too?"

"I've only been here…" Then, noticing Connie's glare, she stood up. "Uh, yeah, I have to leave, too."

When the two women were gone, Aiden sat down.

"I missed you this morning," Harriet told him.

"I was busy," he said without looking at her.

"How'd it go with your sister last night?"

"About how you'd expect."

"Do you want to talk about it?"

"Not really." He was shredding the edge of the disposable puddle pad that had been in Connie's lap when she was holding her charge. He still refused to look at Harriet.

"Are you free for dinner?" She leaned toward him, trying but failing to make eye contact.

"I have to meet with Michelle again. We're going to go through some of my mom's old papers. It will probably take all night," he added before she could ask.

Harriet sat in silence, not sure what was going on.

"Look, I have to go back to work. I'll come get Scooter in twenty minutes, if that's okay."

"Sure," she mumbled and watched him go out the door.

"He's acting like a jerk," Lauren said, reentering the room a moment later.

"Were you outside listening?"

"Not on purpose," she said, crossing the room and picking her scarf up from the floor where it had fallen beside the chair she had occupied earlier. "I didn't want to barge in until you were finished, and there aren't a lot of other places to wait."

"Thanks for that," Harriet said.

"I'm free."

"What?"

"For dinner—I'm free. Want to go to Tico's?"

"Why not?"

"Well, don't hurt yourself."

"I'm sorry, Lauren. Yes, I would like to go to dinner with you. What time?"

"I need to go check my computer. Can we meet there in two hours?"

"Sure. That'll give me time to finish here and unload the new batch of flannel from Marjory."

✄ - - - ✄ - - - ✄

Fred was meowing at the studio door when Harriet came inside.

"What's your problem?" she asked him. "I fed you both canned and dry food before I left."

A gust of wind rattled the window behind her, and Fred made a plaintive yowl.

"I see. You're not liking the storm." She picked the cat up and cuddled him then carried him into the kitchen.

"Don't expect this on a regular basis," she said as she set him on the floor.

She took a can of people tuna out of her kitchen cupboard and scooped a spoonful onto his dish then put the rest in a plastic container in the refrigerator.

"There, that will help with your stress," she said.

Fred only had eyes for his tuna.

She knew she should use the time she had left cutting fabric, but the pounding of the rain and wind was making her feel as restless as Fred. In the end, she went upstairs to the attic to look for the oil lamps she remembered being stored there.

Aunt Beth, who had given her the house when she passed along the quilt studio, had accumulated a variety of the lamps, both decorative and purely functional, over the years. Harriet chose two small models with hand-thrown pottery bases and put them in a bag. She and Lauren were eating early enough she could deliver the lamps to Aunt Beth afterward. Harriet had no intention of allowing her to stay in her cottage, located on the Strait of Juan de Fuca, if the storm did worsen, but she also was aware her aunt might have other ideas, so it was best to make sure she was prepared.

✂- - - ✂- - - ✂

The thighs of Harriet's jeans were soaked by the time she made it from her car to the entrance of Tico's Tacos. Jorge held the door for her then handed her a clean bar towel to wipe her face with.

"Come in, mi'ja," he said. "Your friend is waiting for you. And your aunt is in the back room."

"My aunt is here?" Harriet asked, a little too loud. "What for?"

"What do you think I'm here for?" Aunt Beth shot back as she approached from the rear of the restaurant. "And lower your voice. I didn't raise you to screech like a banshee."

"I'm sorry. I just thought I had heard you say you were going to Connie's for dinner tonight. I was surprised."

"I *am* going to Connie's. I'm here gathering intel from Jorge." She exchanged a glance with the man.

Harriet held her hands up.

"Never mind, it's clearly none of my business."

"It's about Sarah, if you must know."

"What about Sarah," Lauren demanded, getting up from the table Jorge had seated her at and joining them.

"I'm just a little worried about her," Beth said. "I went by the senior care center to visit Millie from church, and Sarah was at the reception desk sewing the binding on a quilt she'd just finished. It was for that boyfriend of hers. He's going south to visit his college roommate while she takes care of his place on the exposed side of Miller Hill."

"Why isn't she going with him?" Harriet asked.

"He didn't ask her," Lauren answered. "I had the same conversation with her the day before yesterday. He told her he doesn't want to leave his place unattended with the storm coming."

"I figured Jorge was the one most likely to have had a chance to observe this joker in person."

"It *is* kind of weird that none of us has met the guy," Harriet said.

"I was just telling your aunt the guy is a perfect gentleman—too perfect," Jorge told her. "There's nothing I can put my finger on, but his manners don't seem natural. It's like he's acting a part. And there is something about the way she looks at him…" He shivered. "There's something not right there."

"I don't like the idea of her being at his house all alone during the storm," Aunt Beth added.

"And I don't like the idea of you being at *your* place alone during the storm," Harriet countered. "I noticed you didn't say anything about your own plan when we were talking last night."

"Who says I'm staying at my house? I don't want to jump the gun, but don't worry—at the first sign that a worse storm is really coming, I'm moving inland, and I hope you don't mind, but I invited Mavis, too."

"I already invited Mavis myself—and Lauren."

"It'll be a regular pajama party," Lauren said without smiling.

"Be glad you have a place to go," Aunt Beth said sternly.

"Yeah, I know, I appreciate it, etc. etc. Can we eat?" Lauren looked at Harriet.

"Sure, lead the way."

Jorge brought a bowl of freshly made guacamole and set it on the table, followed by a basket of warm tortilla chips.

"You want your usual?" he asked Lauren, referring to his chicken burrito platter.

"Is there really a question in there somewhere?"

"You never know. This one ate enchiladas for a long time before I got her to try the special. Maybe sometime you'll try the special, too."

Lauren studied the ceiling silently while Jorge patiently waited.

"Okay," she said with a sigh. "Lay it on me."

"I think you'll like it." Jorge smiled. "And you, chiquita?"

"How can I have anything but the special?" Harriet replied.

Jorge didn't disappoint. When dinner arrived, it turned out to be chunks of pork cooked in a green tomatillo and chili sauce then drizzled with a creamy yet tart sauce of some sort.

"Okay, so the man knows how to cook," Lauren said when she'd tasted the first bite.

"That he does."

"I don't like to stick my nose in Sarah's business," Lauren said when she and Harriet had both eaten enough to take the edge off their appetites. "But do you remember a few months ago when I told you about the bruises I saw on her neck?"

"Yeah, vaguely. But I've not noticed anything like that."

"That's because you're too wrapped up in Aiden to notice anything else."

"That's not true." Harriet was beginning to wonder why she'd agreed to go to dinner.

"Whatever," Lauren said dismissing the protest with a wave. "Ever since I asked her about it, she's worn clothes that conceal almost all her exposed skin. She never wore scarves wrapped so close around her neck before, and now she always wears those half-gloves, and dark tights, and—"

"It *is* winter," Harriet interrupted.

"Is everyone in this town in denial?" Lauren said. "Just because Sarah is probably the most annoying person any of us knows, it doesn't mean she can't be in trouble."

"I'm sorry, you're right."

"What was that? Could you say it again, just so I'm sure I heard you?"

"Very funny. But you're right, it's hard not to let my judgment be colored by her less-attractive behaviors. What do you think is going on?"

"At best, I think her boyfriend is emotionally abusive. At worst, he could be a real danger to her. She's showing all the behaviors of an abused woman. Haven't you noticed how she isn't coming to meetings anymore?"

"She's always been busy," Harriet argued.

"She's always *talked* about how busy she was but then never missed a lunch or meeting or anything. Now, we hardly see her."

"I hadn't thought about it, but you're right. She *has* missed almost everything lately."

"Not almost," Lauren said. "I started keeping track. She hasn't come to anything in almost two months. We see her because we have business at the care center, not because she comes out. And she's not wearing cute clothes anymore. She always used to wear short skirts and flaunt her pathetic cleavage, and now she's wearing turtlenecks and ankle-length skirts."

"I thought she was just growing up."

"It's more than that, and I think her new Mr. Wonderful is the cause."

"What are you thinking we should do?"

"That's your part in this. You're the one with the dramatic past. I figured you'd probably encountered this situation before."

"You give me too much credit," Harriet said dryly. She thought for a moment. "I suppose we should talk to Robin, find out what we can do."

"I don't know why I thought you'd have an idea I hadn't thought of already."

"You didn't. You're human and wanted to share your worries. Don't worry, I won't let your secret out."

They sat in silence as Jorge's waitress cleared away their dinner dishes. When the table was clear, Jorge approached carrying two dishes of caramel-soaked flan.

"Don't argue," he said before either woman opened her mouth. "This may be the last good meal you get for a while if this storm keeps up." He set the desserts on the table and left.

"I guess we wouldn't want to hurt his feelings," Lauren said, pulling one dish toward her and pushing the other in front of Harriet in the process.

"Just don't let my aunt see this," Harriet said and took a bite of the creamy delight.

"May I join you?" said a female voice from the table behind them. Harriet looked up and saw Detective Jane Morse standing in the aisle holding her own dish of flan.

"Sure, pull up a chair."

"Are you ladies ready for the storm?" Jane asked.

"I'm ready to drive to Harriet's," Lauren said. "She has a fireplace, and a gas stove and water heater."

"That sounds comfortable," Jane said and took a bite of her flan. "I'm afraid my apartment has none of those amenities."

"My house didn't start out with all that. My aunt added the propane after a few too many lingering power outages."

"The utility guys told me it's hard to find the faulty power lines when they have to search the feeds that go through the woods," Jane said.

The lights in Tico's flickered but then steadied.

"That can't be good," Lauren said and looked out the window. "The streetlights flickered, too."

"I'm supposed to be going to Everett tomorrow for a task force meeting," Jane said.

"I don't envy you that," Harriet replied. "Will you be driving alone?"

"No, several of us have to go. I'm worried about getting back. We could be driving right through the worst part of the storm."

"Are you meeting about the Interstate Strangler?" Lauren asked.

"I can't really say, but you can draw your own conclusions."

"I feel guilty that I take comfort we aren't close to the interstate," Harriet said.

"Don't worry about it, I feel the same way." Jane smiled. "I was going to call you," she said to Harriet. "I have a quilt finished, and it needs quilting. It's for my niece."

"Do you need it before Christmas?"

"No, whenever you can do it is fine. She picked out the fabric three years ago, so she's not holding her breath waiting. If the power goes out for any length of time, you probably won't be able to quilt anyway. I have it in the car, if you don't mind me handing it off here. I'm not sure I'll have time to bring it to you tomorrow before I leave."

"That would be fine, but eat your dessert first. We're not in a hurry."

"We aren't?" Lauren interjected.

"Do you have somewhere to be?" Harriet asked.

"No, but you didn't know that."

Harriet sighed and noticed that Jane was barely suppressing a smile.

The trio talked about the flannel quilts that had been made for the homeless while they finished their flan.

"I'll go get my quilt," Jane said. "Be right back."

"Isn't she just the chipper one when we aren't involved in one of her murder cases," Lauren commented when she was gone.

"Do you want a cup of tea before we go?" Harriet asked. She knew Jorge kept a good supply on hand in deference to the Loose Threads.

"My goodness, it's wet out there," a slender, middle-aged blonde said as the wind snatched the door from her hand and banged it against the entrance wall. A bearded man in an orange sweatshirt shut it as he followed her in.

"I parked my big rig in a couple of spaces around back," he told Jorge. "Is that going to be okay?"

"Sure. Two for dinner?" He ushered them to a table and poured water into the clean glasses that were already set out. "Would you like some coffee?"

"That sounds wonderful," the blonde said. "The heater on the truck broke, and we were going to try to make it all the way to the interstate, but the windows kept fogging up. We've been in that cold cab for hours."

Jorge brought the hot coffee and took the couple's food order.

"Is there a campground around here where we could stay in our truck?" the trucker asked him.

"Our campgrounds are closed for the winter," Jane Morse said. She'd returned from her car in time to hear the last request.

The man introduced himself as Owen Hart and his blond companion simply as Kate. He explained they were long-haul truck drivers and were returning empty after a delivery to Kalaloch on the Washington coast. He explained their breakdown and his belief that, given some daylight and an open hardware store, he could fix their problem and get them on their way.

"There *is* a large parking lot at Fogg Park," Jane explained. "We keep the restrooms open in the winter for the local homeless camp that's nearby." She pulled a business card from her pocket and scrawled a note on the back. "If a patrol car comes by, just show him this card, and you should be fine." She proceeded to tell them how to find Fogg Park.

"That sounds miserable," Harriet said when Jane returned to their table with her quilt. "I hope he really can fix their problem and get out of the area before the storm hits."

"No kidding," Lauren said.

"Speaking of that and cold people, I'm going to go home and work on rag quilts. There's one that's almost done and a couple of more in progress that could be finished before the worst of the weather hits." Harriet stood up and put her coat on then took Detective Morse's quilt. "Thanks for letting me come to dinner with you," she told Lauren.

"Whatever." Lauren gathered her purse and coat.

Harriet stopped at the table Jorge had seated the truck drivers at.

"My quilting group is making charity quilts for the homeless in Fogg Park. Could you use a warm flannel quilt for your night in the parking lot?" she asked.

"That would be wonderful," the woman said. "Are you sure you can spare one? We'll be okay once we get the truck fixed."

"We'd be happy for you to take one. The only trouble is, I don't have one in my car. My house isn't far from here. Would you mind coming by to pick it up?"

"That's the least we can do. And we'd be happy to give you a donation to buy more materials, if that's okay," Owen said.

Harriet wrote her address and brief directions on a napkin and gave it to them.

"Take your time eating. I'll be sewing for a while tonight."

✂- - - ✂- - - ✂

Fred was waiting in the kitchen when Harriet came in through the garage door, carrying the bag of lamps she'd intended for her aunt. With the wind expected to increase, she'd parked in the garage—she didn't need a tree falling on her car. She was trying not to think about the possibility of one of the tall old fir trees falling on her bedroom.

"Maybe we'll camp out in the hall when the big storm comes," she said to Fred as she scooped a spoonful of gelatinous nutrition onto his food dish.

Three sharp raps sounded on the outside studio door as she entered from the kitchen. *The truck drivers must have taken their food to go,* she thought.

The door pushed opened before she could cross the room.

"Lauren? What are you doing here?"

"Glad to see you, too."

"I'm sorry, come in. I'm just wondering, did we have a plan?"

"Did we need one? You said you have a couple of quilts that could be finished, and my client still isn't ready, so I thought I'd come help you."

"Excuse me if I find that hard to believe, but I'll take the help for whatever reason. You can either cut batting squares at the big table, or there's a stack of blocks ready to be sewn together by the bigger of the two sewing machines."

"I don't know why I bother," Lauren said as she took her coat off and opened her quilting bag.

Harriet was helping her change the bobbin on the sewing machine when another knock on the door interrupted them. She again started for the door expecting the couple.

"Hi," Jane Morse said and walked past her and into the studio. She took her all-weather jacket off and laid it on the wingback chair in the reception area.

"I have your quilt. Did you forget to tell me something?" Harriet asked.

"It sounded like you could use another pair of hands to finish those last quilts," Jane said.

"Come on. All three of us know you're supposed to be getting ready to leave for an out-of-town meeting. Why are you really here?"

"You're really dense for someone who's supposed to be so worldly," Lauren said. "The good detective is here for the same reason I am. You're like a walking teen-age slasher movie."

"What are you talking about?" Harriet demanded.

"You mean, apart from the fact you invited a pair of serial killers to your house where, if it wasn't for us, you'd be home alone?"

"Is that true?" Harriet looked at Jane.

The detective started to say something then stopped, paused and started again.

"Okay, so I was a little concerned. You invited two total strangers to your home, at night."

"I'll be handing them a quilt, not inviting them in."

"I hate to say it, but I agree with Lauren. I know this place must seem pretty tame compared to Oakland. Isn't that where you lived before you came here?"

"Yes, there, and a lot of other places, and Foggy Point isn't what I'd call tame. We've certainly seen our share of crimes in the nine-plus months I've been here, but I'm telling you, that couple just wasn't giving off a danger vibe to me."

"Unfortunately, not all criminals are snarling pit bulls. They come in all sizes, shapes and colors," Jane said.

"I can't believe you invited a truck driver to your house when it's all over the news there's a serial killer operating along the interstate who is probably a truck driver," Lauren said.

"Okay, you're both right. It wasn't a smart move. They just didn't look like criminals to me. I saw her French manicure, diamond earrings and Seven for Mankind jeans and thought 'suburban mom.'"

"What are Seven for Mankind jeans?" Jane asked.

"They're a designer brand that run two hundred a pop," Harriet explained.

"Of course you'd know that," Lauren said. She got up from the sewing machine and crossed to the door.

"That's very observant of you," Jane said. "It raises some questions, but in the future, don't ask anyone you don't know well to come to your house when you're alone. Serial killers or even plain murderers are relatively rare, but robbers aren't. Someone might come back and break in when you aren't here."

A knock on the door saved Harriet from having to make a response. Lauren opened it and let the truck-driving pair into the quilt studio.

"I hope this helps," Harriet said and handed one of the flannel quilts to Kate.

"Thank you, this is great," she said. "The camper part of the truck is pretty well insulated, so usually, we run the heater in there until we turn the lights off and it keeps us warm all night with just a comforter."

"We really appreciate this," Owen said to Lauren. "We were going to try to find a motel, but I hate to do that when we're coming home without a load. We had something lined up, but it fell through, and now we're going to have to pay for a repair, too."

"I'm sure it's tough," Lauren said and eased him toward the door.

"Thank you again," he said to Harriet. "We better get moving and let you ladies get back to your quilting."

"There's something strange going on there, if you ask me," Lauren pronounced when Owen and Kate were gone.

"Since they're not known and loved in Foggy Point, we're probably safe," Harriet said and laughed, thinking of the murders that had happened since she'd returned, all committed by well-known members of the Foggy Point community. "They're gone now, so you two can be on your way."

Detective Morse said her goodbyes and left, but Lauren went back to her sewing machine.

"I hate to admit it, but my social life really is so pathetic I have nothing better to do tonight but help you finish quilts," she said.

Harriet tried not to smile at the admission, but her enjoyment of the moment was interrupted by a loud whoosh. A sustained gust of wind first sucked at the windows until she thought they would come out of their frames then hammered them back into place, pelting them with leaves and tree debris in the process.

"How's Carter handling the storm?" she asked, referring to Lauren's tan Chihuahua-dachshund mix.

"Not well," she said. "He's in his travel bag in the car right now. It seems to calm him to be in a small dark place. That big front window in my new apartment freaks him out when the wind hits."

"You can bring him inside if you want."

"I think he actually prefers the car right now. It's quieter. Aiden told me about a hot pad I could put in his bed. You heat it in the microwave, and it provides heat for up to twelve hours. I'll send you the link for Scooter."

"So, besides thinking I was foolish to meet the truck drivers here alone, what did you think of them?" Harriet asked her.

"I have to admit, she doesn't look like my idea of a truck-driving mama." Lauren slowly stitched through the thick flannel layers. "He seemed a little cleaner than I expected. My image involved older men with big bellies wearing faded T-shirts with beer advertisements and low-slung jeans held up with suspenders."

"That's more like what *I* would have expected. When I was in boarding school, I used to hang out at the horse barn a lot, especially during holidays when the other kids were gone. Delivery trucks would come with hay and grain for the animals, and even adjusting for the fact that we were in Europe, the drivers were a much more rugged lot than the pair we met."

"As far as I'm concerned, the jury is still out on them being serial killers, but even if they're not, there is something going on with that pair besides delivery of goods."

"We'll probably never know," Harriet said.

"Yeah, well, as long as they don't murder me, they're not my problem," Lauren said, ending the discussion.

✂ - - - ✂ - - - ✂

She finished off two more of the incomplete quilts before calling it a night.

"I'm going home," she announced.

"Thanks for helping," Harriet said. "And if we lose power, feel free to bring Carter and yourself over to stay."

"Hopefully, it won't come to that."

She gathered her quilting tools into her bag and put her coat on; Harriet walked out onto the porch with her. Rain hammered the driveway, drenching Lauren as she ran to her car. A heavy drop of rain fell inside Harriet's collar, sliding like an icy finger down her spine. She shivered and went back inside.

Fred rubbed on her leg as she returned.

"You're right. We need to check on Aiden."

She went into the kitchen and dialed Aiden's house number. Carla Salter, his young housekeeper and a fellow Loose Thread, answered.

"Hi, Harriet. Aiden's here, but he's been up in the attic with his sister for hours."

"Don't interrupt, then," Harriet replied with a sigh. They talked about the storm for a bit, and she hung up.

Chapter 6

"Want to meet for coffee?" Mavis asked when Harriet answered her phone the next morning. "Beth and Connie are calling the rest of the Loose Threads."

"What's going on?"

"Nothing, really, it's just with the slide and all, it seemed like a good time to get one more good coffee break in."

"What slide?"

"Haven't you been listening to the radio, girl?"

"No, Fred and I were doing our yoga stretches Robin gave us, so I had on the new age music we're supposed to play when we do them. What happened?"

"It turns out those 'watch for slides' signs have finally born fruit. The road out of Foggy Point is blocked in that wooded stretch before you reach the highway."

"How bad is it?"

"The hillside slid all the way from the top and went across the road and into the river. It only partially blocked the Muckleshoot, but it isn't good."

"Was anyone hurt?"

"One truck was hit, but they were mostly past so it just knocked them around."

"Where are we meeting?"

"The Steaming Cup."

"I can be there in about fifteen minutes," Harriet said; Mavis told her that would be perfect.

✂- - - ✂- - - ✂

Harriet wore a long-sleeved T-shirt, her gray hoodie and jeans under her hip-length Gore-Tex jacket, and she was still cold when she went outside. She'd slipped on the ankle-high rubber-coated boots her aunt had suggested when Harriet was catalog-shopping for winter wear—as usual, Beth had been right. The wind and rain combined with dropping temperatures was brutal, but at least her feet were warm and dry.

The Loose Threads who were still in town were already sitting around a big table in the coffee shop when she arrived. Carla's toddler Wendy sat in Mavis's lap drinking chocolate milk from a lidded cup with a straw.

"Does everyone still have power?" Robin asked. One-by-one the women nodded assent. "Well, at least that's something."

"Go get your drink," Aunt Beth instructed Harriet. "We've got things to talk about."

Like an obedient child, she did as instructed, returning a few minutes later with a large hot chocolate and a warm cinnamon roll.

"So, what do we have to talk about, other than the weather?" she asked when she sat down.

"Harriet and I finished the last two quilts in progress last night," Lauren volunteered.

"There's still a lot of fabric if anyone wants to start more," Harriet added.

"Marjory's in trouble," Aunt Beth said, abruptly changing the subject. "I called her this morning on her cell phone. She'd left town early to drive her mother's car to Seattle. Got out just in time before the slide, too."

"What's the problem?" Connie asked. "Does she need us to take care of the store?"

"I wish it were that simple," Beth said. "It's much worse, I'm afraid. I was talking to her, and then I heard a siren in the background. She said she had to go, that the police were pulling her over."

"Why?" Connie asked.

"How should she know?" Lauren answered. "Beth just said she hung up."

"I didn't say she hung up," Beth corrected. "I said she told me she had to go. She was so rattled she just dropped the phone on the car seat. I couldn't hear clearly, but I got most of it. The policeman said her mother's car had been reported stolen."

"*What?*" Harriet said.

"He said the car had been reported stolen, and Marjory was to keep her hands where he could see them and get out of the car." Beth paused for effect. "Marjory apparently did so, but she was hollering up a storm. She said she was going to kill Pat."

"Who is Pat?" Carla asked in a quiet voice.

"Pat is Marjory's sister," Mavis said. "She's been giving Marjory a hard time about their parents' estate. She's supposed to be coming here uninvited to visit Marjory and talk about it."

"So what happened?" Harriet asked.

"I'm not positive, but I think they arrested her. At the very least, it sounded like they took her into custody."

"Did you call the police?" Robin asked.

"That's why I called all of you," Beth said. "I called Foggy Point Police, and they didn't know anything. I tried Seattle, but all I got was the run-around. I'm pretty sure she wasn't that far, anyway. I don't know what jurisdiction she's in, so I don't know who to call."

"Let me see what I can do," Robin said and pulled her cell phone from her purse before walking away from the table.

"That's really bizarre," Connie said. "What could they possibly arrest Marjory for? It's her parents' car...and isn't she the executor of their estate?"

"If it was really reported stolen, don't you think it was her sister?" Harriet asked. "Who else would be in a position to know Marjory would be driving a car that wasn't hers on this particular day?"

"You mean besides us?" Lauren asked.

"None of us reported that car stolen, and you know that," Mavis said.

"Hey, I was just answering the question." Lauren slouched down in her chair and gripped her mug of coffee in two hands.

Robin paced in the entrance area, her cell phone to her ear. She stopped and opened the door when she reached it, stepping aside to let a small group of people enter. Ronald, Joyce and Duane from the homeless camp stepped to the counter and ordered coffee drinks before crossing the room to the Loose Threads' table.

"Thank you so much for the flannel quilts," Joyce said.

"I slept a lot warmer last night," Duane added. "And I'm pretty sure Brandy did, too."

"We're happy to help out." Aunt Beth said with a smile.

Harriet couldn't help but stare when the trio's drinks were called and Duane retrieved them, bringing back expensive latte and mocha concoctions.

Ronald looked sheepish.

"I know this looks crazy," he said. "But my daughter gave me a Latte Lovers gift card here for my birthday. She had no idea I was losing the house and could have used a night at a hotel, or cold hard cash, much more than frivolous coffee drinks."

"The milk part is nutritious, and they're warming," Joyce said. "And Ronald was generous enough to share with us."

"Which we greatly appreciate," Duane added.

"How did you get here?" Lauren asked. "The park is a long way from here."

Mavis glared at her.

"What my friend is trying to ask is if you'd like her to give you a ride home," she said.

Lauren's eyes got big as she stared at Mavis.

"That would be nice," Joyce said. "We got a ride in from a young couple in a semi. They were on their way to the hardware store to buy parts to fix their heater. They said they'd check to see if we needed a ride back before they left town."

"I hope they were able to fix their heater," Harriet said. "With the slide, they're likely to be stuck here a few days, at least."

"What slide?" Ronald asked.

The Loose Threads told them about the slide that had closed the road in and out of Foggy Point.

"That's terrible," Duane said.

Joyce smiled.

"It's not like we were going to be leaving town anytime soon," she said. "I wonder if the young people got out. The group that was at the church when you were delivering the quilts to us was planning on heading south for the rest of the winter."

Robin returned. The group looked at her expectantly, but she said nothing.

"Come on, fellas," Joyce said. "Let's take advantage of those soft chairs over there." She led the men to a grouping of upholstered chairs on the far side of the room. Aunt Beth smiled thanks at her; then, everyone turned to Robin.

"Well?" Beth encouraged her.

Robin sat down and picked up her cup.

"I called in a few favors and represented myself as Marjory's counsel, which she may or may not back up, but I did find her."

"Where is she?" Beth asked.

"As I said, I had to pull in a few favors, but even then, because of confidentiality laws, my source couldn't directly confirm this information."

"For crying out loud," Lauren snapped, "where is she?"

"I believe she's being held under a fifty-one-fifty order." Several of them began to speak, but Robin held her hand for silence. "Washington State's Involuntary Treatment Act allows designated reporters to invoke a seventy-two-hour hold at a mental health facility on behalf of anyone they believe is a danger to themselves or others. Depending on exactly where they picked her up, she's either at the Snohomish County facility in Mukilteo or at Stevens Hospital in Edmonds."

"You can't be serious," Harriet said.

"How can that be?" Aunt Beth said at the same time.

"Diós mio," Connie said and covered her face with her hands.

"How do we get her out?" Carla asked.

"Unfortunately, until the seventy-two hours are up, we don't," Robin replied. "She can't leave, and she isn't entitled to legal representation until she's been evaluated and then appears in court after the hold expires. And, by the way, the seventy-two-hour clock doesn't tick on weekends or holidays, so I can't even see her until next Monday."

"What do you think happened?" Mavis asked. "Surely, they can't have locked Marjory up because she said she'd kill her sister for reporting the car stolen."

"My suspicion is that whoever reported the car stolen probably also painted Marjory as an unstable person, likely to harm herself or others. Unfortunately, it sounds like she played right into the hands of whoever did that."

"What if the river rises while she's gone?" Carla asked. Wendy squirmed in Carla's lap and tried to get down. Her mother pulled a small wooden puzzle from her purse and dumped the pieces onto the table in front of her.

"Water will fill the basement and part of the first floor at Pins and Needles," Lauren said.

"And unless we move Marjory's fabric, she'll lose it all," Mavis added.

"How are we supposed to do that with her locked in the loony bin?" Lauren asked.

"Don't you think Marjory would want us to break a window or something to get in if it meant we could save her inventory?" Connie pointed out.

"Not when we have a key," Aunt Beth announced.

"We have a key?" Harriet asked.

"Carla?" Aunt Beth said.

Carla reached into her bag and fished around, bringing out a bright-pink rubber keychain. She held it up for everyone to see. She'd worked part-time at Pins and Needles after being laid off from her job at the local vitamin factory the previous spring. Aiden had hired her as his full-time housekeeper when he inherited his mother's large Victorian home, but they'd both agreed she could still work for Marjory a few hours a week while Wendy went to a toddler program at the Methodist church, so Marjory wouldn't be left in the lurch.

"She gave it to me to use in case of emergency." Carla said.

"I think flooding qualifies as an emergency." Lauren took a drink of her latte. "And let's not wait until the water is at the doorstep. It's going to take a while to move that much fabric if we have to go up and down that attic ladder of hers."

"Does anyone know how close to flood stage the river is?" Mavis asked.

Carla pulled a smartphone from her purse and, with a glance at Lauren, tapped on its face. Lauren looked on like a proud parent. She'd undoubtedly had something to do with Carla's newfound technical prowess, Harriet thought.

"Two more feet to reach flood stage," Carla reported, her cheeks turning pink.

"It's another three feet or so to street level," Harriet said. "But once it goes over the street it's right into the basement."

"I didn't know Marjory had a basement," Connie said.

"She doesn't keep anything of consequence down there," Mavis said. "The people she bought it from warned her about the flood potential. She just stores spare shelving and tables."

"I'm with Lauren," Harriet said. "If we're going to have to do a major move, I think we should start sooner rather than later. The rain isn't supposed to let up, and if the windstorm knocks any big trees over the roads or even in the river near here, the shop could be in trouble without much warning."

Ronald had gone for a refill and stopped by the Threads' table on his way back to his chair.

"I couldn't help but overhear your concern about the quilt store flooding. I'd like to offer my services to help move inventory," he said. "I'm sure Duane and Joyce would be happy to help also. It's not like we have homes or families to take care of." His face reddened as he said the last part. "It might help us feel more normal."

"Thank you," Aunt Beth said. "We'll let you know the plan before we all leave."

He went back to his companions and recounted his offer. Harriet saw Joyce nodding thoughtfully as he spoke.

"I guess that's it, then," Aunt Beth said. "When do you all want to start?"

"I'd just as soon get it over with, before the wind picks up," Harriet said.

Connie and Mavis agreed.

"I'll need to check with Aiden," Carla said. "I need to see if he wants me to do anything for his sister now that she's stuck here."

"Michelle is still here?" Harriet felt the muscle in her jaw tighten and willed it to relax.

"She was going to leave yesterday," Carla explained. "But they talked so late last night, she decided to stay over. She was still in bed when Wendy and I left for here."

"Hey, is this a party?" Tom Bainbridge asked. Rainwater dripped from his hair. Harriet had been so focused on Carla's news she hadn't noticed him arrive.

"You're stuck here, too?" Lauren asked.

"I think that's obvious, don't you?" he shot back. "I ran into one of my mom's old friends yesterday and stayed for dinner with her and her husband. I let them convince me it was too late to drive home in all this rain." He gestured toward the chaos outside the window. "So, here I am."

"Want to help move fabric to the attic of the quilt store?" Harriet asked.

"Why not? It's not like I've got anything else to do."

Chapter 7

"Did anyone talk to Sarah today?" Connie asked as the group returned their used coffee mugs to the bar.

"I called to tell her about coffee this morning, but she said she's at her boyfriend's house and he didn't want her to leave his cat alone." Mavis shook her head in disbelief. "Apparently, he thinks the cat is having emotional problems due to his absence."

"Oh, for crying out loud," Lauren said. "I think we need to go check on her. I want to see with my own eyes that cat is the only reason she's not coming to quilting anymore."

"Would anyone care to give us a ride?" Ronald asked hopefully.

"You're going to have to get used to taking the bus," Joyce scolded him. "That's why the church gave us these passes."

"Of course you can ride with us," Aunt Beth said. "I've got room for two people if one doesn't mind crawling into the back seat of my Beetle."

"I've got room," Harriet said, and with the transportation settled, the group drove to Pins and Needles.

✂ - - - ✂ - - - ✂

"How about Lauren and I go up to the attic and see what's already up there," Harriet suggested. "Duane and Rodney could go to the basement and see what's down there. If there are folding tables, they might be useful for stacking bolts of fabric, and at the very least, we could bring them up out of the flood zone."

"Sounds like a plan," Mavis said. "Come on, gentlemen, I'll show you where the basement door is."

"Where *is* the attic access, anyway?" Lauren asked.

"I'll show you," Carla volunteered, and led them to the hallway outside the kitchen at the back of the store. She picked up a broom handle that had a large metal hook in place of the bristles and with a practiced move used it to grab the latch to a set of accordion stairs that folded down from the ceiling.

"I'm not seeing Mavis or Beth going up and down these babies," Lauren said as she stepped onto the first of the steep, narrow steps and began to climb.

Harriet followed and was soon standing in the large attic that covered the entire square footage of the store below. Three eight-foot tables were lined up against the front wall of the building, bolts of fabric wrapped in plastic stacked six bolts high on each table. Plastic storage bins were neatly stowed under each table.

"Here's a bin marked 'tablecloths,'" Harriet said as she opened the container and verified that it was, indeed, full of tablecloths.

"Are we having a party?" Lauren asked as she took the two cloths Harriet handed her and spread them on the floor. Harriet took two more and laid them next to Lauren's.

"Let's stack the tables as high as we can, and then we can start putting bolts on the cloths on the floor."

"Beth told us to bring these tables up to you ladies," Duane said as he fell through the stair opening along with the table he was dragging up the stairs. Ronald followed, dragging another table that was obviously being pushed from below. The two men were red-faced from the effort.

"Thanks, guys. I'm not sure how many more you have, but I think with what's here it'll be enough for now."

Lauren looked at Harriet as she spoke. Harriet was pretty sure they were thinking the same thing she was—the two men looked like heart attacks waiting to happen. Whatever they had been do-ing before they became homeless it clearly hadn't involved manual labor.

"I think we should do some sort of bucket brigade-style line," Tom was saying when Harriet and Lauren returned to the fabric sales room where the others were milling about.

"Tom's right," Beth agreed. "We need an organized plan. Otherwise, we're going to be getting in each other's way."

"Marjory has some wheeled carts we use for stocking," Carla offered. She went to the small room where Marjory unpacked new fabric as it arrived. She came back wheeling a flat-topped cart that could accommodate two stacks of fabric bolts side-by-side lengthwise and fit easily in even the narrowest aisles in the store.

"There are two more of these in the packing room," she said.

Connie quickly organized the volunteer team into four groups. Ronald, Duane, and Beth loaded fabric onto the carts. Joyce and Mavis pushed the carts to the stairs and back. Carla handed bolts to Lauren, Tom and Harriet to carry up the steep stairs.

When Robin arrived, she went into the attic and received the fabric from the person climbing the stairs then put it onto a table or cloth. To the degree possible, everyone was trying to keep groupings of fabric together the same way they were displayed on the sales floor, in the hope that it would make setting up downstairs easier when the flood was over.

"Sounds like it's still raining out there," Harriet said when she reached the bottom of the stairs for what felt like the millionth time.

Tom came up behind her and pointed toward the kitchen window.

"It's getting worse," he said as rain sheeted against the glass.

Before Harriet could look, she heard the jingle of the front door bells and turned to see who'd come into the store. A gust of wind tore the door from the hand of the visitor, slamming it hard against the wall. A large form covered from head to toe in wet yellow oilcloth lurched through the opening, a dark blue plastic bin held with two hands.

Whoever it was set the box down and scraped the hood from their head. Jorge's black hair was plastered against his forehead and his face was wet, but his smile warmed the room.

"I heard you all were rescuing Marjory's inventory from the coming flood, and I thought you could use some sustenance."

"You are a godsend, my man," Duane boomed as he edged closer to the food box.

"Where do you want to eat?" Jorge asked.

"Let's go to the bigger classroom," Robin suggested.

Carla brought paper cups from the kitchen then a pitcher she'd filled from the tap. Jorge unloaded pork tacos, beef taquitos, chicken and cheese quesadillas and a big container of guacamole.

"This is a real nice thing you're doing for Marjory," he said when he'd finished laying out the food. "That river looks real angry. There's a group of people at the Sandwich Board moving stuff. They're hauling tables and chairs away in a truck."

"We appreciate the food," Aunt Beth said.

"It was the least I could do. Robin stopped in to order take-out for her husband to pick up later, and she told me what you were doing. If the power goes out, I'll lose all the fresh stuff anyway, so I might as well let you folks get some good from it."

As the group continued thanking Jorge for the food, Carla tugged on Harriet's arm and glanced toward the kitchen.

"I'm going to make some tea," Harriet said and stood up. "Would anyone like some?"

Several hands went up.

"I'll help you," Carla said.

"Come to *tia*," Connie said to Wendy and pulled the toddler into her lap.

"Me, too." Lauren got up before Harriet could protest. "Okay, spill," she said to Carla when the trio was safely out of earshot in the kitchen.

Harriet filled the electric water kettle and pushed the on button. Carla looked at her, and when she received an affirmative nod, she spoke.

"I came into the front room to get some paper and a pen for Wendy to play with. Miss Beth was in the bathroom, and everyone else was in the hallway or on the stairs or something."

"And?" Lauren prompted.

"And I saw that guy in the purple sweatshirt trying to get into the cash register."

"Are you sure he wasn't just looking for a pen or something?" Harriet asked.

"He was definitely trying to get into the register," Carla insisted, her cheeks turning red as she said it. "He was turning the key and pulling on the drawer."

"Marjory leaves the key in the register?" Lauren said.

"Yeah," Carla replied. "You have to hit a number code to be able to turn the key from locked to unlock."

"I guess we shouldn't be surprised," Harriet said. "He *is* homeless. He's probably desperate."

"It was weird, though. I wasn't sure what to do, so I watched him for a minute, and the other guy saw what he was doing and came over and made him stop. Course, that guy seems like he has better clothes and stuff. Maybe he can still afford a moral compass."

Harriet looked at Carla for a moment without speaking. Her young friend's insights surprised her sometimes.

"When we get back to work, I'll tell my aunt to keep and eye on him," she said. "Thanks for telling me."

Carla looked at her feet.

"It was weird, so I thought you should know."

"You did the right thing," Lauren said and patted her on the back in a rare show of support. "So, who wanted what tea," she asked as the water started boiling.

✂- - - ✂- - - ✂

"What did you find out about Marjory?" Jorge was asking Robin when Harriet, Lauren and Carla returned to the classroom carrying two mugs of steaming tea each.

"Nothing new," Robin said. "I have a call into her assigned social worker, but when you're on a seventy-two-hour hold they cut you off from the outside world. I called a colleague in Seattle, and if we're still stuck in seventy-two hours, he can go to her hearing with her."

"What a nightmare," Tom said. "And you have no idea what happened?"

Robin recounted what they knew, which was not much beyond the fact that Marjory had been stopped for driving a stolen car and had then been taken away on a seventy-two-hour mental health hold.

"Mavis and I are going to stay at Harriet's house tonight for the duration," Aunt Beth announced when everyone had finished eating. "Does anyone else need a more secure place to stay?"

Ronald looked like he was going to speak, but a glare from Joyce silenced him.

"Believe it or not," Joyce said. "Our camp is well-placed. We're sheltered from most of the wind, and thanks to you people, we have tarps to keep us dry and quilts to keep us warm."

"I'm bunking in the restroom when the wind picks up," Duane said. "Didn't the three little pigs find that brick was best in the face of wind?"

Harriet laughed.

"I think you're right."

"Carter is freaking out as the wind picks up, so we'll be joining the party, if the offer is still on the table," Lauren said.

"Of course," Harriet told her. "Connie?"

"Rod has our house sealed up tighter than a drum," Connie replied. "And we have a generator in the garden shed."

"Same here," Robin said. "My kids are ready for a grand adventure. I heard from DeAnn this morning, and we'll check on her house while they're gone."

"Let's get back to work so we can get to those cozy homes," Aunt Beth said.

More than half the fabric in the store had been moved upstairs when the bells on the front door of Pins and Needles jingled again.

"The store is closed," Aunt Beth said without turning to see who'd come in.

"We're not here to shop," said a large woman with short curly gray hair covered with a plastic rain bonnet. She was accompanied by an equally portly man and a sullen-looking younger woman.

"I'm afraid I don't understand, then." Aunt Beth turned to face the visitors. "Oh," she said when she recognized the woman and her companions. "It's you."

"Are you twins?" Lauren asked. "Believe me, I know twins, and you've got to be Marjory's twin." In fact, Lauren *was* a twin—Harriet had met her brother Les in Angel Harbor when she and the Loose Threads attended the folk art school.

"No, we aren't *twins*," Pat said, spitting the last word out as if it were a piece of spoiled food she'd eaten by mistake.

"She is your sister, though." Aunt Beth said. "And I'm guessing you know where she is better than we do."

"I'm sure I don't know what you mean," Pat said, her spine stiffening and her cheeks coloring.

"You did report your mother's car as stolen, didn't you?"

"I did notice it was missing from the driveway. What was I to think, her living near that park and all? The car was missing, I assumed it had been stolen." She stared rather pointedly at the homeless trio.

The looks that passed among the homeless group and the new arrivals were dangerous. Even the usually mild-mannered Joyce was glaring. Carla's eyes widened, and Lauren's jaw tightened. Harriet gently tugged on both their sleeves.

"Let's let Robin handle this," she said in a stage whisper.

"Harriet's right," Connie said. "We'll let Marjory's *attorney* take care of this."

"Let's get back to work," Harriet said, but she hung back as the others went past her and back to their jobs.

"Why are you here?" Robin asked Pat.

"I tried to call Marjory, and she didn't answer. We heard it might flood downtown and thought we should come by and check on her store."

"How did you propose to get in? Did she give you a key?"

"What are *you* people doing here if she's not?"

65

"Looking out for her interests," Robin said. "Now, what are you here for?"

She let the silence stretch to the breaking point.

"We need the key to her house," the bald man said finally.

"And who are you?" Robin asked.

"I'm Richard Reigert, Pat's husband. This is our daughter Lisa. Marjory invited us to come stay with her, and now she's gone, and well, we need to get into her house. She was to have been there when we arrived, but now it looks like she isn't going to be and here we are."

"Marjory's an early-morning person," Robin said. "Everyone knew she was going to Seattle today. You probably thought you'd be here before she drove off into your stolen-car trap."

"If you could just give us the key to her house, we'll get out of your way," Pat said in a conciliatory tone.

Robin put her hands on her hips, a grim smile on her lips.

"I'm afraid we can't do that. I don't have a key."

Harriet noticed that the lawyer in Robin worded her denial carefully, in case Carla or one of the other Threads had one.

"Well, what are we supposed to do?" Pat demanded.

"I suppose you'll have to stay in a motel until the slide is cleared."

"But we didn't bring the sufficient funds with us for a prolonged stay in a hotel," Richard protested.

"The Methodist Church has beds available for people left homeless by the storm," Robin said as she ushered them toward the door. "Now, if you'll excuse me, we've got work to do."

"I'll bet they reported the car stolen before they got to Marjory's and realized she'd left already," Harriet said when they were gone.

"Yeah, and I hope Marjory deliberately didn't leave them a key. She probably thought they were only going to be left cooling their heels for the day while she was gone." Robin said.

"Sticking them in the church shelter is perfect," Lauren said, joining them. "Not that it isn't nice for people who need it," she added.

A blast of wind grabbed the door from Robin's hand and slammed it open against the side of the wall. She wrenched it shut and turned the deadbolt for good measure.

"We better get finished and get out of here before it gets any worse," she said.

"We can't just let Marjory sit there in the hospital," Carla said.

"I'm afraid we have no choice," Robin told her softly. "We really can't do anything else for her right now. Anyway, with relatives like hers, she's probably better off riding the storm out where she is."

"Come on, people, enough with the chitchat," Lauren said. "I need to get home and pack for Harriet's."

A plastic child's wading pool sailed past the window on a heavy gust.

"Lauren's right," Harriet said and headed to the attic stairs.

✂- - - ✂- - - ✂

The group worked for another two hours, carrying bolts of fabric three and four at a time. Carla went into the kitchen and emptied the cabinets below counter level, placing the coffee filters and other supplies into black plastic garbage bags and carrying them upstairs. When she'd delivered the coffee and teapots to Lauren's waiting arms, Mavis stopped her from returning for more.

"Honey, I think you've done enough," she said. "You better get Wendy home."

They both looked at the toddler, asleep in a nest of blankets under the small kitchen table.

"Are you okay to drive?" Tom asked Carla, joining the group in the kitchen and rinsing his coffee cup at the sink. "I could drive you, if you want." He turned to look at Harriet, who was standing in the doorway. "Would you be willing to follow and bring me back to get my car?"

Harriet was going to protest but then noticed the look of relief on Carla's face.

"I'd be happy to, and I agree—it's probably time to call it a day, not only for Wendy but for everyone. The attic is full in any case."

"Where's Terry?" Lauren asked, referring to Carla's boyfriend.

"He was called in to help secure the base."

Terry was a Navy SEAL who worked in some sort of special investigative unit he never quite explained, in spite of Harriet's numerous questions about it. The naval base he worked from was also home to several nuclear-powered submarines. She knew the navy preferred its ships ride out storms in open ocean so he was very likely out to sea, but she wasn't going to mention that to Carla.

"I'll grab my bags then go pick up Mavis," Beth announced and looked pointedly at Lauren.

"I guess I'll be going by the homeless camp before I go get Carter," Lauren said. "Unless you all want to go to the church, which is what I'd do."

"Our camp will be fine," Joyce said firmly.

"I'm going to stop by the vet clinic after I drop Tom back here," Harriet announced to no one in particular.

"It's kind of spooky in here without all the fabric," Carla said and shivered, pulling her sleeping child closer to her chest.

The group filed out in silence, Robin locking the door and returning the key to Carla when the last person was out.

"Take care, everyone," Harriet said as they parted.

Chapter 8

I couldn't help but notice that Aiden hasn't checked in all day," Tom said when he and Harriet were driving back to the fabric store. "I know it's none of my business, but—"

"It isn't your business," Harriet agreed. "And we aren't going to discuss my relationship with Aiden."

"I'm sorry. I said I wouldn't pressure you, and I won't. I'm just surprised he isn't checking to be sure you're okay, or have a plan or anything."

"He knows I'll be with my aunt and we'll be okay."

"If it were up to me, you wouldn't be riding out a major storm with only your aunt for protection."

"Now, that's insulting," Harriet said. "My aunt and I can take care of ourselves, thank you very much."

"I'm doing this badly. I'm just saying, if I had the chance, I'd be there to make sure you were okay. I know you can take care of yourself, but you don't have to always do that alone. You can let someone else help sometimes."

A gust of wind hit the side of the car, causing it to swerve before Harriet fought it back to her lane.

"Can we not do this while I'm driving?"

"Okay. Just don't be surprised if I come calling. The people I'm staying with live near you, I think. Don't you live on the hill above town?"

69

Harriet sighed and gripped the steering wheel tighter.

"Okay." Tom pulled a card from the pocket of his jacket and wrote something on the back of it. "Here's my phone number and the name of the people I'm staying with. Your aunt knows them. If you need anything call...please."

She sighed again.

"Thank you, I do appreciate your concern, but we'll be fine." She pulled to the curb in front of Pins and Needles.

"I guess I'll see you on the other side, then," Tom said, and got out.

She watched until he had turned on his lights and started the engine before she drove to the vet clinic.

✂ - - - ✂ - - - ✂

"Are you looking for Aiden?" Shannon, the receptionist, asked when Harriet entered the waiting area.

"Yes, and I wanted to check on Scooter one last time, if that's okay."

"Sure," the young woman said. "I think he'd like that. We're closing down early so we can all get home before the winds pick up." The plate glass front window rattled hard in its frame. "Well, before they get worse." She gave a nervous laugh. "Do you want to go ahead and go back to the socialization area?"

Harriet followed her to the converted storage room and sat in one of the rocking chairs, shrugging out of her coat as she lowered herself to the seat. Shannon brought Scooter and set him in her lap.

"The vet techs all took off already," she explained as she draped a soft blanket square over him. "I told Aiden you're here. I'm going to be leaving, so he'll have to let you out."

Scooter shivered in that way little dogs do, more a nervous reaction than from a lack of warmth. Harriet carefully settled him closer to her chest.

"Don't worry about all the noise outside," she told the little dog. "It will all be over before you know it. You'll be all set. Aiden said they have a generator here so you'll have all the heat and lights you need. Don't expect that when you come to live at my house. We'll be using oil lamps and wearing sweaters."

"Did Carla go home?" Aiden asked without preamble as he came into the room.

"Yes, Tom drove her and Wendy home a little while ago."

"What's he doing hanging around here in this weather?"

"He's hardly 'hanging around.' He was visiting friends of his mother and got trapped by the slide."

"And he just happened to take Carla home?"

"If you must know, he and a number of other people helped us move Marjory's fabric up to her attic. The weather people are predicting the Muckleshoot will jump its banks within the next twenty-four hours and that could flood Marjory's store."

"Convenient."

"What is wrong with you? Everything was fine, and then all of a sudden you've got an excuse every time I want to see you, and now you pull this jealous routine? You're giving me whiplash."

"I've been busy. You know how my job is."

"It's never caused you to freeze me out in the past. Something else is going on. I can feel it. This isn't you."

"You don't know me. You may think you do, but you don't. I'm not who you think I am."

"Where is this coming from? Is it your sister? What has she done to you?"

"Are you done with Scooter? I need to lock up and get out of here."

"That's it? We've spent almost every day together for nine months, and now I don't know you?"

The muscle in Aiden's jaw pulsed with tension. He picked Scooter from her lap and was out the door almost before his intention registered. She waited a few minutes, but he didn't reappear. She knew employees left by the back door when the clinic was closed.

She put her coat back on and went into a hallway, through the employee locker room and out into the storm again.

✂ - - - ✂ - - - ✂

71

Harriet drove around to her garage and pressed the button on her automatic door opener. She was surprised to find two cars already in the large space. She carefully guided her car into the remaining spot.

Fred meowed loudly when she entered the kitchen.

"Oh, good, you're here," Mavis said. "We were starting to worry about you. A big branch fell onto my car as I was driving home. It like to scared me to death."

"I hope you don't mind, but we told Lauren she could park in the garage, too," Beth said.

Lauren was at the kitchen bar, talking on the house phone.

"With all the trees around this place, we didn't want anyone's car getting damaged," Beth continued. "There are branches and debris all over the road between here and Mavis's." She pulled her sweater more closely around her ample body and shivered.

Mavis rifled through the junk drawer in the kitchen then triumphantly held up a box of wooden matches.

"I want these to be easy to find," she said.

"Jorge says he's coming by with more food," Lauren said and hung up the phone. "I should have asked him to bring nachos."

Harriet went to the closet and hung up her coat. She could tell already this was going to be a long night.

The phone rang, and Lauren answered it.

"Yeah, hang on. It's Carla. She wants to talk to Harriet."

Harriet crossed the room and took the phone, turning her back on her audience. She listened for a moment.

"Sounds like you did the right thing," she said. She listened again for an extended period then recounted her visit to the vet clinic and Aiden's failure to reappear to say goodbye. She listened again. "I'm sure he's fine and will be home soon. He's probably just making sure the dogs are taken care of...Okay...You, too."

She hung up.

"Okay," Lauren demanded. "What was that all about?"

"Lauren..." Mavis scolded.

"I take it Michelle is causing problems," Aunt Beth guessed.

"She doesn't know anything for sure, but that's what she thinks. She says Aiden hasn't been acting like himself. And he's not arguing with Michelle like he usually does. She thinks he's bought into whatever his sister is selling."

"What do *you* think?" Mavis asked.

"I have to agree with Carla. Aiden is definitely not himself. He won't talk to me. He just told me earlier he's not who I think he is."

"Lordy," Mavis said. "What is that girl filling his head with?"

"Are you *sure* we know everything about him?" Lauren asked. "He was gone from here for a lot of years, first to vet school and then his jaunt to Africa."

"We know everything we need to know. He's Avanell's son," Beth said.

"She gave birth to Michelle, too," Lauren reminded her.

Harriet ignored the comment.

"Carla also said she was getting worried people might try to go back to Marjory's store to 'raid the piggy bank,' so to speak. She caught Duane eyeing the register, and she was afraid Marjory's sister and her family might break in. It turns out Marjory just hides the money in a bag in the kitchen when the store is closed. Carla wanted to tell someone that when she went to check on Wendy, she moved the bag to her diaper bag and took it to Aiden's with her."

"I hope she didn't tell Michelle about it," Lauren said.

"As a matter of fact, she made a point of telling me she didn't. It's hidden in her room. She wanted us to know so nobody would think she was stealing."

"It is surely an ill wind that has blown into this town," Mavis said.

As if on cue, the kitchen lights flashed off and then on twice before steadying again.

"Anyone want a cup of tea?" Harriet offered.

"I say get it while we can," Lauren said.

"I agree," Mavis said.

"Me, too," Beth agreed.

"What are we agreeing to?" Jorge said as he came into the kitchen from the studio. "I hope you don't mind I came in," he said. "I knocked on the door, but probably you couldn't hear me over the storm. You need to lock your door, you know? You can't be too careful." He set bags of food on the counter.

"Would you like a cup of tea before you go?" Lauren asked.

Beth glared at her before turning to Jorge.

"Let me take your coat," she said, and took Jorge's wet jacket. She hung it on the back of a chair.

Harriet filled her teakettle and set it on the stove then filled her electric kettle and plugged it in as well.

"Grab those two thermal carafes from under the counter there," Mavis directed her. "We might as well heat the kettles again and fill those up, just in case."

Harriet did as instructed, and she and Mavis filled mugs with tea bags and water then filled the carafes before joining the rest of the group, who had moved to the big table in the formal dining room. A five-branch brass candelabrum sat ready in the middle of the table, flanked by two oil lamps.

"I feel sorry for that truck-driving couple," Jorge said and took a sip of his tea. "They came in and had me make them some breakfast burritos and some chicken burritos for tomorrow in case they can't get around. They were trying to decide if they were going to try to stay in the truck or move into the restroom. I told them they should go to the church, but I guess they wanted to have their privacy."

"They aren't going to find it at the park," Lauren said. "I think some of that homeless bunch is planning on camping in the bathrooms." She tucked Carter into her sweatshirt and partially zipped it.

The group turned and looked up as one as a loud thump sounded somewhere above them.

"That can't be good," Harriet said. "It sounded like something hit the roof upstairs." She got up.

"Don't go outside," Aunt Beth cautioned. "If a tree limb broke off and fell onto the roof, it might roll off just as you go outside."

"Come on, let's go look out the upstairs windows," Lauren suggested.

She and Harriet got up and left the room. They returned a few minutes later.

"It was a broken branch," Harriet reported. "The pine tree outside my bedroom window dropped a limb on the roof. It's now in the flowerbed."

Aunt Beth looked out the dining room window. The sky was a roiling black, the ground littered with debris.

"I'm afraid there's going to be a lot of cleanup when this is all over. The number of the yard cleanup guy I used is on a magnet on the side of the fridge. He does a good job, and he's reasonable," she told her niece.

"I might have a big picture window that could blow in, but at least there aren't any trees at the—"

A huge boom cut off the end of Lauren's sentence. Blue, yellow and white light lit the dining room in rapid succession before the room went dark.

"Here we go," Mavis said.

Harriet got up and went to the window.

"The whole hill is dark," she reported.

Aunt Beth lit the candles and the oil lamps.

"Do you have wood?" Jorge asked.

"Yes," Harriet said. "There are fireplaces in the living room and the bedroom directly above it, and I have wood all set up in both."

"I'll go light them," he said.

Lauren pulled a hand crank radio from her purse and turned it on. She listened for a few moments then turned it off.

"Hope you've got room for one more," she said to Harriet. "And I hope Jorge didn't have anywhere he needed to be, either. The radio said a tree fell on the power line at the bottom of this hill. It broke the lines and tore up the power pole. They're closing the street for a quarter-mile on each side. The radio signal was cutting in and out, too, so they may not be good for much longer."

"That blue flash was more than a power line going down," Mavis said sagely. "Mark my words—that was a transformer."

"It doesn't really matter which it is," Beth said. "No power is no power, whatever the cause. I say we get our hand stitching and move to the living room in front of the fireplace. I think we have enough light to do our work."

75

"I've got an LED light on one of those elastic headbands," Harriet said. "I hang it around my neck, and it's just the right level to shine on my stitching."

"Aren't you the clever one," Aunt Beth said.

"I have something similar," Mavis said. "Only mine was *meant* to hang around my neck."

"My radio has an LED flashlight on one end," Lauren said.

Jorge came downstairs in time to hear the discussion.

"Don't worry, Señora Beth," he said. "I forgot to bring my stitching, so my hands are free to hold your light for you." He smiled at her.

Harriet raised her left eyebrow and looked at Lauren, who gave a barely perceptible shrug.

"Anyone need a refill on hot water before we move to the other room?" Harriet asked.

Everyone agreed to nurse the tea they already had in their cup, so they all migrated to the living room and found seats.

Lauren was cutting out small green leaves, her arms stretched around Carter, who was still tucked in her sweatshirt. The dog quilts the Threads had donated to a silent auction that benefited a dog adoption program had generated a number of requests for commissioned quilts. Lauren was making a variation on their hand-appliquéd quilt that had featured Yorkshire terrier faces in wreaths of green leaves. This one would feature West Highland white terrier faces, but was otherwise the same.

Harriet had needed to cough to cover her gasp at the price Lauren had quoted the woman who requested the quilt after the silent auction had concluded. She was equally shocked when the woman didn't bat an eye but instead pulled out a checkbook and asked how much of a deposit she wanted to get started.

"I still can't believe how much that woman is paying for that quilt," she said now.

"I figure if everyone who worked on the original one does their same part on this one, we can split the money and it will go a long way toward paying for our trip to the quilt show next year."

"Maybe we should make another one and enter it in the quilt show as a group project," Mavis suggested.

Whatever the group thought of that idea was lost in a roar that sounded like a freight train going through a long tunnel. It ended as the windows on either side of the fireplace bowed in and then out violently.

Harriet put the kaleidoscope block she was piecing down on the foot stool in front of her.

"I can't concentrate on stitching with that going on," she said and gestured toward the window.

"Maybe we should play cards or something," Aunt Beth suggested. "That's what we used to do when you were little, remember?"

"Now you're talking," Jorge said. "Where do you keep the cards?"

Aunt Beth pulled open a drawer in the lamp table next to the recliner she'd bought to replace her own favorite chair, which she'd taken to her smaller house when she'd downsized.

"What are we playing?" Mavis asked. "Canasta? Bridge?"

"Poker," Jorge said as he carried the cards and an oil lamp back to the dining room.

"Deal me in," Lauren said and followed him.

✂ - - - ✂ - - - ✂

The raucous card game was just the distraction everyone had needed. Jorge commandeered one of Aunt Beth's old sun visors he'd seen in the coat closet and used two rubber bands as sleeve garters on his white shirt to dress the part of a Vegas dealer. Harriet donated the jar of change from her bedroom dresser in lieu of poker chips, and the game was on.

In spite of Mavis's tamer card game suggestions, she turned out to be quite the card sharp and ended up with the lion's share of the money by the time the rest of the group gave up several hours later.

"It must be time to eat," Jorge said. "These bands are squeezing the feeling out of my hands. I need to cook while I still can."

He took off his visor and the bands and headed to the kitchen. Rain was hammering the windows, but the wind had eased slightly.

"I'm taking Carter out whether he wants to go or not," Lauren said.

"Let me go get Curly, and I'll join you," Mavis said. "Beth, you want me to bring Pamela down?"

"Thanks," Beth said. "I'm sure she'll come out from under the bed if Curly leaves the room."

The rescued dogs were all dealing with the storm noises in their own way. Curly had holed up in her carry bag while her sister Pamela had retreated to the dark space under the bed. Lauren's Carter was the only one of the dogs who was willing to tough it out with the humans. For his part, Fred was meowing a running commentary on the storm's progress.

✂ - - - ✂ - - - ✂

"Between the storm settling, Jorge's wonderful meal, and all the poker frivolity, I think I can sleep, so I'm going to turn in unless anyone needs something," Harriet said when they'd finished the delicious pork burritos.

Jorge had insisted he would sleep on the sofa downstairs so he wouldn't displace any of the women upstairs.

"I think it's because he snores," Aunt Beth said with a knowing glance over the banister as she and Harriet climbed the stairs behind Lauren and Mavis.

Harriet hoped she was merely speculating.

Chapter 9

The first thing Harriet noticed when she woke up was the silence. The second was Fred sinking his needle-sharp claws into the calf of her right leg when she attempted to move.

"Stop," she said and batted him away. She listened again. The wind had stopped.

She shivered as she got out of bed and into her bathrobe then started for the window. She turned at a knock on her door.

"Come in."

Aunt Beth came in carrying two mugs of steaming tea.

"Don't look outside," she said. handing one to her niece.

"Well, now I have to, don't I? I mean, you can't say something like that and seriously think I won't look."

"Let me rephrase," her aunt said. "Brace yourself."

"That bad?"

"Worse. Go ahead and look."

Harriet went to the window and pulled the curtain aside. Beth was right—nothing could have prepared her for the scene outside.

Broken limbs and branches littered her driveway and the road beyond, but that was to be expected. As she looked down at the neighborhood that stepped down the hill below her house, what she saw looked like a scene from a made-for-TV disaster movie.

Her view used to include red and black and brown rooftops protruding through the canopy of trees. Today, foliage and roofing were all jumbled together, with trees broken and jutting through segments of roofs or tangled in torn power lines. It looked like the older Victorian houses with their multiple steep roofs had fared better than the newer flat-roofed contemporary homes that had been built lower down the hill. Two streets down, she saw a red sports car with its top caved in by an iron shepherd's hook that had formerly held a large peat moss flower basket, which was now neatly deposited in the front seat of the small car.

A cloud of smoke floated up from the downtown area. It was unclear whether it was vigorous fireplace output or a burning building. Harriet hoped for the first.

Mavis shuffled into the room in her plaid wool bathrobe and fleece-lined moose-skin slippers, a ceramic mug grasped in both hands.

"This is the worst I've seen in at least twenty years, maybe more," she said.

"How'd Curly do last night?" Harriet asked.

Mavis crossed the room and looked out.

"See for yourself." She gestured toward the window. Jorge was on the grassy area to the inside of the circular driveway, a dog leash in each hand, Curly and Brownie tugging hard in opposite directions, their noses to the ground.

"Okay, they don't look worried," Harriet said. "Unlike Fred, who was up and down all night. I don't suppose the power came on, did it?" Harriet asked sent a hopeful look at her aunt.

"You did just look out the window, didn't you?" Beth asked.

"Is this a slumber party?" Lauren asked as she came in. She wore her zip-front sweatshirt over her pajamas, her little dog tucked between. "Power is the least of our problems. I listened to the Seattle news on my radio, and they said the Muckleshoot is over its banks."

"Did they say if it's over the bridge?" Harriet asked.

"I said I listened to the *Seattle* news. We're lucky they even mentioned the Muckleshoot, much less Foggy Point and our bridge. They did say more rain is expected—a lot more."

"That's all we need," Mavis said.

"Speaking of water," Lauren said. "What's the situation on ours?"

"There's a fifty-gallon drum of water in the garage we can use for bathing, if the water system is contaminated." Beth said. "You'd think they could have found a better place for the municipal water source—somewhere that wasn't right in the middle of the Muckleshoot's flood plain."

"If I remember right, when this came up before, they said it was located there because they're drawing water from wells and that's where they found water," Mavis explained.

"I've got three cases of individual bottles and ten one-gallon jugs in the garage for drinking." Harriet added.

"Mavis and I brought our camping showers over," Aunt Beth continued. "We can heat water on the gas stove and put it in the solar shower bag and hang it from the shower head in the bathroom. It only takes three to four gallons for a shower, and that includes washing your hair."

"I'm impressed," Lauren said.

"This isn't our first rodeo," Mavis told her. "You should have seen it back in nineteen-ninety. All the rivers flooded in November."

"Yeah, they lost the span of bridge on I-Ninety between Mercer Island and Seattle," Aunt Beth said.

"And then we got eighteen inches of snow in December," Mavis continued. "And I had all the boys at home back then. We were without power for a week. I dug out the camping equipment, including the sun shower, and it was a lifesaver."

"How's the food situation?" Harriet asked.

"Heaven knows," her aunt replied. "That man won't let us in the kitchen."

✄ - - - ✄ - - - ✄

"I wonder how the homeless camp fared," Harriet said as she joined the rest of the Loose Threads, who were drying their hair in front of the fireplace.

"Sit here," Lauren said and got up from the footstool she was sitting on. She ran a wooden-handled hairbrush through her long, blonde hair. "I have to go check Carter. He wouldn't eat with the other dogs, so I shut him in the downstairs bathroom with his dish."

Mavis had wound her hair on curlers and was bent over at the waist, exposing the top of her head to the heat.

"We did what we could, but until the roads are clear Joyce and the others are on their own," she said.

"And we did offer to take them to the church," Aunt Beth pointed out. "They turned us down flat. There's not much we can do if they don't want help."

"Your breakfast is served in the dining room, ladies," Jorge called from the next room.

Harriet was impressed. He had made cheese omelets and hash brown potatoes and served them on plates with cut-up apples, oranges, bananas and toast points.

"This looks fabulous," Mavis said. "How did you make toast without any power?"

"You have a gas stove. What more does a person need?"

"I'm not trading my toaster in anytime soon," Lauren said as she returned, Carter again tucked into her sweatshirt.

A knock on the front door interrupted them before they started eating. They looked at each other.

"Who on earth could that be?" Lauren wondered.

"Let's find out," Jorge said and went through the entryway and opened the door.

"How's it going?" Tom Bainbridge asked as Jorge led him to the dining room.

"What are you doing here?" Harriet asked.

"Hello to you, too," he said with a grin. His normally neat hair hung at a rakish angle over his hazel eyes. He was dressed in brightly colored all-weather pants and a matching jacket. "Excuse me for checking to see how you all are doing."

He set a heaping plate, covered in waxed paper on the table.

"Mrs. Renfro baked for days in preparation for the storm, and there's just the two of them. Even with me, we can't possibly eat it all. Turns out Mr. R had an off-road utility vehicle hidden in the garage, so they unleashed me to spread baked cheer around the neighborhood. I have dozens more where these came from."

He pulled the paper off with a flourish, revealing large peanut-raisin-chocolate chip cookies.

"I take it back—I don't care why you're here, you can stay if we can keep the cookies," Harriet said.

"We can save these for lunch," Aunt Beth said with a meaningful glance at Harriet. She claimed the plate and carried it to the kitchen.

"Well, she's no fun," Tom said when Beth was out of the room. "I guess you do have plenty of food, though."

"You want to stay for breakfast?" Harriet asked. "I'm sure the neighborhood can survive without your sugary goodness for a few minutes."

"Thanks, but I'm going to try to make it to the homeless camp. During normal weather, Mr. and Mrs. R volunteer delivering meals to those folks. Mr. R was going to try to take them food this morning, and ten or fifteen years ago that would have been a good idea. I'm pretty sure eighty years are in his rearview mirror, so I'm thinking him and the Quad are not a good combo. Since Mrs. R had to dig the keys out of a bag of sugar in the pantry, I think she agrees."

"Did we just steal the homeless people's cookies?" Lauren asked.

"No, she really did bake a bunch, and she did send that plateful for you all. I just came by to see if Harriet wanted to go to the homeless camp with me." He looked at Lauren. "Sorry, the Quad only holds one passenger."

"Like that would matter." Lauren took a bite of her omelet. "Hey, there's no sense in letting the food get cold," she added when Mavis looked at her.

"I'd love to get out of here," Harriet said with glance at her.

"What's everyone looking at me for?" she protested.

"Let me get my coat and hat," Harriet said.

"I hope you have helmets for that thing." Aunt Beth said as she returned from the kitchen.

✂- - - ✂- - - ✂

The Quad turned out to be some strange combination of a golf cart and a motorcycle.

"They're called MUVs—multi-utility vehicles," Tom explained. "It's an offshoot of an all-terrain vehicle."

The small vehicle bore some resemblance to a miniature Jeep; it had a bench seat big enough for two people in the front and a small cargo bed behind. Tom assured her it could hold a thousand pounds of cargo and was currently filled with cases of canned food and bottled water destined for the homeless camp.

"Is that gas strapped to the back?" Harriet asked, noting two square red plastic cans behind the flats of food and water.

"Yeah, Mr. R said the last time the power went out for an extended period, everything ground to a halt due to an inability to pump gas. He said the town has generators in place and a supply of gas to run them, but he thinks they're reserving that capability for emergency vehicles."

"Seems like they would have planned for that a long time ago," Harriet said.

"You would think that, but I guess not. Or maybe they haven't had storms of this magnitude since people became so dependent on fossil fuels. I'm sure there was a time when they saddled up the family horse after a storm if they wanted to check on things."

"I guess so. Do we really have to wear helmets?" she asked when Tom handed her a red motorcycle one, donning a black one himself.

"This thing looks like a small car of sorts, but it really is closer to a motorcycle, and we are going to be going off-road, so, yes, we do need the helmets. Besides, I'm not crossing your aunt if I don't have to."

He helped her climb into the passenger side of the vehicle and strapped her seatbelt across her lap, returning to the driver's side and repeating the process.

"I'm worried about those people at the homeless camp," he said, a serious note in his voice.

"They should be okay if they went into the restroom. It's floor-to-ceiling cement."

"Some of them probably did, but I'm guessing the young drug addict didn't, and if she didn't, the older woman probably didn't, either. And neither of those two older guys looked like rugged outdoorsmen."

"You're right. Joyce seemed a little more skilled at camping."

"Camping is one thing, but I'll bet it's going to turn out we had eighty- or ninety-mile-an-hour winds."

Tom started the MUV, backing it up then turning to go down the side of Harriet's driveway that was free of larger tree limbs. They started downhill, and Harriet glanced back past her house to the forest at the end of her street. As they turned onto the pavement, she caught sight of Aiden's tall slender form emerging from the trees.

Chapter 10

The trip to Fogg Park and the homeless camp behind it would have taken no more than fifteen minutes under normal conditions. This time it took just over two and a half hours.

"At least it will be quicker on the way home," Tom said as he got back into the driver's seat after they had stopped for the umpteenth time to drag a large tree limb to the side of the road. The entrance to the park was visible in the distance.

"I'm just glad we didn't have to saw that one," Harriet replied. "My arms are getting tired."

"I'm glad Mr. R had the foresight to pack that little chainsaw in the cargo box."

Tom reached over and gently wiped her cheek with his thumb. She started to reach up to stop him, but he halted her hand.

"I'm not putting the moves on you. You've got mud on your cheek."

"Oh, of course. Sorry." She ducked her head to hide her embarrassment.

"Would it be that bad if I *was* touching your cheek for other reasons?" he asked softly and cupped her face in his hand, tilting it up until she couldn't avoid looking at him.

He leaned in until their lips were nearly touching. Harriet closed her eyes, but Tom pulled back.

"I promised myself I wouldn't pressure you, and I won't—but you are so beautiful," he said with a sigh. "It's taking every bit of restraint I posses." He turned away from her and steered their vehicle back onto the road.

Beautiful? she thought. Covered in mud and sweaty from the hard work, and he thought she was beautiful. She tried to remember the last time Aiden had called her beautiful—or even anything.

✂- - - ✂- - - ✂

"Oh, thank heaven you've come," Joyce said as she rushed to Harriet before she could even untangle herself from the MUV's seatbelt and get out. Tom had just pulled into the parking space closest to the restroom building.

"What's wrong?" Harriet asked. She put her arm around the older woman to steady her.

"It's just awful," Joyce said as tears began streaming down her deathly white face.

"Here, sit down." Harriet eased her into the seat she'd just vacated. Tom opened a bottle of water and handed it to her without saying anything. Joyce took a small sip, paused then took a longer drink.

"Can you tell us what's upset you?" Harriet asked in a calm voice. She put her hand on Joyce's shoulder.

"Dead," she stammered. She looked from Harriet to Tom and back to Harriet again. "Dead," she repeated.

"Joyce," Harriet said. "Look at me." Joyce complied. "Who is dead?"

Joyce started to cry again but then stopped and took a deep breath.

"Duane," she said. "Duane Cunningham."

"Where is he?" Tom asked.

Joyce pointed to the building. Tom and Harriet both looked just in time to see Ronald stagger out of the men's side and lean up against the outside wall, his red Gore-Tex jacket a stark contrast to the pitted gray cement. Tom sprinted to his side and eased him into a sitting position, loosening his jacket and then his shirt collar as he did so.

Harriet joined Tom, quickly followed by Joyce.

"Ronald, what is it?" Joyce asked. Ronald's face was pale and clammy and his breath rapid.

"Medicine," Ronald croaked.

Harriet immediately started patting his pockets, finding an amber plastic pill bottle in his right pants pocket on her third try. She glanced at the label then popped the cap and shook out a small white pill. She pressed it to Ronald's lips, and he quickly sucked the pill into his mouth and under his tongue. Slowly, the color returned to his face, and his breathing became slow and regular.

"Okay," Harriet said. "Can one of you tell us what's going on?"

"It's Duane," Joyce said again and gestured toward the men's room door.

"He's dead," Ronald finished for her.

"I'm so sorry," Harriet said.

"You don't understand." Ronald leaned forward, holding his head in his hands. "He's...*dead.*"

"What Ronald is trying to say," Joyce said, "is someone has killed Duane."

"Are you sure he didn't have a heart attack or something?" Tom asked.

Ronald looked up and tried to speak and then dropped his head again.

"We're sure," Joyce said. "Several of our group slept in the bathrooms last night. Brandy was up wandering around. She was out of it so I stayed out here with her. I finally got her to sleep it off, but the storm was over by then.

"I figured everyone would need coffee, so I built a fire and made a pot. Slowly, people came out and joined me. No one got much sleep last night. We talked, and people drifted back to their own spaces. I checked on Brandy, and when it started to rain I went back to my bed and fell asleep.

"When I woke up again, I fixed breakfast." She sighed. "I tried to find Duane to see if he wanted some and...well." She paused, searching for words. "No one had seen him since last night. Ronald went into the men's room to see if he was in there, and he found him."

"He was in his sleeping bag," Ronald said. "I thought he was asleep."

"Weren't there other people in there with him?" Harriet asked.

"We were spread out," Ronald said. "Some were in the women's room, some the men's and everyone staked out their own space. Duane was in the handicapped stall."

"Was anyone else in there with him?" asked Tom.

"No." Ronald wiped his face with his hand. "It was so much quieter in there—I fell asleep as soon as I got my sleeping bag settled. When I woke up again, I smelled Joyce's coffee so I got up and went out. It seemed like everyone else was still asleep."

"So, who else was in there?" Harriet asked.

"Well, me, of course, and the truck drivers. And some other big guy I'd never seen before, and his lady friend. They left at first light."

"Someone needs to call the police," Joyce said. "Does one of you have a cell phone?"

"Unfortunately, our phones don't work when the electricity is out over a wide area," Harriet told her.

"We can drive back by the police station if the bridge isn't out," Tom offered.

"Do you have any duct tape in the vehicle?" Harriet asked him. "We need to seal off the area to preserve the crime scene as best we can."

"Sure," he said and went to retrieve it. "Here." He handed Harriet the roll when he returned. "I'm coming in with you. It's probably not reasonable under the conditions to block people from the whole restroom. If he's in the handicapped stall, maybe we can just tape it shut."

Harriet agreed and led the way into the small building. The area smelled faintly of bleach and pine cleaner. She supposed either the park or the homeless people kept it cleaner than a usual public facility because of their daily use of the space. The outside temperature was running only a few degrees above freezing, so they wouldn't have to worry about Duane's decomposition for a while.

"We can tape the door shut without looking, you know," Tom suggested.

"I'm sorry, but I need to have a look," Harriet said with a weak smile.

She pulled her gloves from her pocket and put them on before carefully opening the stall door and leaning her head in. At first glance, you couldn't tell anyone was under the pile of blankets next to the toilet. She recognized one of the Loose Threads' flannel quilts on top. She stepped in and gently pulled the corner of the quilt away from the top end of the pile, revealing the remains of Duane.

In what she now realized was a bout of magical thinking, she had hoped Ronald had been so overcome he had exaggerated the situation, and that Duane was either asleep or perhaps had hit his head or had some other less fatal misadventure. One look at the cord wrapped around Duane's neck beneath his blue face, and she knew there had been no mistake. Duane was very definitely dead.

"Come on," Tom said and gently pulled her back out of the stall. "We've seen enough. He's gone."

He shut the door, took his gloves off and began sealing the door with the duct tape.

"Why on earth would anyone want to kill such a sweet old man?" Harriet asked.

"Why does anyone kill anyone? Besides, maybe he *wasn't* a nice old man. You've only known him, what? A few days?"

"I guess. It's still sad, though. At least he had a nice flannel shroud."

"That's something, anyway. My mother would have thought so," he said.

"We probably should unload the food and get on to the police station."

"If we *can* get there," he cautioned.

Chapter 11

Tom pulled the red MUV to a stop on the approach to the bridge over the Muckleshoot River, facing downtown Foggy Point on the opposite side. Harriet took a deep breath. The air smelled of pine from all the broken trees and the associated debris.

The drive from the homeless camp had been more exciting than she had anticipated. Downed power lines lay across roadways, still tangled in the trees that had pulled them down. They'd passed workers from the Foggy Point PUD at one point, chainsaws in hand, trying to restore order to the mess. After cautioning Tom to give any downed wires a wide berth, they'd reported that, in reality, there wasn't much danger until someone was able to locate the break in the main feeder line that provided electricity to the whole peninsula, which could take days.

"We can still turn back," he offered as they watched the Muckleshoot River rush by, lapping at the edge of the bridge on both sides. "If we go across, there's no guarantee we can get back."

"I guess we better hurry, then," Harriet said.

Without a word, he released the brake and crossed the bridge.

Driving in the downtown area was slightly easier, since there were fewer trees to drop broken limbs, but there was still plenty of debris on the ground. A few shopkeepers were out surveying the damage and clearing the sidewalks around their businesses. Tom quickly guided their small vehicle to the Foggy Point Police Department.

Harriet hopped out and went to the door as soon as Tom had stopped. Officer Hue Nguyen met her at the door. He was obviously leaving.

"I hope you've come to volunteer," he said with a glance at the all-terrain vehicle they had arrived in.

"I'm afraid not," Harriet told him. She had met the young Asian officer earlier in the year when she'd been assaulted.

His jaw tightened in preparation for what was probably going to be bad news of some sort.

"We've come to report a murder," Harriet went on. "At the homeless camp."

"Oh, geez. Who was killed? Do you know what happened? Was it a fight?"

"We don't really know anything," Tom said. He'd joined them after securing the MUV. "We went there to deliver supplies from my hosts, and the residents had just discovered one of their group dead."

"You said murder," Nguyen said. "Are you sure?"

"The guy has a wire wrapped around his throat, so, yeah, I'm pretty sure it's murder," Harriet told him. "We looked, just to be sure, and then we taped the bathroom stall he's in closed and came here."

Nguyen ran his hand through his short black hair.

"No one's here but me. The detectives all went to what was supposed to be a daylong task force meeting about the killings along the interstate, and then the slide happened, and the last time we were able to speak, they were stuck there. I talked to them on the satellite phone, but they don't have power yet either. No one is willing to pay for a helicopter to fly them back, so I guess we're on our own for now."

"Where are all the other *officers*?" Harriet asked.

"Stuck at home, I guess. No one has a satellite phone at home, and our cell phones aren't working, so I came down here, hoping someone would show up."

"Do you want me to run you up to the homeless camp?" Tom asked. "After I take Harriet home."

"Thanks, but I rode my off-road bike down here," he said and pointed to a muddy blue motorcycle parked near the door to the station. "I'll go by the camp on my way to check on my mother. You should probably get back across the bridge before it floods out."

"I want to go check the fabric store for Marjory before we leave," Harriet said.

"Be quick about it," Nguyen ordered. "I think most people have already left for higher ground. I wouldn't want to see you get stuck here."

"Thanks for the advice," Tom said as he and Harriet turned to go back to their vehicle. "Might be fun," he mumbled.

"What did you say?" Harriet said.

"You heard me. I said it might be fun being trapped alone with you."

"You're crazy." She climbed back into her seat and strapped on her seatbelt.

It took less than five minutes to drive to the quilt store. Tom kept glancing nervously back toward the river, but he didn't suggest turning around. As they turned the last corner, Harriet could see two figures huddled at the door to Pins and Needles.

"What are those people doing?" she wondered.

"Let's find out." Tom slid out of the driver's seat. "Hey, what are you doing?" he shouted as he approached the pair.

They turned, and Harriet saw it was Marjory's sister and brother-in-law.

"What are you doing?" she demanded.

Pat's hair hung in limp curls on her neck. She was wearing the same clothes she'd had on the day before, now considerably more wrinkled.

"We wanted to make sure Marjory's shop survived the storm," Richard answered. A screwdriver dangled from his left hand. He belatedly looked for someplace to conceal it with no luck.

"So you thought you'd just break in?" Tom pulled out his phone as if to dial 911.

"Marjory's not in any position to let the police know you aren't common criminals, so I guess you're on your own," Harriet said.

"Now, wait one minute," Richard said, pulling himself up to his full, not very impressive height. "It's not like we've done anything, here. We just were looking in the window."

"You were here yesterday. You know we've already moved her inventory up to the attic," Harriet pointed out.

"Okay, you've got us—we're hungry," Pat said. "We're stuck here, and we're hungry. We were trying to get in to see if Marjory had any food inside."

"Didn't you go to the church shelter?" Tom asked. "They have food."

"No," Richard answered. "We decided to stay in our car."

"Lisa didn't want to sleep in the same room with strangers," Pat explained.

"So, she'd rather be hungry?" Harriet asked.

"We thought we'd be able to go to the church in the morning," Pat replied. "We tried, but…" She spread her arms out to indicate the mess around her.

Harriet just shook her head.

"You're going to have to get to a shelter," Tom told them. "I haven't seen any open stores. You need to get across the bridge before the river swamps it then see if you can make your way to one of the churches or schools."

"What if we can't get to one?" Pat asked, a real note of panic in her voice for the first time.

Harriet's shoulders sagged, but before she could speak, offering Pat and Richard a place at her house, Tom said, "I have a nice plate of cookies to tide you over until you make your way to a shelter. Wait right here."

"What are *you* doing here, anyway," Pat asked, recovering her composure. "Didn't Marjory tell me your aunt has a big house up on the hill?"

"Yeah, if the river is so dangerous, why are you here?" Richard said.

"If you must know, my friend and I were delivering supplies to the homeless camp. One of their members didn't survive the night.

We came to notify the police, and thought we'd check and see how Marjory's store fared. As we all know, she's not able to do it herself."

"Was it one of the people who helped you pack up the shop yesterday?" Richard asked.

"What's it to you? Why the sudden interest in the homeless people?"

"Was it?" He pressed, a steely tone entering his voice.

"As a matter of fact, it was—one of the men."

"Which one?" He leaned toward her.

"The guy with the deep voice," she said, stepping away. "Duane."

Richard sighed and rocked back on his heels, his gaze far away from Pins and Needles.

"Did you know Duane?"

"Me?" Richard asked. "Of course not. I just noticed the two fellows in the shop yesterday."

Harriet tried to think back to the day before to remember if she'd noticed any interaction between Richard and the homeless trio, but too much had happened since then.

Tom returned a moment later with one of the plates of cookies from his hostess, and it was as if Richard's intense interest in the homeless man had never happened. He grabbed the cookies from Tom's hands and barely let Pat have a crack at them. It would have been funny if it hadn't been so pathetic.

Tom took her firmly by the arm and started to lead her away, but she stopped and turned back to Pat and Richard.

"You're wasting your time, you know."

They looked up at her, crumbs trailing from both their mouths.

"Marjory doesn't leave any cash in the shop when she isn't there," she lied. She turned away from them and hurried toward the MUV.

"What was that about?" Tom asked her when she was back in her seat.

"Oh, I was just trying to discourage Richard from his larcenous inclinations."

"Good luck with that. He looks like he was born sleazy." He turned the MUV on. "We need to get you home," he said.

Chapter 12

I 'm starving," Harriet announced as she came into the kitchen from the garage. She was carrying a bottle of water in each hand.

"Is Tom with you?" Aunt Beth asked, eyeing the extra water.

"No, he went back to check on the Renfros." She looked down at the extra bottle she was holding. "I'm just really thirsty." She sat down at the breakfast table and opened one of the bottles, nearly draining it before setting it down again.

"How was it out there?" Mavis asked as she joined them.

Harriet sagged back in her chair.

"It's awful."

"That bad, huh?" Lauren asked, as she, too, entered the kitchen. "So, spill," she said and slid into the chair opposite Harriet. "What was the worst you saw?"

"That would be Duane." Harriet sighed. She looked up gratefully as Mavis slid a plate with half of a peanut butter-and-jelly sandwich on it in front of her.

Aunt Beth lifted the lid of a large pot that was simmering on the stove, and the room was filled with the spicy smell of chili.

"We're having dinner shortly," she said as she stirred it and replaced the lid. "We thought we'd eat before it gets dark."

"Not that it ever really got light," Mavis remarked, looking through the window at the gray sky outside.

"Come on, throw us a bone," Lauren said. "What happened to Duane?"

"He's dead."

"*What?*" Aunt Beth exclaimed. "Did he have a heart attack or something?"

"It was more in the 'or something' category."

"Don't be a drama queen." Lauren prompted. "Spit it out."

"Someone strangled him during the storm."

"Who?" Lauren asked.

"Do you think I'd have said 'someone' if I knew who'd done it?" Harriet snapped, more sharply than she'd meant to.

"Sorry," Lauren said, dragging the word out in a way that indicated she was anything but.

"Settle down, you two," Mavis said sternly. "Eat your sandwich, and then you can tell us everything."

✂ - - - ✂ - - - ✂

A half-hour later, Harriet was settled in front of the living room fireplace in a fresh set of clothes, a cup of tea clutched in both hands, a soft old quilted lap robe around her shoulders.

"First of all, the Muckleshoot was just starting to flow over the bridge when Tom and I came back. We barely made it across in time." She paused and took a sip of tea. "Second, it took us more than two hours to get from here to the homeless camp. We cleared tree limbs and debris as we went, but there are wires down everywhere. We passed utility workers, and they said they're doing repairs on the power lines in anticipation of the main feeder line break being found and fixed, but it's anyone's guess when that will happen."

"Oh, dear," Mavis said.

"We got to the homeless camp just as Joyce and Ronald found Duane. They thought he was sleeping in after being awake all night, but eventually, they checked and he was dead."

"Was he in his camp?" Lauren asked, looking at Mavis the whole time to see if a reprimand was coming.

"No, he was in the handicapped stall in the men's room. I guess several people rode the storm out in the bathrooms, but they took different stalls or corners for privacy. Joyce stayed out all night to keep an eye on Brandy, who was too out of it to come in, so she doesn't know what happened indoors. Ronald said he slept through it all, but he knows the truck-driving couple and some other couple no one knew were in there, too. Joyce went to sleep after the storm broke, so Brandy was on her own during that time." Harriet shook her head then shivered. "It was awful. And he was covered with one of our quilts after the fact."

"You're not suggesting our quilt had anything to do with it, are you?" Lauren asked.

"Of course she isn't," Mavis said. "It was just an observation, I'm sure."

"We dropped the supplies Tom had and then went to the police station. Officer Nguyen seems to be the only law enforcement in town—I guess the detectives got stuck on the wrong side of the slide while they were at their task force meeting. Nguyen hadn't been able to reach anyone else in town."

"Wow," said Aunt Beth. "I wonder who'll investigate the murder."

"Tom and I used duct tape to seal off the bathroom stall, and I'm sure Joyce will do her best to keep people away. It's certainly cold enough in the bathroom to preserve Duane for a while."

"Well, that's just terrible," Aunt Beth said. "It must have been very upsetting."

"It was a shock, that's for sure. But that wasn't the end of the fun on our adventure. Tom took me by Marjory's shop so we could see if it had made it through the storm in one piece and..." She went on to describe their encounter with Marjory's family.

"Richard reacted strangely when we told them about the death at the homeless camp. The fact that he reacted at all was strange," Harriet said. "I think they slept in their car last night, and they were pretty hungry. I was going to cave and invite them here, but Tom wouldn't let me. He gave them some cookies and told them to go find a shelter."

"You've had an eventful day," Mavis said.

"Anyone hungry?" Jorge called from the kitchen. The smell of cornbread greeted them as they made their way back to the kitchen.

"Did you make that on top of the stove?" Lauren asked.

"Yes, I did," Jorge said. "There is only an electric oven under the gas cooktop, unfortunately."

"Aren't you tricky," Lauren said. "And here I thought you only cooked Mexican."

"I am a man of many secrets," Jorge said with a knowing smile and scooped his spicy chili into ceramic bowls. "The grated cheese, sour cream and green onions are on the dining table with honey and butter for the bread," he said.

"This is fabulous," Harriet said as she took the bowl he handed her and made her way to the other room.

Everyone agreed, if the subsequent empty dishes were any indication.

Aunt Beth and Mavis insisted on washing the dishes, leaving Harriet and Lauren to sip their after-dinner tea in front of the fireplace in the living room. Jorge went outside to bring more firewood into the garage to dry, a task made more difficult by the elderly electric door opener needing to be operated manually using a temperamental pull cord.

"So, who do you *think* did it?" Lauren asked without preamble. "I mean, you were there. You must have some idea."

Carter was in his usual position with only his head peeking out from her sweatshirt.

"I'm trying not to think about it," Harriet admitted.

"How's that working for you?"

"Not too well, actually."

"That's what I thought. I think you'll feel better if you talk about it."

"I'm sure you do," Harriet said with a sigh. She pondered the bottom of her teacup for a few minutes, but no answers were revealed there, so she finally spoke. "There are quite a few possibilities, and no real way to sort them."

"You said the truck-driving couple were in the same bathroom, right?" Lauren mused. "Seems like that would be too obvious, though."

"Sometimes the simple answer is the right one," Harriet cautioned.

"What about the unknown couple?"

"That's all they said—a man and his companion who left first thing in the morning. I get the feeling that transient visitors aren't unusual at the camp."

"Who else should we consider?" Lauren asked. "Didn't you say Joyce went to sleep for a while?"

"Yeah. She and Ronald both say they were asleep for portions of the night. And Brandy was 'out of it,' but I'm not sure exactly what that means. I don't know if she was passed out or merely uncooperative. In any case, no one can say what she was doing when the others were asleep."

"I wonder if Darcy and her bunch will be able to determine the time of death when they're finally able to get here." She meant crime scene investigator and sometime Loose Thread Darcy Lewis.

"The real question is, where *is* Darcy?" Harriet sat up in her chair. "If she's trapped in town like us, maybe we can get Tom to fetch her to the crime scene."

"What do you suggest? Smoke signals?"

"Let's see if we can figure out where she lives." Harriet got up from her chair.

"You might as well give me the dogs before I come in. I can't get any wetter." Jorge called from the kitchen.

Lauren handed a frightened looking Carter to him as Mavis snapped leashes onto the collars of Pamela and Curly.

"Who are you trying to find," Aunt Beth asked when Harriet asked where she might find a phone book.

Harriet had lived in the house for most of a year, but she still didn't know where everything was.

"We were wondering where Darcy lives, and if she's around. Officer Nguyen said he hasn't been able to reach anyone. He seemed pretty overwhelmed before we told him about Duane. He might not have called Darcy yet," Harriet explained.

"We know he didn't call her," Lauren said. "Unless she has a satellite phone. But maybe *he* knows where she lives."

"I can tell you that," Aunt Beth answered. "She lives in one of those duplexes on the other side of Miller Hill."

It might as well be a continent away, given the conditions, Harriet thought.

"Well, it was a good idea," she said. "We were thinking there won't be much forensic evidence by the time the power is back and the roads are clear."

"I'm sure the scene has pretty well been contaminated by now anyway," Mavis said. "I'll bet everyone in the homeless camp has been in there to look."

"You're probably right."

Lauren picked up her radio and began winding the crank on its side. After a minute, she stopped and turned the radio on.

"Shhh," she said, even though no one was speaking. "Listen."

She turned up the volume, and a scratchy voice came from the small speaker.

"What was that?" Mavis asked. "What did they say about water?"

"We have to boil it," Lauren translated and clicked the radio off with a snap.

"Great," Harriet said.

"You should be grateful," Aunt Beth scolded. "At least we have a gas stove to boil water with."

"Yeah, as long as the propane lasts," Harriet shot back.

"What was that about the propane?" Jorge asked. He'd just come in from outside, Pamela and Curly on their leashes, Carter held in one large hand. "Everyone did their business," he said as the women took their respective pets from him. Water ran in rivers down his face, dripping from his dark hair onto the collar of his raincoat. "Boy, it's raining to beat the band out there."

"Did you see Aiden this morning?" Harriet asked him.

"No, I've been here all day," he said as Aunt Beth brought him a towel to dry his hair and Mavis took his wet coat and carried it off, presumably to hang it on a chair in front of the fire.

"He didn't come to the house around the time I left?" Harriet pressed.

"No. Why do you think that?"

"As Tom and I were driving away, I looked back, and he was coming out of the woods at the end of the street."

"Oh," Jorge said. "I'm sure that didn't please him—seeing you drive away."

"Probably not," Harriet said.

"I don't like him being stuck with that sister of his all this time. She is *not* a good influence on the boy."

"Me, either, but there's not much I can do about it. He won't talk to me."

"That Michelle is up to no good," Jorge said.

"Yeah, but what can we do about it?"

"Maybe the roads will be clear enough for us to pay a visit over there tomorrow. In the meantime, there's nothing you can do about it." He put his arm around her shoulders and gave her a squeeze. "Let's go play cards," he said. "Come on, Blondie, you, too." He looked over his shoulder at Lauren.

Aunt Beth and Mavis declined the offer of cards and took one of the oil lamps to Harriet's studio. They said they were going to sit in front of the window and see if they had enough light to work on their hand-stitching projects for a while.

"Do you ladies know how to play a game called scat?" Jorge asked.

Harriet and Lauren shook their heads.

"You are in for a treat, my friends," he said and ushered them toward the living room. "We can pull that little table in front of the fire and play where it is warm." He indicated a low coffee table.

Lauren brought the candelabrum from the dining room and relit the candles after setting it on the table.

"Okay, big guy, show us how it's done," Lauren said and sat down across the table from Jorge.

Chapter 13

*H*arriet had lost all her pennies and Lauren was down to one when someone knocked on the front door.

"Who could that be?" Harriet wondered. "No one comes to the front door."

"One way to find out," Lauren said and started to get up, but Jorge beat her to it and opened the door to discover Carla and Wendy.

"Come in, niñas," he said. He took Wendy from Carla and helped the toddler slip out of her wet jacket. "It still rains very hard out there." He shook his head. "We are not out of the forest yet, ladies."

"How did you get here?" Harriet asked Carla. "It's almost dark."

"I drove Aiden's Bronco," she said. "And I didn't ask first, either." Her face was livid in spite of the cold temperature outside.

"Oh, dear," Mavis said as she and Aunt Beth heard the commotion and came to see the new arrivals.

"What's wrong?" Harriet asked.

"Are the roads clear?" Aunt Beth asked at the same time.

"Let's let the poor child get out of her wet coat and get settled," Mavis said. "Go get her some tea, Harriet. And you..." She gestured at Lauren. "...go upstairs and get one of those fleece throws from the TV room."

"I'll take the niñita to the kitchen for some warm apple juice," Jorge said then tickled Wendy, causing her to giggle.

"Can you tell us what happened?" Aunt Beth said in a soft voice after they had Carla settled in front of the fireplace, wrapped in the throw and with a cup of tea held in both hands.

"It's that woman," Carla said. "I couldn't take it anymore. I had to get out of there, even if it is bad outside. I was afraid I was going to kill her."

No one had to ask. They all knew she was talking about Michelle.

"What's she doing?" Lauren asked.

"'Carla, be a dear and get me some coffee. Carla, dear, could you warm my sweater in front of the fire? Carla, could you carry more wood up to my bedroom? And make the fire bigger while you're up there, it's getting chilly.'" Carla said all this in a voice intended to mimic the affected tone Aiden's sister used. A blush crept up her neck to her face. "When she expected me to heat the antique iron and press her 'favorite linen tablecloth,' I couldn't take it. There were three other tablecloths that were already ironed and looked fine," she finished with righteous indignation.

"That's just terrible, honey," Mavis said.

"And she made Wendy cry," Carla added.

"I'd of killed her for that," Harriet said. She'd become quite fond of the toddler since Carla had joined the Loose Threads, and couldn't imagine anyone mistreating the good-natured little girl.

"I know I shouldn't have driven with Wendy in this weather, but I did put her carseat in the back seat and everything."

"How were the roads?" Aunt Beth asked for the second time.

"They weren't as bad as I expected," Carla said. "People have been out clearing downed limbs. You can see lots of freshly cut wood at the sides of the road. And the power company was working at the bottom of your hill. They were letting people go off-road to get around the mess if you had four-wheel drive. Most of the way was okay, though."

"Well, I'm glad you were able to get through," Beth said. "That woman could drive anyone to drink."

"That's not the worst of it," Carla said. "She's playing with Aiden's head something awful."

"Have you heard what she's saying to him?" Harriet asked.

"Not much—she shuts up around me, except for orders. But when she made Wendy cry, she was working on some kind of craft project. She left it on a table in the nursery, and Wendy touched her paper, and she came in and screamed at her."

"What kind of craft project?" Harriet asked. "And why was she doing it in the nursery?"

"I don't know. She ordered Wendy and me out of the room, and when I went back to get Wendy's toy that she'd dropped, everything was gone."

"I thought Aiden let you have the nursery for Wendy." Lauren said.

"Not when Michelle's there, I guess." Carla said. "Whatever it was involved little scraps of paper and some sort of glue."

"That is very curious," Aunt Beth said.

"Last night, I heard Aiden say 'So, you're telling me all my work here has been for nothing?' but I couldn't hear what she'd said before that and I didn't hear her reply."

"I wish we knew more about what she was up to," Mavis said.

"I could try to find out," Carla offered.

"We wouldn't want to get you in any trouble," Aunt Beth said. "But it would sure help to know a little more about what angle that girl is trying to play this time."

Everyone sat, lost in her own thoughts for a few moments.

"I think I know a way," Harriet finally said.

"Well, don't just sit there," Lauren said. "Enlighten us."

"Carla, do you still have the extra baby monitor you had when Kissa was staying at Aiden's?"

"Yes. In fact, I have another one Terry made that filters out background noise so I can hear Wendy more clearly."

"Do any of them use batteries?"

"Sure, all of them can operate on battery power. I think it's one of those safety things."

"Perfect," Harriet said. "Do you think you can conceal a unit in whatever room Aiden and Michelle spend most of their time in?"

"Totally," Carla said, her expression brightening. "That will make it a little easier to go back there, too."

"Do any of you ladies have the old-fashioned kind of phone?" Jorge asked as he carried Wendy back into the living room, a pink sippy cup clutched in her chubby fingers. "You know? The kind with just a cord that plugs into a wall jack, but no electric cord."

"We do," Harriet said, excitement in her voice as she realized what Jorge was saying.

"Why didn't we think of that?" Lauren said. "Old school phones often work even when the power is out because the electrical power for the phone lines is separate from the regular power system," she explained to Mavis and Aunt Beth. "Of course, that's if the phone lines are intact."

"That will only help us if the people we're calling have them, too," Aunt Beth pointed out.

"I passed several phone company vans on my way here," Carla said.

"We've got more than one old school phone," Harriet said. "I replaced the ones upstairs with a cordless set when I moved in. The old Princess models are in a box in the TV room closet."

Lauren left the room, returning a few minutes later with a phone in each hand.

"These babies are museum-quality," she said and set the two units on the coffee table.

"Perfect," Aunt Beth said. "We can send one with Carla and plug the other one in here. There should be a phone jack in the baseboard there under the window." She pointed to a spot on the exterior wall.

"There's probably a phone jack in either your bedroom or your sitting room," Mavis told Carla. "Plug this in as soon as you get home."

"Don't put it out in the open," Harriet warned. "Until we know what Michelle is up to, we don't want to put her on her guard. From what I've seen of her, though, she'll never suspect you could be watching her or gathering evidence of whatever she's doing."

"Still," Mavis said, "it pays to be cautious. And don't take any chances. She's a mean one. She used to pick on Aiden something awful when he was a little guy."

"I'm just so happy to be here with you guys for a little while, I'll do anything." Carla sighed. "It's been a really long couple of days."

"Okay," Harriet said and picked up the watch Jorge had laid on the table for communal use. "Let's wait until nine p.m. to make contact. They shouldn't be looking for you to any chores by then."

Carla looked at her like she had to be kidding.

"You call me so we won't have to worry about the phone ringing on your end when someone else is around," Harriet went on. "If you can't get through, try again before you go to sleep."

"And, honey, if it gets to be too much for you over there, you just call and we'll get you out of there," Mavis said.

"Thanks, but I'll be fine now," Carla said, her eyes shining with unshed tears. "I just needed some sympathy."

"I'm going to drive you home," Jorge insisted. "I need to see how bad the river is. If it was at the bridge when Señor Tom brought our Harriet home, I'm sure its worse now, but I need to see it myself."

"Thank you for that," Aunt Beth said. "I don't like the idea of Carla driving around alone in this weather."

"I should go back before they notice I'm gone," Carla said. "Michelle will start screaming for me as soon as she gets hungry."

"How's Jorge going to get back here?" Lauren asked.

"Are you afraid *you're* going to go hungry?" Harriet asked with a grin.

"Aiden will loan me a car," Jorge said. "Let me get my coat, and we'll be on our way."

"Call us as soon as you can safely do it," Harriet said again.

"Hang in there," Mavis added. "You did the right thing coming to us."

108

Chapter 14

J orge had not yet returned when the pink Princess phone in the living room started ringing. Lauren and Harriet were straining to read years'-old issues of a quilting magazine Lauren had discovered when she was upstairs getting the phones. The light from one oil lamp and the fireplace were barely adequate to look at the pictures. Reading the articles was out of the question.

"Are you going to answer that?" Lauren asked Harriet.

Harriet gave her an exasperated look as she got up and crossed to the table by the window. Rain was lashing the windowpanes again.

"What's happened?" she asked when she picked up the phone. "It's nowhere near nine o'clock." Something had to be very wrong for Carla to be making contact so soon after she arrived home. "Oh, I'm sorry, Detective Morse, I was expecting a call from Carla...Well, I...not this soon, but later. So I was surprised...I'm sorry, I'm babbling. What can I do for you?" Lauren was gesturing frantically at her. "Excuse me a minute. This thing doesn't have a speaker option. I'll tell you what she says after," she told Lauren, a note of annoyance creeping into her tone.

"Yes, I was at the homeless camp earlier," she went on.

"Who was there?" Jane Morse asked.

"Joyce Elias, a woman they call Brandy, a stranded trucker couple, and Ronald Bachman said a couple came late and left early.

He didn't seem to know who they were. I guess that isn't uncommon there."

"I wish I could interview the truckers. If they could prove they were out of the area on a couple of critical dates, they could be eliminated as suspects."

"Which dates?" Harriet asked.

"Why?" Morse shot back.

"Just curious," Harriet said.

Morse recited the three dates.

"I'm sure they wouldn't be suspects, but Marjory Swain's family was roaming around town, too. They said they spent the night in their car, so they could have gone to the park to use the facilities at some point, too."

"I doubt they're serial killers, but everyone's a suspect in Duane's murder until we eliminate them. Why didn't they go to the shelter at the church?"

"I asked, and they said something about needing privacy."

"So, they'd rather be killed in a storm?"

"Hey, I'm just the reporter here," Harriet said.

She heard Morse sigh.

"Some days I'm amazed the human race has survived all these years. Speaking of survival, are you ladies doing okay?"

"We're fine. My aunt has been through a lot of storms, so we were prepared. And Jorge couldn't get home, so he's here cooking for us."

"Oh, good. I just wish there were some way for me to get there. The Coast Guard said the water is still too rough for us to come by boat, so we're stuck here going over and over the slim facts we have on the serial killer. At least I brought an appliqué project with me."

"I'd be happy to talk to the folks at the camp for you," Harriet offered, "if that would help."

"Let's leave the police work to the professionals. You just make sure your aunt and the rest of the Loose Threads are okay. I'll try to check in with you all again if this continues. On this end, they're saying it's going to be days before they can clear the slide. The news said they're looking for a break in the power transmission lines, but it's somewhere in the forest and the going is slow."

"We appreciate the contact with the outside world," Harriet said.

They chatted for another few moments then said goodbye.

"Okay, what was that all about?" Lauren demanded.

"Let's get Aunt Beth and Mavis so I don't have to say this all twice," she said.

"Get us for what?" Aunt Beth asked as she and Mavis came in from the studio.

"We thought we heard the phone," Mavis added. "You heard correct," Lauren said. "Detective Morse just called, and sometime in the next decade, Harriet is going to tell us about it."

"Morse is still stuck on the other side of the slide along with the other Foggy Point detectives. Apparently, Officer Nguyen reached her on his satellite phone after we saw him. By the time he got done doing whatever she told him to do to secure the office, he couldn't get back over the bridge, so he's holed up in the upstairs of the building. One of the other officers came in while he was there, so there are now two of them trapped there. She says the office is current on all its disaster planning, so they have food and water available."

Harriet went back to her chair by the fire. Lauren sat on the stool she had pulled as close to the heat as she could stand.

"She said she got hold of that skinny blond officer we met that one time, but she had a tree fall on her house and her leg. Apparently, there's a doctor on her street who was able to put a splint on her leg, which is broken, but she can't do anything but sit with it elevated."

"And?" Lauren prompted. "Get to the punch line."

Harriet started to say something, but Aunt Beth put a hand on her arm, silencing her. She took a deep breath.

"The upshot is, the only officers Morse can get hold of are out of commission. She asked a lot of questions about what Tom and I saw at the homeless camp. I think her concern, along with the task force group she is with, is that the highway serial killer is trapped here with us. All indications are that the killer—or killers—drives a semi."

"Oh, honey, don't tell me she wants you to get involved in *those* murders," Mavis protested.

"No, not exactly," Harriet said choosing her words carefully to avoid having to tell an outright lie. "I could tell she was reluctant to ask us to go anywhere near the homeless camp..." That part was true, Harriet thought. "...but she can't raise anyone else."

"What does she want us to do?" Lauren asked, leaning toward her.

"She wants to know where the truck-driving couple was on three dates—the last week of August, September seventeenth and Halloween. If they were any distance from Highway One-oh-one or Interstate Five then they can't be the serial killers Morse and company are looking for."

"How does that help us with Duane's murder?" Lauren asked.

"Morse said before that most murder victims know their attacker. The likelihood of a second serial killer operating in our area is slim to none, so if the couple is eliminated as possible suspects than our danger level drops dramatically."

"And if they are the serial killers?" Lauren persisted. "What's that do for our danger level?"

"I'd like to hear the answer to that one myself," Mavis said.

"It sounds like a terrible idea to me," Aunt Beth stated.

"I'm sure we'll be safe if several of us go. She didn't seem to think Duane was a serial killer victim, and according to the paper, those victims were always alone when they were last seen."

"I can't believe a police detective would make such a request," Aunt Beth said.

"Believe me, she needs this information. She said they're all getting antsy sitting there at their hotel. The task force has a limited budget, and the non-Foggy Point members don't want to spend the money to get a helicopter so they can interview the couple themselves, and it's not guaranteed they could even *get* a helicopter. The Coast Guard won't bring them.

"She said the task force members from Seattle are sure 'their' serial killer couldn't possibly be someplace as mundane as Foggy Point. They're still working on other possibilities, but it would help Jane if she could eliminate our pair."

"So, 'eliminate' sounds like she doesn't think they're the killers," Mavis said.

"She said they've been operating under the assumption they're looking for a lone killer, but she said the profiler on the team says they can't rule out the possibility the killer has taken on a partner. I guess it's rare, but it does happen," Harriet reported.

"We need to make a plan," Lauren said. "You know, figure out who is going to say what when we go up there."

"I think we should decline her request," Beth said. "I can't imagine what she's thinking, suggesting we put ourselves in harm's way."

"I ran into her at the Steaming Cup a couple of weeks ago, and we had coffee," Mavis said. "I think the male detectives aren't giving her the kind of support they would if she were also a man. She didn't come straight out and say as much, mind you—it's just the feeling I got."

"That might explain it," Aunt Beth said. "If she's being left out of the loop, she might need to come up with something—you know, to prove she's as good as the guys are."

"Morse said the victims so far were last seen traveling alone at night on either Highway One-oh-one or the interstate. If we go as a group during the day to the camp, where there are additional people, we'll be fine."

"Easy for her to say," Mavis said. "I'm with Beth—good reason or not, I don't like it."

"Would you feel better if we took Jorge or Tom with us?" Harriet asked. "I'm sure either one of them would be up for the adventure."

"I think it's none of our business," Aunt Beth said.

"I'm sure Detective Morse wouldn't want us to do this if she felt there was any risk," Harriet insisted. "You know how conservative she is."

"If you gals are determined, I guess we better work on our story," Mavis said with a sigh. "Anyone want a cup of tea?"

✄ - - - ✄ - - - ✄

"I think we should bring up Halloween first," Harriet said for what seemed to her like the hundredth time. The women had been suggesting and rejecting scenarios for more than an hour. "We don't need them to have alibis for all three dates. If they were elsewhere for any one of the dates they can't be the killers. Halloween is an easy date to talk about."

"Harriet's right," Mavis said. "We can talk about the quilts we made for Halloween."

"I still think it's like poking a hornet's nest with a stick," Beth said when they'd all agreed on a plan.

"And what would that be?" Jorge asked. The four women had been so intent on their plan no one had noticed that he'd come into the kitchen from the garage. "I can tell from the look on Señora Beth's face I'm not going to like this."

"Detective Morse called, and she wants this bunch to go questioning people at the homeless camp about the murder up there," Aunt Beth explained in an exasperated tone.

"Don't worry, Señora, I'll keep them safe." He looked at Harriet. "Do not even think about going without me there to protect you."

"I wouldn't dream of it," Harriet said with a sigh. "I was hoping you were going to offer to drive anyway."

"I saw you have a bag of pinto beans in your pantry. I can make some bean-and-rice burritos for the people."

"I don't have that many tortillas," Harriet protested.

"Please do not insult the cook," he shot back. "You have a large bag of flour—that's all I need."

"That will give Jorge a good reason to be there and maybe give him a chance to poke around a little," Mavis pointed out.

"I'll put the beans in to soak," Jorge said and turned toward the pantry to get the ingredients he'd need.

"You'll probably want the canning kettle to cook that quantity," Beth said.

"I'll get it," Harriet offered and got up.

She had just returned to the kitchen carrying the large pot when the phone rang in the living room. She set the kettle on the counter and continued on to answer it.

Lauren and Mavis followed her and stood expectantly in front of the fire.

Harriet listened for a few minutes then said, "Good work...No, that's great. We can't expect they'll tell all just because we started listening. Keep up the good work, but don't put yourself in jeopardy. Okay, talk to you tomorrow." She turned to the group. "That was Carla."

"No joke," Lauren said, and Mavis poked her.

"What did she say, honey?"

"She hasn't heard much yet. Aiden said he wished Michelle had some proof to back up what she was saying, but neither one of them said what that was."

"That's it?" Lauren said.

"She hasn't been able to place her second set of monitors yet. She said she's waiting until everyone goes to bed; then she can put the two wireless remote units in play."

"I'm going to take the dogs out and head up to bed," Mavis said. "You want me to take Carter?"

"No, I'll come with you." Lauren jostled the little dog out from her sweatshirt.

"I'll see you ladies in the morning," Harriet said. "I'm going to go read."

She truly had intended to read, but she couldn't concentrate on her novel and instead lay awake in bed going over and over the events of the day in her mind. When she finally fell into an exhausted sleep, Duane was still dead, and she had no idea who was responsible.

Chapter 15

I t was after nine o'clock when Harriet came downstairs the next morning. She had gotten up and done what she hoped was an adequate rendition of her exercise routine. It was an activity she usually did with the guidance of a muscular young man named Lars who slept in her DVD player, awaiting the summons of the remote control to spring into action.

She'd followed her workout with a warm shower, thankful that someone else must be up and feeding Fred—he'd left her during sit-ups, an activity he normally felt required his supervision.

"Where is everyone?" she asked Mavis, who sat alone with a cup of tea at the kitchen table.

"Your aunt is taking her shower, and Jorge went for a drive to see how the roads are and whether the Muckleshoot is down enough for him to cross the bridge and get to his restaurant. Lauren and Carter went with him."

The aroma of cooking pinto beans filled the air, and a stack of handmade tortillas sat waiting on a plate at the side of the stove.

"Jorge's been busy," Harriet said.

"He does like his cooking. And he's a bit of a ham, I'd say."

"What do you mean?"

"He's been practicing his questions for the truckers. He's changed clothes twice, an activity that was hindered by the fact he's limited to the ones he had in his truck and we don't have the means

116

to either wash or iron them. He's redone his hair three times and might have gone for a fourth, but Beth told him to stop wasting water."

"If he goes too overboard he's going to blow it for us. They aren't going to talk to us if he goes in like some sort of beggar from *The Threepenny Opera*."

"You can try to talk to him if you want, but I wouldn't get my hopes up." Mavis returned to reading the week-old newspaper that lay on the table.

"I'm sure Lauren wouldn't mind if you used her wind-up radio to hear something a little more current."

"It's not the same," Mavis said and readjusted her glasses before returning to her reading.

"Okay, fine," Harriet muttered to herself.

She was about to get her jacket and go outside when the phone rang. She dashed for the dining room and managed to pick up the receiver before it quit.

It turned out to be Carla.

"It sounds like she's trying to talk him into going back to Africa," she reported. "She told him that going far away was the only real way he could start over. I don't get it. Why does he need to start over? He's barely gotten settled here."

"Think about it," Harriet said. "If he goes back to Africa on a permanent basis, he won't need his big house and cars."

Carla gasped. If Aiden didn't live in his big house, he wouldn't need a housekeeper.

"I didn't mean to scare you, but I'm thinking this is Michelle taking another run at getting her hands on Aiden's money."

"Can't he see what she's doing?" Carla asked.

"Ordinarily, yes, but she's obviously found something to scare or intimidate him with. That's what we need to figure out. What does she have on him?"

"She doesn't give up easy, does she?" Carla said. "He's turned down her calls for money a lot just since I've been working there."

"She's determined, I'll give her that."

"Why doesn't she just work?" Carla wondered. "Isn't she some kind of attorney?"

"Yes, and she works at it, but Aiden said it's simple—she spends more than she and her husband make. He said she was like that as a kid, too. She was always trying to con him and his brother out of their allowance."

"But she's older than him," Carla protested.

"You got it. He was in grade school, and she was in high school, talking him out of his lunch money, according to my aunt."

"That's awful."

"Yes, it is. That's why I'm sure she's running some sort of scam on him, using his goodness and loyalty to get him to leave town and hand over his money. Your mission is to listen more and see if you can figure out what her angle is this time."

Carla agreed to do to her best and rang off.

Harriet again turned, intending to get her jacket and go outside to start assessing the cleanup that would be needed, when the phone rang again.

"Oh, good, you do have a working land line," Tom Bainbridge said in place of a greeting.

"Hello to you, too. What's up?"

"I'm going a little stir-crazy here and was wondering if you wanted to take another ride out to the homeless camp with me."

"There's a lot of that going around," Harriet said. "I'd love to go. Jorge and the rest of my crew here are planning on taking a hot lunch of bean-and-rice burritos to the homeless folks in just a while."

"Do you need to go with them?"

"Not at all. In fact, I think a little space would help us all. I'm ready whenever you want to leave."

"In that case, I'll be there in less than thirty minutes. I'll be driving my host's pickup this time, so we'll be a little more comfortable."

✂ - - - ✂ - - - ✂

True to his word, Tom arrived a half-hour later. Harriet met him in the driveway, a dog leash in each hand, Curly and Pamela circling and scratching in the leaves under one of the trees that lined the drive.

"Looks like you have your hands full there," Tom said as he got out of the red pickup. The cargo bed had several cases of water and canned goods and more plastic-wrapped plates of homemade cookies.

"Wow," Harriet said. "Is there no end to your host's stockpile?"

"Doesn't seem like it, does it?" Tom said. "They're good people, but they like to be prepared for any eventuality, up to and including nuclear holocaust. And, yes, they do have full chemical/gas protective suits, complete with tanks of oxygen."

"Wow," Harriet repeated.

"They really are nice people, apart from the disaster preparation thing. And you sort of forget about it once you get used to them."

"If you say so," she said with a smile.

"So, what's the plan?"

"Jorge and Lauren and Aunt Beth are driving to the camp to deliver the burritos, and we all thought we'd see if we could help with cleanup. I already put some rakes and trimmers and stuff like that in the back of Jorge's truck."

"Good, I could use the exercise. Mr. and Mrs. Renfro have been playing cards endlessly. Judging by the running score of five thousand, six hundred forty-five to four thousand, nine hundred seventy-seven, I'm pretty sure they do this even when there's power. They're so competitive, I find myself watching for hours on end when I'm supposed to be sketching buildings or something."

Harriet filled him in on the Loose Threads' alleged assignment from Detective Morse.

"Sounds like you've got all the necessary roles cast, but if I can help, count me in."

"Let me take these two back inside," Harriet said indicating the dogs. "Mavis is going to stay home with all the critters and to keep the home fires blazing. Literally."

✂ - - - ✂ - - - ✂

"Connie's going to meet us at the camp," Aunt Beth said when Harriet came inside. "Her hubby is working with a group of volunteers removing downed trees from streets and driveways."

119

"I'm going on over to the park with Tom," Harriet told her. "He's got some water and other supplies for the campers."

"I'll be another few minutes more with the burritos," Jorge said. He was systematically rolling them then wrapping the finished product in foil. "But you go on ahead." He gave her a quick wink.

✄ - - - ✄ - - - ✄

"Okay," she said as she got into Tom's borrowed truck, "we're free to go. Jorge said they'll be along in a few minutes."

"So, we're free till then?"

Harriet studied him for a long moment.

"Ye-e-es," she said slowly. "May I ask why that matters?"

"Oh, we're just taking a small detour."

Harriet raised her left eyebrow.

"Relax, I'm not kidnapping you or anything. We can't leave Foggy Point, remember?"

He guided the truck to the Strait of Juan de Fuca, taking numerous detours around downed trees and small slides before pulling into a wayside viewpoint, parking and getting out. Harriet followed him to a small stone enclosure. A brushed-steel sign was mounted flat to the back of the space and described the seabirds that frequented this point. A roughhewn bench spanned the covered space.

"Wait here," Tom said and, when Harriet sat, jogged back to the truck then returned with one hand held behind his back.

"What's going on?" Harriet started to stand.

"Relax," he said, and she sank back onto the bench as he swept his hidden hand into view, presenting her with a bunch of flowers. At least, it resembled a bunch of flowers.

"What is this?" she asked as she took the cellophane-wrapped bouquet of holly that was brightened with what turned out to be carefully crafted origami flowers.

"I just thought you might need something to brighten your day," he said with a smile. He sat down beside her.

"Did you make these?" She bent to sniff them out of habit and was surprised to find they smelled faintly of roses.

"Don't sound so surprised. Mrs. R taught me how to make them the first day, in between card games. She has lots of craft supplies. She also provided the rosewater. She said her grandkids and great-grandkids have given her enough cologne to float an ocean liner."

Harriet laughed.

"What? A guy can't make paper flowers? It's not that different from making architectural models. Paper is paper."

"This is very unexpected…and very sweet," she said and bent to smell them again.

She felt a gentle touch on her chin. She turned and as she did, Tom brushed his lips against hers. When she didn't resist, he put his arm around her shoulders and pulled her closer, deepening the kiss.

He broke contact and pulled back, using his fingers to brush her bangs away from her face. He searched her eyes with his.

"Are we okay?" he asked in a quiet voice.

Harriet's cheeks had turned pink, and she could feel the heat all the way to her toes.

"We're fine," she said and smiled. Only a little twinge of guilt twisted her stomach.

Tom took her free hand and pulled her to her feet.

"We better get to the camp before your aunt sends a search party out after us."

"You're right—and, Tom…" She paused for a moment. "Thanks for bringing me here."

He put his arm around her shoulders and walked her back to the truck.

"I designed that," he said as he was turning the truck onto the road again.

"The bench thingy?"

"I believe the proper term is *kiosk*, but, yes, the bench thingy."

"I'm impressed."

"It was a long time ago, while I was still in college. We all had to submit designs for scenic wayside kiosks. I was lucky—mine was chosen to be implemented."

"Now I'm *really* impressed."

"It's not like I saved the life of a tortured animal or anything."

"Hey," Harriet said and reached across the center console to touch his arm. "This isn't a competition, and I certainly don't choose my friends based on their work output." She was quiet for a moment. "I do like your bench thingy, though."

Tom glanced at her with a grin.

"I feel like I'm back in high school."

"As you pointed out a few days ago, I don't seem to have a committed relationship with anyone, so I'm free to have as many friends as I want. Can we just leave it at that?"

"As long as I get to see you, I'm fine with leaving things as they are," he said. "For now."

Chapter 16

Jorge's truck was already parked near the restrooms when Tom pulled in. A blue Peterbilt truck sleeper was at the far side of the area. The couple, Harriet assumed.

Aunt Beth, Lauren and Connie stood in a half-circle near the tailgate while Jorge handed pans of food and bags of paper goods to the group from the bed of the truck.

"Did you get lost?" Aunt Beth asked.

"It's my fault," Tom explained. "I wanted to show Harriet a sample of my work, and we had to take a pretty long detour to get there."

"Uh-huh," Beth said. "We certainly didn't see any of your work at your mother's place."

Harriet glared at her.

"Can we help you unload Tom's truck?" Connie asked. "Come on, Lauren," she added before Lauren could add her own comment about Harriet and Tom's delay.

Joyce came out of the ladies restroom and smiled when she saw the group slowly making their way toward the trail behind the building.

"We brought you a hot meal." Jorge raised his pan slightly.

"Oh, my," Joyce said. "You *are* a welcome sight. We've been living off what Tom and Harriet brought, and we're only eating two meals a day."

"What would you have done if we hadn't showed up?" Lauren asked.

"Lauren," Harriet warned and glared at her.

"I'm just curious about how this all works. I'm self-employed—you never know what's going to happen. I mean, I could end up down here with them. I need to know what preparations I should make. You know, just in case."

"Yeah, right."

"Did you tell the police what happened here?" Joyce asked Tom.

"We did," Harriet answered. "They've got their own problems—all the detectives got stuck on the other side of the slide. We reported to the officer at the station, but he's stuck downtown with another guy because the river overflowed the bridge right after we left. Anyway, without being able to access the station and with little communication, the police aren't going to be any help anytime soon."

"What are we supposed to do?" Joyce asked. "Should we bury him?"

"*No!*" Harriet and Lauren and Beth said at the same time.

"You can't destroy the evidence," Harriet added.

"I know it seems disrespectful," Aunt Beth soothed her. "But the best thing for your friend is to figure out who killed him, and to do that the police need all the evidence they can get."

"It doesn't seem right to leave him lying there," Joyce protested.

"Has anyone gone in to that stall in the restroom?" Harriet asked.

"We haven't been using the men's room at all, but you can see how it is. Anyone could go in if they wanted to. All they'd have to do is wait until everyone is asleep or in their own area."

"Great," Lauren said.

"My food is cooling," Jorge reminded everyone.

"Oh, my, yes, let's get the food to the group before it's cold," Joyce said. "I'll call everyone while you set up. Could someone go across the parking lot and tap on the truck door?"

Tom turned and headed back. Jorge led the parade down the trail to the common area. He set his pan of burritos on the table then took the bag of paper goods from Connie. He pulled napkins and forks from the bag and set a stack of plates beside the burrito pan. Aunt Beth opened a quilted bag and drew out a carton of sour cream, two jars of salsa and a bottle of hot sauce.

"Sorry we didn't have chips or cheese on hand," she said.

"This looks wonderful," Ronald said as he joined them.

"Thank you for doing this," they heard Kate say to Tom.

"Thank the big guy," Tom replied as they came into view—accompanied by Marjory's family.

"What...?" Lauren started to say.

"They came here to use the restrooms," Tom told her as he came to stand by Harriet. "They were getting out of their car when I was coming back by with Kate and Owen. I told them they could have a burrito."

Harriet looked at him, and he shrugged.

"I was feeling good and wanted to share the joy," he said in a quiet voice only she could hear. Her cheeks reddened, but she didn't say anything.

"As long as you're here, I guess you can eat with us," Beth said.

Harriet had seldom seen her aunt angry enough to deny food to hungry people, not that this particular situation had ever come up before.

Joyce returned, pushing and guiding Brandy to the table. Jorge removed the lid from the big pan and unwrapped two burritos onto a plate. He put a daub of sour cream and a splash of salsa beside them and handed the plate to Joyce. When she and Brandy were settled on a log by the fire, he prepared plates for the rest. Pat pushed Lisa up to the table, but she and Richard showed amazing restraint and went to the back of the line.

"Don't be shy," Jorge said and waved the group forward.

Ronald took a plate, then Owen and Kate. Joyce urged Richard and Pat to the table, and when they'd gotten their food, they went to the stump bench and started to sit down next to the truckers. Owen stood up and pulled Kate up with him, almost dumping her plate in the process.

Harriet watched the interplay between the two couples. Lisa and Pat seemed confused, but there was no mistaking the look of absolute hatred on Owen's face as he glared at Richard. For his part, Richard studied his burrito, refusing to make eye contact with the other man.

"I forgot to lock the truck," Owen said coldly, and they left the clearing.

Everyone was silent for a moment.

"These are delicious," Joyce finally said. "Thank you so much for thinking of us."

"Yes," Pat said. "Ummm…thanks," It seemed to pain the woman to say the word.

"Did you stay dry?" Aunt Beth asked Joyce. "During the storm and after?"

"I was up for most of the storm, so I got a little wet, in spite of my wet-weather clothes. Brandy stayed dry as a bone. And the quilts are wonderfully warm. Thank you all so much."

"Step up," Jorge announced. "I made enough for everyone."

The Loose Threads and Tom helped themselves to burritos, and once they all had been served, Jorge fixed himself a plate and sat down with them.

"We thought we'd help you-all clean up the area while we're here," Tom said when they'd finished eating. Jorge poked at the remains of the fire, making a space between logs to feed the paper plates into the flames.

"We can definitely use the extra sets of hands," Joyce said. "Everyone's space has some amount of branches and debris that were blown in, and the trail has become a river of mud."

"We brought some tools," Tom said. "A couple of saws, some shovels, stuff like that."

"I've got a wheelbarrow in my truck," Jorge offered.

Joyce enlisted Harriet and Lauren, and they took the wheelbarrow into the woods to gather leaves and needles that could be used to recover the muddy trail. Tom and Jorge would take shovels and attempt to scrape the slurry from the top layer of the path, hoping to expose some of the buried rock beneath.

Ronald pulled a mop bucket and toilet brush from behind the log bench and stood up.

"I'll go swab the ladies' loo," he announced and went down the trail toward the restrooms.

Connie and Aunt Beth began collecting errant branches from the common area, stacking them in a pile at Joyce's direction.

When everyone had begun their tasks, Richard cleared his throat. When everyone ignored him, he went and stood in front of Joyce.

"What shall *we* do?" he asked.

Harriet and Lauren paused at the edge of the common area to observe the interchange.

"It looks like it's hurting him to offer," Lauren said with a smirk.

"I'm sure it is. Notice his wife and daughter aren't joining him."

The two women were, in fact, headed back toward the parking lot.

✂ - - - ✂ - - - ✂

Harriet and Lauren filled their wheelbarrow several times, dumping the debris on the freshly cleared trail each time. The third time they returned, Tom stopped them before they could tilt it onto the trail.

"We're going to see if we can shore up this muddy stretch with some of the sticks your aunt and Connie are stacking up," he said.

"Maybe the ladies can take a small break while we find a saw and prepare our branches," Jorge suggested.

Connie and Beth joined them in the common area. Joyce brought everyone bottled water from one of the two cases Tom had brought.

"The bathroom is sparkling clean," Ronald said and collapsed onto the long bench next to Connie. His face was red from the exertion of walking back from the bathrooms. "I hope you don't mind if I join you."

"Here, have some water," Harriet said and offered him a bottle. "Are you okay? I mean, do you need to see a doctor about your heart? We could give you a ride somewhere."

"Thank you for your kindness, but I'm fine. Well, not fine, exactly, but I'm stable. I'm supposed to avoid stress, but as you can see, my life hasn't cooperated with my doctor's orders. In fact, I no longer have health insurance and, therefore, no doctor, so there is no one left to order my heart around."

127

"I'm sure Joyce and the others don't want you killing yourself just to keep the bathrooms clean," Harriet told him.

"Of course we don't," Joyce agreed.

"Everyone is expected to do their share of the work around here—it won't work any other way. Keeping the bathroom clean is the least rigorous task we have."

Joyce looked exasperated but kept quiet.

"Maybe you could go at it a little slower," Connie said.

"Go at what a little slower?" Tom asked as he and Jorge came back to the common area with Owen and Kate. Richard trailed them by a few feet, lingering out on the trail.

"Nothing," Ronald said. "The ladies and I were just nattering on about our little society here." He spread his arms wide, indicating the camp around him. "Did you come up with a saw?"

"As a matter of fact, we did," Tom said. "We not only have the two crosscut saws I brought…" He held up two common-looking saws. "…but Owen here had a bow saw and not one but two folding pruning saws."

Owen held up the smaller saws.

"We aim to please," he said. "I had these in my truck in case we passed a good U-cut Christmas tree lot in the upcoming week or two."

"Owen likes to put a tree on the back of the truck for the holidays," Kate explained.

"Most drivers put a wreath on the front of their truck, I try to be original," Owen said and looked at his feet. "Seems kind of trivial about now."

"I think it sounds nice," Aunt Beth said.

"We want to help with the cleanup," Kate said.

Owen glanced toward the main trail, but Richard was no longer in sight.

"We need two teams of people," Jorge said. "One group needs to cut some of the smaller branches into pieces to use for trail repair work, and the other needs to use the bigger saws to cut apart the larger limbs that are blocking the path."

"I'll be working on trail repair," Tom said and took the bow saw and one pruning saw from Owen.

Harriet and Lauren stood up and crossed to stand beside him. Aunt Beth and Connie went with Jorge.

"I think Ronald needs to rest for a bit," Joyce said after a long look studying the man.

"I agree," Aunt Beth said. "There are more of us than we need for trail repair anyway."

"Richard could take over our leaf-gathering," Lauren suggested with a sly grin.

"We left the wheelbarrow down the path, just beyond Brandy's spot," Harriet added, and put her hand up for a high-five when Joyce went to tell him. Lauren slapped her hand, and they turned to follow Tom back toward the parking lot.

"Señora Beth, Señora Connie, Señor Owen, would you care to join me behind the restrooms? I think that tree we all crawled over coming in here is our first opportunity."

Owen passed his remaining pruning saw to Aunt Beth.

"Since you seem to have a full crew, I think I'll go try to repair my truck heater again. I thought of another trick that might work until we can get downtown and get a replacement unit," he said.

✂- - - ✂- - - ✂

Tom handed Harriet a retractable tape measure and the pruning saw when they reached the pavement.

"Cut pieces of branch in two-foot lengths. To the degree possible, have the whole length be the same diameter—between one and two inches. I realize the branches are not straight, but do the best you can with them."

Once the women started working and Tom had proclaimed them trained, he began cutting larger pieces.

"Do you and Owen come this way very often?" Harriet asked Kate as they held opposite ends of a long stick while Lauren sawed on it.

"This is my first time. I've only been riding in the truck with Owen for a few months."

"It must be romantic," Harriet said. "Going wherever the wind blows you."

"Not really. You go where the work is, and sometimes you get stuck for days in some truck stop along the interstate, waiting for the next load to be ready."

"That must wreak havoc with your holidays," Lauren said.

"Except for the Christmas tree on the truck, we don't really celebrate the holidays," Kate admitted.

They worked in silence until they had used all the fallen branches in the immediate vicinity. Lauren straightened her back and stretched.

"I need a bathroom break," she said and headed for the ladies' room. A slow drizzle had begun to fall.

"I think I'll join you," Harriet said. She'd planned to talk to Lauren about another approach to the Halloween discussion.

An inhuman scream pierced the quiet of the park.

"What was that?" Lauren asked.

"I don't know, but it didn't sound good. We better go check."

Another agonized scream pierced the air, and their whole group ran for the encampment.

Joyce was wrestling with a highly agitated Brandy when they reached the common area. Tom took over restraining the younger woman, who let loose with another earsplitting shriek.

"Calm down," he soothed in a neutral voice.

She kicked him in the shin. He pulled her backward and sat on the bench, pulling her onto his lap, his arms wrapped around her. He continued speaking in a calm, steady tone.

"Brandy," Joyce said in a clear voice. "Stop. Now. This man is not trying to hurt you." She reached out and took Brandy's hands and leaned in close to the girl's face. "Look at me." When Brandy finally complied, she continued. "What has gotten you into such a twist?"

"He's dead," Brandy said in a voice only slightly slurred by alcohol.

"Who is dead?" Joyce asked, keeping a firm grip on her hands.

"The man," she said, "the man in my bed."

Harriet looked at Joyce.

"She has delusions sometimes—snakes, spiders, that sort of thing."

"Not a big stretch, given where we are," Lauren said in a murmured low enough only Harriet heard her.

"She's never mentioned a man before," Joyce continued, "but she does have these spells."

"If she can calm down, I'll go check her space, if you think that would help," Tom offered.

"What are you talking about?" Brandy slurred, her voice rising, a sheen of sweat on her forehead. "There is an awful man with blue lips in my bed."

Joyce looked at Tom and then Harriet and Lauren.

Tom loosened his grip slightly and paused to gauge Brandy's reaction. When she didn't move, he released her and stood up, setting her on the bench.

"I'll be right back," he said.

"Brandy, dear," Joyce said. "Take a deep breath and try to relax. Good. Now another one."

Harriet was surprised to see Brandy follow Joyce's instruction, taking several deep breaths then letting them out slowly.

"Now," Joyce said. "Tell me what happened to frighten you so."

"After we ate, I went for a walk," Brandy said in a voice only slightly clearer.

"Right," Lauren whispered to Harriet. "Straight to her stash of alcohol."

Harriet poked her with an elbow, silencing her.

"And then what happened?" Joyce continued in her almost hypnotic tone.

"I tried to lie down in my bed." Tears started to dribble from Brandy's eyes, mixing with the raindrops.

"You say you tried. What prevented you from lying in your bed? Did a branch fall onto it?" Joyce tightened her grip when Brandy tried to jump up but continued her steady stream of questions.

"Unfortunately, no, it wasn't a tree," Tom said. He came to the center of the common area. His face was pale, without its usual hint of humor.

"What?" Harriet asked.

Tom looked at Brandy.

"There is, in fact, a dead man in her bed," he said quietly.

131

Lauren and Harriet both started to speak, but he held his hand up.

"It's Richard."

Joyce put her arm around Brandy's shoulders.

"What about Ronald?" she asked.

"He's in his tent, asleep, but very much alive, earplugs and all—I checked after I saw Richard. I didn't see any reason to wake him. We don't need him having a heart attack on top of everything else."

"You're sure Richard is dead?" Harriet asked.

"Yeah, I'm sure."

A vision of Duane's strangled body flashed through her mind.

"I think we need to leave," Tom said, "and I suggest you…" to Joyce "…do the same."

Brandy staggered to her feet.

"I'm not going anywhere with you."

Joyce looked at the others, but if she hoped someone was going to talk Brandy into going, she was disappointed.

"I can't leave her here by herself," she said. "She's vulnerable in this condition."

"Unless she's the killer," Lauren mumbled.

"Would you hush!" Harriet snapped in a low tone. "What about Ronald?"

"What about him?" Lauren countered.

"We need to tell him what's happened," Harriet said. "I know he's not doing well but finding himself alone with a dead body isn't going to help his heart any."

"I'll go get him," Jorge volunteered.

"We could drive all of you to the church shelter," Connie offered. "You would be safe there."

"I'm. Not. Leaving," Brandy shouted, dragging out each word.

"Calm down," Joyce said. "No one is making you do anything you don't want to do."

They stood in silence until Jorge returned, supporting Ronald with an arm under the older man's elbow.

"I knew losing my house was going to mean some changes, and I knew there would be some danger in living out-of-doors, but I never imagined this," Ronald stammered.

"Relax," Jorge said. "We're going to take you to the church shelter. You'll be safe there, and with any luck, they will have someone who can give you medical attention."

Ronald swiped at his forehead with his hand.

"I think that would be for the best. I thought I was in good condition for a man of my age, but this lifestyle is a little more difficult than I could have guessed."

"Don't worry," Jorge said. "We'll get you inside, and when downtown is open again, we'll get you set up with someone who can find you transitional housing of some sort."

"Thank you. I'd appreciate that."

"I'm not going anywhere," Brandy insisted when Joyce tried to get her to stand up.

Joyce turned to Aunt Beth and Connie, who were now sitting on the bench on either side of her.

"Maybe you should take Ronald to the church without us. Let me take some time to explain things to Brandy without the pressure of all you people standing around watching her."

"You mean to let her sober up," Lauren said to Harriet.

Harriet ignored her. "That's a good idea. That will give us a chance to call Detective Morse and also to see if any police officers are sheltering at the church."

"Someone needs to tell Marjory's sister and her daughter, too," Connie said.

"Oh, my goodness," Aunt Beth said. "I'd almost forgotten they were here."

"I'm sure that was the plan," Harriet said. "They retreated to their car as soon as lunch was over."

"They may not be the people we would wish Marjory's sister and niece to be, but they loved Richard and no one deserves this," Aunt Beth said. "No matter what they did to Marjory, they need our support now. And I know Marjory would expect us to be here for them."

Harriet sighed but kept her mouth shut. She looked at Lauren and could tell she was biting back whatever sharp-edged retort had formed in her brain, too.

✂- - -✂- - -✂

Connie's husband Rod had just gotten out of his car when Harriet and Lauren, followed by Jorge, Aunt Beth, Tom and Connie came out of the woods behind the restroom building.

"Where'd Kate go?" Harriet asked.

"Probably back to the truck," Lauren answered. "She didn't follow us when we went to see what all the screaming was about."

"Leave them be," Aunt Beth said. "We've got enough to worry about here."

"So, who's going to deliver the news," Lauren asked, nodding toward Richard's car.

"Señora Beth and I will tell them," Jorge volunteered. "We'll drive them to the church and bring their car. Señora Connie, can you and Rod bring Ronald and get him settled? See if you can locate a doctor or nurse at the shelter to keep an eye on him."

"I'll take Harriet and Lauren home," Tom said. "I can come back and get Joyce and Brandy."

"I wouldn't bother," Harriet said. "Brandy isn't going to leave. She knows they won't let her bring the stash of alcohol she's got hidden in the woods. We'll check at home and see if Detective Morse has called again and find out if there is any news on the slide or the river level. Connie, maybe you and Rod can come by my house when you're done with Ronald and we can figure out what to do next."

Connie nodded, and they separated to go to their vehicles.

Chapter 17

The sky unleashed a deluge before Harriet, Tom and Lauren reached the borrowed truck, soaking them. Mavis had hot water in the thermal carafe and warm cookies cooling on a wire rack on the kitchen counter when Harriet led the soggy procession through her studio and into the kitchen.

"How did you pull off baking cookies?" Lauren asked.

"If Jorge can make toast on the stovetop, I figured I should be able to bake cookies there also." Mavis tapped on a covered cast iron skillet. "My last batch is cooking now. Anyone care for some tea?"

"I'm about tea-ed out," Tom said. "Have you got any coffee?"

"Sure."

She pulled a bag of ground coffee from the freezer compartment and got a single cup and a cone-shaped filter holder from the cabinet under the counter then inserted a white filter paper into the holder.

"How strong do you like it?" she asked when she had the cone assembly balanced on a coffee mug.

"After today, I think I need a double," he said.

Mavis put three scoops of coffee into the filter then poured hot water over the grounds.

"Anyone else?"

She made tea while Lauren took Carter out to do his business and Harriet went upstairs to change clothes. When they'd returned, they all joined her in the living room.

"Detective Morse called while you were gone," Mavis reported. "She said she'd call back later. How did it go at the camp?"

"As bad as it *can* go," Lauren said.

"Is everyone okay?" Mavis asked.

"All of *us* are," Harriet answered. "Unfortunately, the same can't be said for Marjory's brother-in-law."

Mavis pulled Curly up onto her lap and waited.

"Richard is dead," Harriet continued, "It happened while we were all working."

"It looked like someone whacked him in the head pretty hard," Tom explained.

"That could have been us," Lauren said, realizing for the first time Richard was last seen doing the job she and Harriet had abandoned. She hugged her little dog to her chest, and he attempted to worm his way under the flannel shirt she'd put on while her sweatshirt was drying on the back of her chair in front of the fire.

"I'm pretty sure his death had nothing to do with us or our leaf-gathering."

"And that would be why?" Lauren asked. "Did some cone of enlightenment come down from above for your ears only? Haven't you ever learned the rules of group thinking? First you brainstorm, listing all possible ideas. Only when you have all those out do you start eliminating options. And then you need some plausible reason to do so."

"Well, excuse me for using common sense," Harriet shot back.

"Will you two behave?" Mavis scolded. She turned to Tom. "Perhaps you can fill me in without all the color commentary."

"We don't know what happened. We divided up into work groups and dispersed to do our jobs. Richard was down the trail, scooping up leaves and needles to be used on the trail to sop up mud. We were in the parking lot, cutting up branches for the same purpose, when we heard Brandy scream, and when we investigated, it turned out she'd found Richard—dead."

"My goodness," Mavis murmured. She shivered and tugged her knit shawl closer around her shoulders. "Who would want Richard dead?"

"Who wouldn't?" Harriet asked. "If he was as charming to everyone else as he and his family were to Marjory, I imagine he had more than a few enemies."

"But which enemies were at the camp with us?" Lauren asked.

"You're assuming our group is the only possibility. We don't know where the trail through the camp goes, or if there's another approach to the woods from the other side of the park."

"Score one for Harriet," Lauren said.

"It's a good point," Tom agreed. "Someone could have followed Richard and his family to town. Maybe they were just waiting for an opportunity."

"In the middle of a storm?" Harriet asked.

"Why not?" Lauren said. "It would be the perfect cover."

"Well, Richard and Pat did seem pretty anxious to get their hands on a bunch of money for reasons unknown. Marjory even said so. They had been riding high—too good for their relative in Foggy Point, until suddenly they weren't. They were broke and desperate for money any way they could get it, including sending Marjory to lockup."

"So now we have two murder victims, both found at the homeless camp," Mavis said.

"Makes you wonder what they had in common." Harriet took a sip from her tea.

"It does seem like a bit of a coincidence," Tom said.

"Duane could be anybody," she mused. "We know nothing about him, other than that he was homeless and then he was dead."

"The same could be said of Richard, it sounds like," Tom pointed out. "By the way, Owen happens to have a roll of electrical wire that looks a lot like the wire we saw wrapped around Duane's neck in his toolbox."

"That's interesting," Harriet said.

"I guess we'll just have to tell Detective Morse when she calls back," Mavis said. "Anyone for more tea or coffee before I go upstairs?"

"I'd love to, but I better go check on the Renfros. They're probably doing better than we are, but I don't like the idea of leaving them with no way to call for help if they need it. Besides, someone has to make a dent in all the brownies they've stockpiled."

"You have brownies?" Lauren's voice took on a shrill quality.

"If you behave yourself, I might be persuaded to bring some by tomorrow."

"Are they the cake kind or the chewy kind?"

"Chewy."

"You're killing me."

"I'll see what I can do," Tom said. "I better run. Thank you for the coffee, Mavis."

"You come for coffee anytime," she answered then turned to Harriet. "I might close my eyes for a few minutes. If I'm not back by the time the rest of the group arrives, would you come wake me?"

"Sure." Harriet turned to Tom. "I'll walk you to the door."

Lauren wrapped the tails of her shirt around Carter and pulled him close to her body again, her long hair forming a curtain around him.

✂ - - ✂ - - - ✂

"You really know how to show a guy a good time," Tom said when they had made their way to the studio door.

"I'm really sorry about all that."

"Hey." He put the tips of his fingers under her chin, turning her face toward him. "This isn't your fault."

"Sometimes I wonder," she said. "I mean, Foggy Point was a peaceful place before I moved back. Now all of a sudden there's a crime wave."

"But you didn't kill anyone. As near as I can tell, you didn't even know these two victims until this week, which is when all the rest of us met them. You can't possibly believe you have any connection to all of this."

"No, I know I don't. It's just a weird coincidence, but I find it rather creepy."

"I think you're thinking about it too much," Tom said and gently pressed his lips to hers. He pulled back and looked in her face. "You're not alone here. None of this is your responsibility."

He pulled her into a gentle embrace, his arms wrapped around her, his chin on the top of her head. She leaned her head on his shoulder. Without conscious thought, her arms went around his waist.

He smelled like freshly cut wood. She breathed deeply.

"You smell good," she said in a husky voice.

Tom kissed her again, this time longer, deeper. Then, he pulled away, catching her hand in his and holding it.

"If I don't leave now, I can't be responsible for what might happen," he said with a rueful grin. He brought her hand to his mouth, kissed it, and let it go. "See you tomorrow."

He went out the door.

The ringing phone saved Harriet from having to explain the high color on her cheeks when she came back into the living room. She was pretty sure Lauren knew the score anyway.

It's Detective Morse, Lauren mouthed when she handed her the receiver, as if there were dozens of people calling during the storm.

"Oh, where to begin," Harriet replied to Morse's query how things were going. She decided to start at the action point and gave the detective a concise replay of the afternoon's events.

"Where's the body now?" Detective Morse asked.

"Still at the homeless camp. He's in a sleeping bag but otherwise in the open."

"You did the right thing, leaving him there," Morse replied. "I'll call the fire station and see if they can get paramedics to go pick him up. They're trained in how to preserve evidence. If I can raise them, I'll get them to pick Duane up, too."

"Is there anything we can do?"

"No," the detective said. "Staying safe is the best thing you can do. The Coast Guard thinks there might be a window between storms tomorrow that could let them fly us in by helicopter."

"That would be great," Harriet said.

They exchanged storm stories then rang off, with Morse promising to call again tomorrow.

Lauren had left the room while Harriet was talking to Morse. She returned a few moments later with a cookie in each hand.

"Here," she said and handed one to Harriet. "Mavis cooked dinner, but I don't think we get to eat until everyone else returns. Who knows when that will be?"

"I wish we knew how the other serial killer victims were killed," Harriet said.

"I don't. I don't want to know anything about the serial killer. It's none of our business."

"If they were killed with electrical wire wrapped around their throats, it might explain Duane's murder."

"And make Owen and Kate killers." Lauren handed a bite of cookie to Carter.

"Did you catch the bad blood between him and Richard?"

"You mean that stare-down when Jorge was handing out the food? Yeah, I noticed."

"It doesn't make sense. If Owen is the serial killer and he killed Richard, why didn't he strangle him?" Harriet wondered. "And how on earth do they know each other?"

"Maybe he didn't expect to run into Richard, who recognized him and therefore had to be killed. He saw an opportunity and took it."

Harriet took a bite of her chocolate chip cookie and chewed thoughtfully.

"Owen's truck was right there. He and Kate went back to it before Richard went missing. Why wouldn't he get a length of the wire then?"

"You think the truck driver is the murderer?" Mavis asked

"I thought you were napping," Lauren said.

"I couldn't get to sleep. Curly kept squirming around trying to get under the quilt, and as soon as I let her under it, she was circling and digging until she worked her way out again. And then I was thinking about Marjory's sister-in-law. I know she's a difficult person, but no one deserves to have her husband killed like that. And then there's that poor spoiled daughter."

"I know," Harriet said. "This is going to devastate both of them. They seemed pretty dependent."

"Maybe they killed him," Lauren suggested.

"Lauren," Mavis scolded.

"What?"

"She has a point," Harriet said. "Everyone is a suspect until we prove otherwise, and if they were as broke as Marjory thinks, and Richard had life insurance, he might be worth more to them dead."

"I suppose there's no doubt it was murder," Mavis said. "Is there any chance he had an accident? Or even did himself in?"

"Tom said he'd been hit in the head," Harriet reminded her. "I suppose it's possible he could have fallen on something, but he was in Brandy's bed."

"I suppose you're right," Mavis said. "At this point, anything's possible."

"I'm going to get my stitching," Lauren said and stood up. "We might as well do something useful—we're getting nowhere as crime solvers."

Harriet followed her to the studio where they'd both stored their projects.

Chapter 18

*L*auren and Harriet were sitting in front of the fireplace, the candelabrum and two oil lamps arranged around them providing a warm light. Lauren was cutting more leaves for her appliquéd wreathes from a piece of hand-dyed green fabric. Harriet was using scissors to cut small flannel squares from the scraps left over from the rag quilts they'd made. Mavis was rattling pots in the kitchen.

"Okay, I give," Lauren said after watching Harriet closely for a few minutes. "What on earth are you doing?"

"I'm doing an experiment. One of my customers showed me pictures she'd taken at the Quilt Festival in Houston. They had a category for doll beds with doll quilts."

Lauren stopped working and stared at her.

"You know, with all that 'poor me, I went to boarding school' business you're always making us listen to, I never pegged you for the doll type."

"Who said anything about dolls," Harriet said. "And I've hardly mentioned boarding school at all."

"Yeah, but it's the excuse your aunt uses every time she's trying to explain away your bad behavior."

Harriet took a deep breath. She was determined not to let Lauren bait her into an argument.

"I'm seeing if I can make a miniature rag quilt from the leftover scraps from the homeless quilts. Before his sister came to town, Aiden was going to let me look at the toys in the attic at his place. He said he thought there was some doll furniture his mother had brought with her from France."

"Good luck with that. That shark that passes for a sister has probably sold off anything of interest or value."

"I wish Carla would call with an update. I'd like to know what kind of head game Michelle is playing on him."

"She'll call. I'm sure she's waiting for an opportunity when they won't notice, which means when Michelle is unconscious because that one doesn't miss much."

"You're probably right," Harriet said.

"Could you say that again?" Lauren prompted. "'Lauren was right about something.' Say it."

"Don't press your luck," Harriet said, smiling in spite of herself.

✂ - - - ✂ - - - ✂

Carter barked and licked Lauren in the face.

"I think that's his signal for me to carry him into the other room to see who drove into the driveway," she said and stood up.

Harriet set her flannel and scissors down on the table.

"I'll come with you. It has to be Jorge and Aunt Beth."

Instead, Connie and Rod stood on the porch outside the studio when she opened the door.

"Your aunt and Jorge will be along in a few minutes," Connie said. "They just got Reverend Hafer to take over with Pat and Lisa at the shelter. We found a nurse to take care of Ronald. He had another episode where his face suddenly turned bright red and he started sweating."

"Did he take his medicine?" Harriet asked.

"He did," Rod answered. "Little white pill?"

"Yeah, that's what he took after we found Duane when he almost fainted on us."

"Don't just stand there," Mavis called from the kitchen door she was holding open with one hand while the other held up a ceramic mug. "I've got coffee and tea."

"That sounds good," Connie said and led the way into the kitchen. Rod came over and petted the still-barking Carter, eventually taking him from Lauren and holding him inside his down vest. Carter quivered with joy as Rod patted his little head and spoke to him in crooning tones.

"He's a master with puppies and small children," Connie said with affection.

"Get your drinks," Mavis said. "We're starving for information here. And I've got beef stew for everyone when Beth and Jorge get back."

They didn't have to wait long. Beth came into the kitchen before Connie had taken her place at the table with her coffee mug.

"Jorge is bringing some wood from the stack outside into the garage to dry before he comes in," she said.

"Does he need help?" Rod asked.

"I don't think so. He was only bringing in a couple of armloads. We've got three cars in the garage, so there's not room to bring much in at any one time."

They discussed the rain, the river and the few tidbits of storm-related gossip that had been learned from people at the church shelter until Jorge was inside and holding a hot cup of coffee.

"I've got beef stew here," Mavis announced. "Grab a bowl and help yourself. There's warm bread wrapped in foil in the pot at the back of the stove."

"Let's eat at the dining room table so we have a little room to spread out," Harriet suggested. The antique dining room set could easily seat ten people and could accommodate twelve without much crowding, so it was definitely more comfortable.

"I'm sure you're all anxious to hear how it went at the shelter," Aunt Beth said when the initial feeding frenzy had passed. She proceeded to recite the events from the time she and Jorge told Pat and Lisa the sad news until they left them in Reverend Hafer's capable hands. There didn't seem to be any revelations that were useful in solving either of the murders.

"Do they have any idea who could have killed Richard?" Harriet asked.

"If they did, they weren't telling us," Aunt Beth said. "And we did ask."

"More than once," Jorge added. "According to them, Richard was a hardworking saint with no enemies."

"I find that hard to believe," Lauren commented.

"Before we report on Ronald, I'd like to say thank you for the wonderful stew," Connie said. "It was a pleasant surprise on a cold, powerless day."

"It's an interesting combination of ingredients," Jorge said. "Was that parsnips I tasted?"

"Yes, it was, along with Italian kale, turnips and a green pepper. I brought the fresh veggies from my house when I came over, and Beth did the same, so I used some of everything we had left," Mavis explained.

"Well, it's a very pleasing combination."

"Now, about Ronald," Connie went on. "We didn't learn much from him, either. He says he put his earplugs in and crawled into his sleeping bag and didn't hear a thing until he was awakened by us with the news about Richard."

"He says he'd never seen the man before coming to Foggy Point," Rod added.

"That doesn't help us much," Lauren said.

"And probably isn't true, either," said Harriet.

"What isn't true?" Lauren shot back.

"I'm not sure, but I can't believe they're all that innocent. We all know Richard wasn't a prince. And if Ronald was such a saint, what's he doing living in a homeless camp?"

"Now, honey," Mavis said. "We all know that simply having poor judgment where money is concerned doesn't make a person a criminal."

"We were talking earlier, and Harriet and I both noticed an exchange between Richard and Owen, the truck driver. There was definitely bad blood between that pair," Lauren said.

"Ronald was worried about his safety," Connie said. "He thinks the killer was targeting middle-aged men at the homeless camp and figured Richard was killed because he was in the wrong place at the wrong time."

"That gets back to our 'stranger in the woods' theory," Harriet said. "If it isn't the truck driver then the only option left is some unknown person hiding in the woods."

"That conclusion assumes we've eliminated all the women," Aunt Beth pointed out. "Joyce, Brandy, Kate and, for that matter, Pat and Lisa, were all there at the critical time."

"Kate was with us," Harriet reminded her. "We were in the parking lot when Richard was killed."

"Joyce was cleaning up the common area," Beth conceded. "Anyway, she's so small I have a hard time seeing her kill a guy as big as Richard. But she *was* out of our sight, so she has to remain a suspect."

"Same with Brandy," Harriet said. "She was out of sight, and I could definitely picture *her* chunking a rock into someone's head."

"And crazy people have that superhuman strength thing going on, too." Lauren observed.

"That what?" Harriet said.

"You know. You always read stories about crazy people summoning superhuman strength and breaking out of the loony bin."

"In the grocery store gossip rags, maybe," Harriet said. "I don't think that happens in real life."

"Still, I think she could have done it." Lauren said as she readjusted Carter's position, the little dog having returned to her lap.

"I agree. Not the strength part. I just agree she could have done it."

"She gets extra points for being in the same vicinity, too," Aunt Beth said. "Owen was working on his truck, but did any one of us actually see him?"

"The restroom blocked our view of the truck," Harriet told her.

"Same for us," Beth said. "We were behind the building, so we couldn't see anything."

"He would have had to go through the woods to get back there without any of us or Joyce seeing him." Lauren observed.

"But again, there's no reason he couldn't have done it. We don't know how many trails cut through the woods in that park. I'm willing to bet there's more than one."

"We don't know enough about these people to figure anything out," Aunt Beth decided.

"I made some chocolate chip cookies," Mavis said. "Would anyone care for some dessert?"

The phone rang, and Harriet went into the living room to answer it.

"Hello?" She listened while Carla spoke. "Wow. Did they expand on that?" She twisted the coiled cord around her finger. "Good work. See what else you can find out."

She then related the events at the homeless camp.

"I'm glad I wasn't there with Wendy," Carla said, "even if that did mean we were here all day with the witch. Aiden went to the clinic, so he wasn't here to rein her in. It was a nightmare, but nothing compared to finding a dead guy."

"I'm going to try to come to the clinic and see Scooter tomorrow," Harriet said. "Maybe I'll have a chance to see him and find out what's really going on."

"Good luck with that," Carla said. "Uh-oh, gotta go, she's calling for me again."

Lauren was standing in front of the fireplace when Harriet hung up.

"So?" she demanded.

"Let's go back with the others—Aunt Beth and Mavis and Connie need to hear this. That was Carla," Harriet said when they'd rejoined the others.

Mavis slid a cookie on a napkin in front of her.

"She had a bombshell to report. She said she was listening to Aiden and Michelle while they were eating breakfast this morning. He said he believed she was just trying to scam him into giving her more money, which their mom had explicitly said not to do, and unless she could produce evidence, he didn't believe anything she said.

"Carla said she heard rustling noises and then what sounded like the turning of pages. At any rate, they were silent for a few minutes. Then Michelle said 'Read right here,' and then she heard Aiden suck in his breath. Then he said, 'So, it's true. Our mother was a murderer.'

147

"She thinks he stormed out at that point. She heard the door slam, and then Michelle mumbled something, but Carla couldn't make it out."

"Wow," said Lauren. "That's a bombshell, all right."

Harriet picked up her cookie and took a bite. For once, her aunt didn't make a comment. Beth and Mavis were looking at each other.

"Clearly, there's a story here," Lauren observed.

"I suppose we're going to have to tell them," Mavis said to Beth.

"Tell us what?" Harriet asked, looking first at one then the other.

"Many years ago..." Aunt Beth began.

"...While they still lived in France..." Mavis added.

"...Aiden's mother was involved in a car accident," Beth continued. "It was dark and raining..."

"...The visibility was nonexistent..." Mavis said.

"...And a girl ran out into the street. She was running away from her controlling boyfriend and darted out in front of Avanell without warning."

"The police didn't cite her or anything," Mavis noted.

"The girl suffered a fatal head injury but was not taken off life support for a long, agonizing month."

"Diós mio," Connie said. "I never knew."

"Avanell was trying to put it behind her. That's why they moved to America—to try to get a fresh start. But she was haunted by it," Aunt Beth said.

Mavis took up the story.

"It didn't help that the family sued Avanell in the French equivalent to our civil court. They were in total denial that their daughter was in an abusive relationship. The suit was found to be without merit, but they appealed and dragged things out for years—long after Avanell came here. She kept having to go back and relive it."

"That's horrible," Harriet said.

"She felt terrible, even though there was nothing she could have done," Beth said. "There were witnesses who testified at her various proceedings that she couldn't have done anything. I think they were really the only thing that got her through it. That and

148

Aiden—she had him after they came here, and with a new baby, she couldn't dwell on things too much."

"It's also why she was always giving money to charities that provide services to troubled girls," Mavis added.

"That's a sad story, but what does that have to do with Aiden?" Lauren asked.

"Come on," Harriet said. "You can imagine what Michelle is doing with this. She's probably telling him that with both his mother and his uncle being killers, he's doomed. That's why she's suggesting he go back to Africa. She's probably telling him he needs to go to keep us all safe from him."

"And since he's not going to be here, why does he need a house or money," Mavis finished the scenario for her.

"She's a real piece of work, that girl," Jorge said. "Her parents took her to counselors, you know. It just didn't seem to help."

"Poor Aiden," Harriet said. "I've got to go see him tomorrow."

"You better wear your armor," Jorge said. "The boy is stubborn. If he believes what *la diabla* said, he will be hard to reason with."

"Carla said she seemed to be showing him something," Harriet reminded them.

"I wonder what it was." Lauren said.

"She said something about Michelle doing a craft project in the nursery the other day," Harriet remembered. "I'll bet she phonied up something. She worked in the nursery because she knew Aiden had given use of the room over to Carla, so he wasn't likely to happen on her creating the fake."

"What a witch," Lauren said.

"Always has been difficult," Mavis concurred.

"We better get back to our house," Rod announced. "We need to turn the generator on again to run the freezer and the water heater. What are the plans for tomorrow?"

"I'm going to the clinic to see Scooter and to try to talk some sense into Aiden," Harriet said. "Then I'd like to go to back to the homeless camp and look around. There has to be something we're missing."

"Jorge and I told Reverend Hafer we would come manage lunch at the shelter to give him and his wife a break," Beth said.

"Many people are willing to work for their food, but unfortunately, most don't have experience in a commercial-sized kitchen," Jorge added.

"Let us know if we can do anything to help," Connie said.

"There is one thing," Lauren said. "We haven't heard from Sarah. She's at her boyfriend's place on Miller Hill."

"By herself?" Rod asked.

"We tried to talk her out of it," Lauren explained, "but the jerk has her brainwashed."

"Do you have an address?" Connie asked, pulling a small notepad from her purse. Lauren scratched the address on it.

"I searched this out on the internet, but I think it's current."

"We'll see what we can do," Rod said.

The phone rang again while everyone was saying goodbye to Rod and Connie.

"Hello," Harriet said.

"I know I said I'd call tomorrow," Detective Morse told her, "but we have a plan of sorts in place, and I wanted to let you know and ask you a favor."

"Sure, what do you need?"

"I'm coming in by Coast Guard helicopter tomorrow along with another detective and some emergency medical personnel. They'll be landing us at the grade school. My apartment is on the downtown side of the bridge, so I won't be able to get home or get a car. Could you give me a ride to the shelter at the church?"

"Of course, but why don't you come stay at my house? We're having a sort of ongoing pajama party. My aunt and Mavis and Lauren are here, along with Jorge."

"It sounds like you have a full house already," Morse said.

"We still have room. I've got several of those blow-up beds, and I have a whole attic that no one is staying in. It may not be the Ritz, but with a down sleeping bag and the airbed I think it will be as comfortable as any of us are without power. And we have a gas water heat and a gas stovetop."

"How could I refuse an offer like that?" Morse asked. "Their target landing time is noon, but it could be plus or minus an hour. Come at your convenience—I won't be going anywhere."

"We'll be there at eleven, just in case."

"I did get the fire department to pick up your bodies."

"Hey, they aren't my bodies," Harriet protested.

"I know, but you reported them, and we have to call them something. In any case, they're chilling in the fire station garage. It's the coolest protected place they could access. We've managed to get hold of a few more officers since we talked, too. And the guys downtown requested permission to take a kayak from the mercantile and use it to paddle out."

"Have you been able to reach Darcy?" Harriet asked.

"Yes, she checked in just before I called you. She'll be heading up to the homeless camp tomorrow to see what, if anything, she can come up with. We don't expect to find much useful forensic material at either site after all this time, but we have to try."

"I'm glad you're coming back," Harriet said.

"See you tomorrow," Morse said and hung up.

Harriet turned to her roommates, all of whom were currently standing in front of the fireplace, rears to the heat. They'd probably come into the room more for warmth than a pressing need to hear who had called, but she told them what Detective Morse had said without prompting.

"Well, I'm glad she's coming back," Aunt Beth announced.

"Me, too," Harriet agreed.

"Since when?" Lauren said.

"Since we aren't police officers, and it's their job, not ours, to figure out who killed Duane and Richard—two men we barely knew, I might add."

"Did Morse brainwash you?" Lauren asked.

"Since when did you become the gung-ho private eye?"

"Are you trying to tell me you're not the least little bit curious about who killed those two men, practically right under our noses?"

"Of course I'm curious," Harriet said. "I just don't think it's our place to interfere in a police investigation."

"I'm glad you've come to your senses," Aunt Beth said then turned to look Lauren squarely in the face. "You would do well to learn from Harriet."

Harriet raised her eyebrows and grinned at Lauren from behind her aunt's back. Lauren narrowed her eyes, but kept her mouth shut.

"Anyone interested in a friendly game of cards?" Jorge asked.

Everyone was, and he offered to take all the dogs out before they started.

Chapter 19

Weak light oozed through the kitchen window when Harriet came downstairs the next morning. Day three with no power had begun, and the whole slumber party/campout bit was starting to be not so much fun.

"I want my power back now," she complained to Aunt Beth and Mavis, who were sitting side-by-side at the kitchen bar. "I'm not out of clean clothes yet, but my dirties are stacking up, and I don't want to find out how the pioneers dried their laundry in the winter."

"You don't want to know what the pioneers did," Mavis agreed.

"You want some tea?" Aunt Beth asked. She had already filled the thermal carafe with water and set out clean mugs and a basket of assorted teabags.

"Sure," Harriet agreed. "Were those waffles?" she asked, pointing at the crumbs on the mostly empty plates in front of the two older women.

"You should know," Mavis said. "I found them in your freezer in the garage. I was looking for dinner meat to start thawing, and I found a package of frozen waffles. We heated them in the iron skillet and put the remains in the freezer compartment."

"You want some?" Aunt Beth asked.

Harriet did, and a few minutes later she sat down to hot tea and waffles with warm maple syrup.

"Yum," she said when she'd finished eating. "That really hit the spot."

"Well, we thought you'd need fortification if you're going to go see Aiden," Beth said.

"Where's everyone else?" Harriet asked.

"Lauren is up in the attic sweeping, and then she's going to set up the air-bed," Mavis said. "Jorge's outside with the dogs."

"He said he would drive you to the animal hospital when you're ready," Aunt Beth added. "He said there are a couple of places where the water is over the road."

"You ready to head out?" Jorge asked a few minutes later when he returned with the dogs. "Let me get these girls settled, and I'll be ready." He stooped to unhook the leashes.

Harriet got her coat from the kitchen closet and put her waterproof boots on.

"Wish me luck," she said to Beth and Mavis as she followed him out the door.

"Go easy on the boy," Jorge recommended when they were in the truck. "If you go at him with both guns blazing, all he'll do is argue, no matter how right you are."

"How can I make him see that Michelle is trying to use him?"

"The best thing is to try to get him away from her, somehow. He knows how she is. The only reason she's having success at all is because the storm is keeping him from talking to anyone else."

"But this started before the storm. She was here, and he was listening."

"He would have come around if he'd had the chance to talk to you and me and your aunt."

"We'll see," Harriet said. "I've at least got to try."

She spent the rest of the trip staring out the window at the storm carnage that had yet to be cleaned up. For his part, Jorge was kept busy dodging debris, standing water, and minor mudslides.

"Here we are," he said finally as he pulled off the road in front of the vet clinic.

A large Douglas fir had fallen across the front corner of the parking area, blocking the entrance, so Harriet would have to walk the rest of the way in. The offending tree was large enough it would require commercial equipment to cut it up and remove it.

"I'll be back in an hour," Jorge said as she got out of the truck.

"Thanks for driving me," she said and pushed the door shut.

"Hi, Harriet," one of the clinic vet technicians said from the front desk when she walked in. "Did you come to spend some time with Scooter?" The young woman was dressed in mismatched scrubs, her blond hair scraped back in a severe ponytail.

"Yeah, I thought he might like a little company. Besides, I can't work without power."

"We're all getting a little tired of this storm. We have a generator going in the back to keep the patients warm and do their laundry, but we're running it one hour on, one hour off to preserve fuel and it only runs two circuits. You can go on back. I'll tell Aiden you're here."

Harriet went through the door the tech held open for her then down the short hall to the converted storeroom. The tech brought in a space heater and plugged it into an extension cord that trailed down the hall and out the back door.

"You're lucky it's an 'on' hour," she said as she flicked the heater's power switch. Aiden came in a few minutes later, Scooter in one hand, a fuzzy lap pad in the other. He deposited both in Harriet's lap and turned to leave.

"Wait," she said. "Can't you stay and talk a minute?"

"I've got work to do," he said, opening the door, then hesitating.

"Please," she said in a quiet voice.

"There's no point," he told her without turning back around.

"Can't you at least tell me what's going on?"

"If I talk about it, you'll try to tell me I'm wrong, and then we'll argue and I don't want to remember us that way."

Harriet could feel the heat rising up her neck, flushing her face.

"*Remember* us?" she snapped, her voice rising. "I have no say in this matter? You've just decided we're done, and I don't even get to know why?"

She stood and put Scooter and his pad down in her chair then grabbed Aiden's arm and spun him around. She started to speak, but hesitated when she saw the pain etched into the lines of his face.

"Please," she pleaded. "Talk to me,"

"It won't change anything," he said, letting the door shut.

"What sort of lies is your sister filling your head with?"

"My sister is not telling me lies. She's just helped me see things more clearly."

"Are you sure that's what she's doing? *Helping* you? Think about it. When has she ever helped you?"

"I know my sister is greedy and self-centered, but that doesn't mean she's wrong about this. She knows our family, and more important, she knows me."

Every fiber of Harriet's being was screaming out that she knew Michelle was conning him because Carla had heard them, and Aunt Beth and Mavis had told her the truth, and she was certain Michelle had faked her proof, but she couldn't betray Carla so she kept her mouth shut.

"Can't we talk about it," she pleaded, "and figure out *together* if we should keep seeing each other?"

Aiden jerked his arm free.

"There's nothing to discuss. I'm sorry things didn't work out. You tried to tell me all along we shouldn't be a couple, and now I agree. Just let Shannon know when you're done with Scooter."

"Wait"...

He opened the door.

"Good-bye, Harriet."

Tear filled her eyes as she picked Scooter up and put him and his blanket in her lap again. The little dog licked her face, his tail wagging his whole body. He did his best to charm her. He tried to chew on her earring; he pawed at her fingers until she petted his head. And he sneezed repeatedly if she stopped talking to him for more than a minute.

"If you're trying to distract me, it's working," she told her little companion. "Maybe you're the only man I need in my life—well, besides your feline brother Fred. I bet you'll never leave me without notice or reason."

156

Scooter licked her face again then began barking at the sound of a knock on the door.

"Come in," she called when the door didn't open immediately.

It was Shannon.

"I just wanted to let you know it's time to turn the generator off again. It's going to get cold in here. We have microwave heating pads in the animal cages that will retain the heat for an hour, so I'm afraid this little guy needs to go back."

Harriet glanced at her watch and was surprised to see her hour was almost up.

"My ride is going to be here any minute anyway. Thanks for taking such good care of Scooter."

"No problem," Shannon said with a smile. Harriet didn't know if the young woman had heard any of her discussion with Aiden, but her slightly awkward manner suggested she had.

She waited until Shannon and Scooter had left the room then put her coat on and walked out through the reception area and into the cold parking lot. Jorge's pickup was parked at the side of the road, across the street from the clinic.

"How did it go?" Lauren asked when Harriet got into the truck.

"Let her be," Jorge said when he saw Harriet's face. "Is there anywhere you'd like to go? We've got about thirty minutes before we need to pick up the detective."

"How's that going to work?" Harriet asked. "I mean, where's she going to sit?"

Lauren answered for him.

"I had the same question, but it turns out there are two little seats in back that face each other and have seatbelts and everything."

"We could swing by the homeless camp," Harriet said. "According to Morse, the paramedics took the bodies away, and Darcy was supposed to be trying to collect evidence. Maybe she's still there."

"The park it is, then," Jorge said and turned the truck toward Fogg Park.

"Aiden is being totally dumb," Harriet said, answering Lauren's earlier question. "I can't believe he's willing to listen to his sister's nonsense. I mean, what if his mother *was* a murderer, and his uncle, too? It doesn't make sense for him to just give up his life and go hide in Africa, does it? Does that make sense to anyone?"

"If your family was psychopathic serial killers, wouldn't that give you just a little pause," Lauren asked. "I mean, wouldn't you at least wonder if you were capable of turning into a killer?"

"But the very fact he would worry enough to want to break up and leave means he couldn't be a psychopath."

"Oh, so now you're an expert on criminal behavior?" Lauren asked. "You see it on TV all the time—serial killer lived on our street and we never suspected anything, he was married with two-point-four kids."

"And of course everything you see on the television is true."

"As true as—"

"Ladies," Jorge said, cutting Lauren off. "We're here,"

He stopped near the restroom building. A red Jeep sat sideways across two parking spots, the back hatch open. Darcy was here.

Harriet got out of the truck; she zipped her coat as a slow rain started falling.

"I'm going to see Señora Joyce," Jorge said and headed for the trail.

"Darcy?" Harriet called out as she and Lauren headed toward the restroom door.

"In here," Darcy answered from the men's side. "Don't come all the way in."

"How's it going?" Harriet asked from just outside the door.

"I'm not getting much done on that quilt I'm making for my niece," she said. "Hopefully, I can still get it done in time for Christmas."

"I'll hold a spot for you if you want me to quilt it," Harriet offered.

"Of course I do," Darcy said. "I don't quilt anything bigger than a table runner on my own sewing machine anymore."

"When the power comes back, call me with your best guess on timing, and I'll put you on the schedule."

"Thanks, I will."

"Are you finding anything?"

Darcy was in the stall, paper booties covering her feet, a large black camera in her hands. She focused the lens and snapped a rapid succession of pictures.

"You know I couldn't tell you if I did. But I *can* tell you this—the scene was compromised. Not only from people coming in to look at the vic, but a lot of fine debris blows into the bathroom through the vents during this type of storm." She pointed up at a series of screened openings above each stall.

"It doesn't look like anyone disturbed the body before the paramedics got here, but who knows. I'll have to compare my pictures with the ones they took and see what story they all tell us."

"I didn't see any footprints when I came in here the first day," Harriet offered.

"Whoever did this was careful," Darcy said. "But with all the mud from people coming in and out before and after the crime and the open environment, he didn't have to worry too much."

"He?" Lauren asked.

"Or she," Darcy said. "And that's all I'm saying." She started picking up paper bags she'd filled with samples and evidence then closed her camera into its case. "I've got to go check these in to the temporary storage area at the fire station," Darcy said. "Do you all have food and water and batteries and stuff?"

"Yeah, we're good. My aunt and Mavis stocked my house before the slide. I think we're good for another month or so. How about you?"

"I went to stay with my folks. They're doing fine, but I wanted to be there, just in case. Besides, they have a woodstove with a flat top, so my mom is cooking all kinds of yummy stuff in her iron pots while it warms the whole house."

"Let me know about your quilt," Harriet said as Darcy went back to her car. "We're going to go see how the homeless folks are doing." She headed around to the back of the restroom and the trail into the woods. "I hope Darcy can come up with something."

"She didn't sound very hopeful," Lauren said.

The two women walked the rest of the way to the camp's common area, each lost in her own thoughts. They found Joyce and Jorge laying a quilt from the plastic storage bin onto the table.

"Well, that's weird," Joyce said. "We're missing a quilt. I was going to send one of the two extra we had left to Ronald at the church. Jorge said he would take it to him."

"What happened to the one we gave him?" Lauren asked.

"I'm sure it's in his tent, but I don't feel like I should break in just to get a cover."

"Break in?" Harriet asked.

"He has a little combination lock on the zipper. I know it isn't much, but we all lock up what we can. It won't stop a determined thief, but it does deter the casual one."

"Did you look in any of the other areas? I understand you had some transient people who stayed here the first night of the storm."

"They may have had extra people in the restrooms, but the people who were camping here went to the church shelter that afternoon."

"Have you looked in Duane's space?"

"No, I haven't. That young woman from the police went back and looked around, but she didn't bring anything out that I could see."

"Do you mind if *we* look around a little?" Harriet asked.

Joyce nodded her agreement.

"Didn't Duane have his quilt with him in the restroom stall?" Lauren asked.

"He did, but remember, he didn't take one at first so we left the extras with Joyce, and I specifically gave her one for him. It was one of the quillows. But you know, now I think about it, the one that was covering him in the restroom didn't have a pocket on it. At least, not that I could see."

"Who knows what goes on when we aren't here," Lauren said. "Maybe they did something crazy, like trade their blankets. Perhaps the one you thought he was getting didn't match his decor, so he traded it with one of the other inmates—I mean, residents."

"Would you lower your voice?" Harriet muttered through clenched teeth as they walked farther into the woods.

Duane's space looked much as it had when the Loose Threads had helped set it up several days earlier. His sleeping bag lay on the brush-pile bed covered by one of the tarps they'd made. There was no sign of a flannel quilt.

"Let's take a peek at Ronald's area," Harriet said and led the way deeper into the forest.

"Not much to see here," Lauren proclaimed when she came up beside her in front of the tent. As Joyce had told them, it was buttoned up tight, with a small luggage lock holding the two ends of the zipper system in its grip.

Harriet turned to go, but Lauren didn't join her.

"You aren't going to just walk away from this, are you?" she asked.

"I most certainly am," Harriet answered. "Just because his home is outside doesn't mean it wouldn't be breaking and entering."

"You're no fun," Lauren griped, but she backed away from the tent.

Brandy was nowhere to be seen as they walked back on the trail, so Harriet stopped at the entrance to her area and listened for the sounds of someone breathing.

"Is she in there?" Lauren whispered.

"I don't think so," she answered in the same tone. "Let's check it out."

They crept as quietly as they could into Brandy's camping area.

"What have we here?" Lauren asked in a normal voice.

Piled on Brandy's bed were three quilts, one with the distinct quillow pocket on its top.

Harriet picked up the quillow, and when she did, a cell phone fell out onto the bed. She dropped the quilt and picked up the phone.

"Jackpot," Lauren said.

Harriet pushed the power button, but nothing happened.

"This probably ran out of juice a long time ago," she said. "Let's go back to Duane's and see if he has the charger cord in his things. I'm not sure how it's going to help us, unless it has a place for notes and he used it. But if he was doing something that got him killed, he probably didn't spell it out for us."

"Geez, don't you ever go to the movies?" Lauren asked. "There's always some cryptic clue left behind at a crime scene. Are you going to take it with us?"

"I probably should leave it and tell Detective Morse about it."

"With Brandy on the loose, we might never see it again." Lauren pointed out.

"You're right. We need to protect the evidence." Harriet tucked the phone in her jacket pocket, and they made their way back to Duane's area. "We can give this to Morse when we pick her up."

"Speaking of which," Lauren said looking at her watch, "we need to go."

"Hold on." Harriet ruffled Duane's bedding with her hands. Nothing there. She paced around the space, looking first down and then up into the tree branches. "Got it," she said, and unwound the cord from a small limb that also held a damp washcloth and an equally damp towel. "We probably should leave the quilts and just tell Joyce where they are. She seems to know how best to deal with Brandy."

Lauren led the way through the forest and back to the common area of the camp.

"We found the quilts," Harriet told Joyce.

"Brandy has them," Lauren added. "They're on her bed."

"Are you señoritas ready to go pick up the detective?" Jorge asked.

They said goodbye to Joyce and assured her they would check in again the following day.

"I don't like those two women staying out here alone with a killer in the area." Jorge said when they were on the way back to the parking lot.

"They aren't alone," Harriet reminded him. "Owen and Kate are here, too."

"I didn't see their truck," Jorge said. "They may have decided to park in the church parking lot. There are a number of RVs there already."

"Or maybe they went for a drive," Lauren said, "because they could."

"Did Joyce have anything to report?" Harriet asked as Jorge guided the truck out of Fogg Park and headed for the grade school.

"Nothing to help your investigation," he said with a smile. "She's worried about Brandy. I guess the girl wanders out into the forest for hours at a time, and Joyce doesn't really know where she goes or what she does, and she doesn't want to follow her to find out."

"I think we can guess, based on the pile of bottles in her living space," Lauren said.

"Which kind of makes you wonder where she gets her supply," Harriet mused. "I can't imagine she could be walking to town and back in the hours she's not accounted for, but she has to be getting it somewhere."

"It still boggles my mind that they all live out there without transportation of any sort except their own two feet."

"Chiquitas, you are selling our fine community short. We have public transportation. The bus comes right to the park at least twice a day, maybe more."

"Really?" Harriet asked. "I've seen them around town, but I didn't realize they came out to the park. That adds a new dimension to our situation."

✂ - - - ✂ - - - ✂

She heard the *whoop-whoop-whoop* of the helicopter before she saw it, lowering to the playground pavement like a giant insect and coming to rest on a large white X that had been spray-painted onto the black surface. Jorge parked the truck a safe distance away, and the trio got out to wait for the passengers to disembark.

Harriet waved when Detective Morse climbed out the door, hunched over, one hand holding her hair away from her face, the other one gripping a large shoulder bag close to her side. She hurried out from under the rotor wash then walked to the truck.

"Well, that was nerve-wracking," she reported. "If anyone tells you the storm is over, don't believe them."

"I'm glad you made it," Harriet said.

"And I'm glad you're here, too," Jorge said. "Maybe you can talk some sense into those two ladies who insist on staying in the park while someone is running around killing people."

"Thanks," Detective Morse said to Harriet. "And as for the homeless people—I can't make them leave the park if they don't want to go. They have legal permission to camp there. And you know better than anyone that I don't have any officers to spare to protect them. Frankly, at this point, they're not cleared as suspects."

"You can't believe either of those two women is the killer," Jorge protested.

"Maybe they're a team," Morse said with a grim smile.

"Yikes," said Harriet.

"You gotta admit," commented Lauren, "if they are the killers, they've got a good cover act going on."

"But why would they want Duane and Richard dead?" Harriet asked. "One guy lived with them, and the other was just there by chance one afternoon."

"That's why they call us detectives," Morse said. "We get to figure that kind of stuff out. But I didn't say they were the killers. I just said they haven't been eliminated yet. No one has. I'm going to have to talk to everyone who's been to the camp since this all started, including all of you."

"Let's go back to my house and get you settled," Harriet said. "Then, if you want, you can talk to all of us. If not, Jorge can probably drive you wherever you need to go."

"Sure," he agreed.

"Sounds good to me," Morse said and climbed into the truck.

Chapter 20

I really appreciate you letting me stay here," Detective Morse said an hour later when she came back down from the attic space Harriet and Lauren had set up for her.

"We've got some sandwiches in the dining room if you'd like to have a snack with us before you get on with things," Mavis offered.

"That sounds good. And maybe you can fill me in on what's been happening here while we're eating."

Harriet started by describing her visit to the homeless camp with Tom right after the discovery of Duane's body and finished with Richard's death.

"I'm afraid we don't know much more than that two men are dead," she said when she was done. "Oh, and Tom mentioned that when he went to Owen's truck with him, he noticed a spool of wire that looked a lot like the wire that was wrapped around Duane's throat. We do know that Richard was in town because he was having money troubles and was trying to get money from Marjory."

"Our Marjory?" Morse asked. "Quilt store Marjory? Does she have the kind of money someone would come after?"

"Yes, our Marjory," Mavis explained. "And she has a small inheritance from their parents."

"So, I take it you didn't identify or catch the serial killer when you met with the task force," Harriet said.

"No, 'fraid not. Everyone shared their information on killings in their respective jurisdictions, and we compared similarities and differences and came up with a list of what are almost certainly victims of the killer and eliminated a couple of others. We spent a lot of time talking about how we would share information. And we tried to figure out what our killer's signature is. There is some disagreement, but we think we came up with a victim profile."

"Do Duane and Richard fit the profile?"

"Duane's not a perfect fit, but he does have some of the traits. Richard I don't know enough about, but on the surface I'd say no. These victims tend to be vulnerable in some way—homelessness puts Duane in that category."

"Great," Lauren said. "So, we didn't learn anything." Carter licked her face as if in sympathy.

"Sorry to disappoint." Morse got up and crumpled her napkin before carrying it to the fireplace and throwing it in. "If you're still willing, I think I'd like to go to the fire station and check in with the rest of my team," she said to Jorge.

"Sure. Anyone else want to go along for the ride?"

"I'll go," Lauren said when no one else offered.

✄- - - ✄- - - ✄

"How would you feel about driving, honey?" Aunt Beth asked Harriet. Jorge and Lauren had been gone for half an hour, and Harriet had spent the time pacing between the kitchen and the fireplace. "You're going to wear the carpet out if you don't stop that dancing around."

"I'm not dancing," Harriet said.

"You're not doing anything productive, either."

"What did you have in mind?"

"Mavis and I were thinking we'd really like to get up to the church and see how things are going."

"We realized that we've already started taking donations for the clothing drive," Mavis said. "And we're betting some of the people didn't bring extra clothes with them."

"Plus we always buy new underwear with donated money, and we've already purchased them," Beth continued. "We're thinking people might be real happy to get a fresh set of those."

"We'll suggest they donate a new set when things get back to normal." Mavis finished.

"Sure," Harriet said. "I'd like to see if the Owen and Kate are there. They kind of disappeared."

"You don't think someone killed them, do you?" Aunt Beth said, concern in her voice.

"No. At least, I didn't until you just mentioned it. That's a horrible thought."

"Oh, honey, I'm sure they went to the church for a hot meal or something like that. Or maybe they just wanted a change of scenery." Mavis said.

"One way to find out," Harriet said. "The bus leaves in five." She headed upstairs to brush her teeth and get a sweatshirt.

✂ - - - ✂ - - - ✂

"I hope the girls will be okay here by themselves," Aunt Beth said as she climbed into the passenger seat of Harriet's car.

"They'll be fine," Harriet assured her. "You and Mavis spoil those two rotten."

"You just wait until you get Scooter home," Mavis said from the back seat.

Harriet was relieved to see the familiar semi truck in the church lot when she turned in and parked.

"Well, that answers one question," Aunt Beth said. "Let's go inside and see what else is going on."

"How are the streets out there?" Reverend Mike Hafer asked Aunt Beth when they came into the church gymnasium.

"Passable," Aunt Beth said. "The Muckleshoot is still over the bridge to downtown, but folks are getting the streets cleared."

"How are you holding up?" Mavis asked.

"We're doing fine," Mike replied. "We were pretty well prepared, and people keep dropping off food and supplies. The children are getting cabin fever, but we've got some teachers here holding classes of sorts, and we have board games and the church library to help them learn about how people spent their leisure time before the days of television and video games. I just thank the Lord there weren't any serious injuries due to the storm."

Aunt Beth explained her intention to make up more newcomer kits in case anyone else came to the shelter. Mavis told him their plan to raid the clothing drive closet.

"That's a good idea," Mike said. "We're continuing to have people arrive as they run out of fuel and supplies at home. And I know we have people who arrived with just the clothes on their backs."

"If you think of anything else you'd like us to do while we're here, let us know. Otherwise, we'll get to it,' Aunt Beth said.

"Thank you for coming today. I know you're living in less than ideal conditions yourselves."

Mavis and Aunt Beth headed toward the doors across the gym that led to the interior of the church and their destination.

Harriet spotted Kate standing at a roll-up window that separated the kitchen from the gym. The church volunteers had set up a coffee station on the counter with multiple large thermal carafes with pump spouts.

"Hey," Harriet said as she approached her. "How's it going?"

Kate attempted a weak smile.

"It's going," she said.

"Is this a permanent move?" Harriet indicated the gym around them.

"Nothing is permanent in our life," Kate said and took a sip from the paper cup she clutched in both hands.

"Is that a bad thing?" Harriet asked. "I mean, that must go with the territory when you decide to become long-haul truckers."

Kate squeezed her cup so hard the hot liquid spilled over the lip and onto her hand. She dropped it and grabbed for a napkin. Harriet handed her napkins from a nearby table and put several more on the spilled coffee.

"I'm sorry," she said when she'd cleaned up the spill. "I didn't mean to upset you."

"It's not you," Kate assured her as she took a fresh cup and poured it half-full of coffee. "It's our situation. It's just so frustrating. And it's our own fault. Well, not our *fault*, really, but our stupidity."

Harriet waited for the woman to elaborate and began to think she wasn't going to when Kate sighed.

"This is so embarrassing, but…we *live* in our truck…because we lost our house. In fact, even the truck isn't ours. It belongs to Owen's brother. He has a trucking business, and if he hadn't let Owen drive for him, we'd have been in a homeless camp somewhere, too, just like Joyce and Brandy."

Harriet wasn't sure what the appropriate response was in this sort of situation.

"Like I said, it's our own fault. We had a custom cabinet business in Sequim. We weren't rich, but we did okay. One of Owen's suppliers told him about this financial fund that seemed too good to be true. He said he'd been investing his money there for ten years, and it was as near to bulletproof as a fund can be. He told Owen that not just anyone could put their money in it. You had to be nominated by a current investor and had to meet a rather high minimum deposit. To meet that minimum, we had to use all our money."

"I'm guessing things went bad when the economy tanked."

"As bad as it can go," Kate admitted. "We lost it all. It turns out we had given our life savings to a Ponzi scheme. We later learned this sort of scheme always has a few people who actually are paid their earnings. The people who run it choose people who will be withdrawing money from their account. The investors are so amazed by the returns they're willing to sell the fund to their friends. And of course, the company had all kinds of dummy reports and full-color glossy brochures.

"So, for those lucky few, it was the deal of a lifetime. It's the rest of us poor schmucks who got shafted. Owen and I were in that majority who had their money in the fund for the long haul. We marveled over how rich we were each month when we opened our statements, but we never tried to withdraw any of it." She made a strangled noise that Harriet thought was supposed to be a laugh. "We were so naive." Tears welled in her eyes.

"I'm so sorry," Harriet repeated. "Is there no way to recover any of your money?"

Kate shook her head. "We don't even know who was in charge of the fund. The government white-collar crime people are trying to untangle the mess, and there's some small hope they'll be able to find whatever remains of the funds, but even if they do, it will be pennies on the dollar."

"I don't know what to say," Harriet said. "That's just awful."

"You can imagine how we felt when everything started happening at the homeless camp. Things will never be the same for us, but we'd been starting to achieve some sense of normalcy. Owen's brother keeps him busy with driving jobs and pays him a decent wage, so with that and the sale of our business and home, we've managed to pay the debts we ran up when the housing bubble burst. We were living on credit when the jobs dried up, thinking that either the work slump would end or we could cover our debt with money from our investment fund.

"I thought we'd finally turned a corner. Then we had the misfortune to have our heater break in Foggy Point, Washington. What seemed like it was going to be a fun adventure has turned into a nightmare. I know it may seem cold, and I'm really sorry those two men died, but frankly, I can't cope with any more bad news. I just want to get as far away from here as fast as I can."

"I can't say I blame you," Harriet said.

"I'm starting to feel like this big black cloud is following us around and we don't know why. We're not bad people. We pay our taxes, go to church on Sundays. We both have good relationships with our families..." she trailed off with a sigh.

Harriet stood with her for a few minutes, neither of them speaking. She hoped it was helping in some small way. She was staring into her own coffee cup, lost in thought, when Aiden came striding up to them.

"I need to talk to you," he said in a cold tone, his jaw so tense she could see the muscle jump. He grasped her arm in a rough grip and pulled her toward the door.

The moment they were out in the hall, he whirled around to face her.

"Is it true?" he demanded. "Are you involved in not one but *two* murders? Again?"

"So what if I am? What business of yours is it? You've made it very clear—we're through. I get it. I don't like it, and it took me a few tries to hear the message, but I finally did. Aiden and Harriet are no more. So, again, what business is it of yours if I'm involved in two murders or twenty murders or anything else, even?"

"Just because I said I can't be with you doesn't mean I don't care about you. I don't want to see you get hurt, by me or anyone else. That's the whole point of all this."

"All what?" Harriet said in a louder voice than she'd intended.

"Don't change the subject. What about the dead guys? Why are you involved?"

"I'm not involved, not that it's any of your business."

"You *are* involved. I came here to take care of a dog and a cat that got into a fight. The two owners were talking about the people who had arrived from the homeless camp. They mentioned you by name. They said you were there when they found both bodies."

"That's not exactly true, but again—not your business." Harriet whipped around, pulling her arm from his grip and went back inside the gymnasium.

"What's wrong, honey?" Mavis asked when she spotted her leaning with her back against the wall just inside the gym door. Harriet wiped at the tears that streaked her face.

"Aiden's here," she said and took the tissue Mavis pulled from her sweater pocket

"Come on," she said and led Harriet out of the gym again. Aiden was no longer in the hallway. "Here." She guided Harriet into the closet where she and Aunt Beth were sorting through the donated clothing, looking for items that might be useful to the displaced people in the gym.

Aunt Beth stuck her head out from behind a rack of coats. She started to say something, took one look at Harriet and Mavis and retreated around the rack.

"I'll be back here if you need anything," she said.

"Do you want to talk about it?" Mavis asked.

"No," Harriet said. "Yes. I don't know."

"Take a deep breath," Mavis said in a soothing voice.

"I can't figure out what sort of game Aiden is playing. At the clinic, he told me we are through and offered no explanation. Of course, I couldn't confront him with what we've learned from Carla, so I just had to let it go at that."

Mavis handed her a bottle of water from her tote bag on the floor. Harriet opened it and took a long drink.

"A few minutes ago, he came storming in here and grabbed me by the arm. He dragged me out in the hall and started yelling about my being involved in the two murders. He said just because we can't be together doesn't mean he doesn't care. What am I supposed to do with that? He cares, but we can't be together?"

"Sounds like the boy's confused," offered Aunt Beth from behind her rack of coats.

"Oh, for Pete's sake, if you're going to horn in on our conversation, you might as well come out in the open and quit hiding." Mavis told her.

"I was trying to give you two some privacy, but I can't believe Aiden is pulling that old saw on you. 'I love you, but I'm not good enough, so I'm setting you free.' If I didn't know the boy better, I'd say he was having an affair. But since I do know him, I have to believe he's incredibly misguided. We have got to confront him about that nonsense his sister is feeding him."

"Hold on a minute," Harriet said.

"Yeah," Mavis added. "Hold your horses. It's not our job to interfere with Harriet's relationship with Aiden."

"Not that I have one," Harriet pointed out. "But I agree. Aiden has to figure this out on his own. Otherwise, we'll be doing this again and again with Michelle."

"I think it would help Aiden see the light if we could prove to him that Michelle's evidence has been fabricated," Beth said.

"Maybe," Mavis agreed. "But we can't put Carla's job in jeopardy."

"I'm getting a little tired of all the drama," Harriet muttered.

"Does that tired have anything to do with a certain out-of-town visitor?" Aunt Beth asked.

Harriet was quiet for a moment.

"Would it be terrible if it did?" she said finally.

"I suppose that would be up to you," Beth said.

"Let's take these bundles of clothes out to the gym. Julie Swendsen is setting up a table for us to put them on," Mavis said. She handed Harriet a paper shopping bag filled with packages of underwear. "Let's deliver this stuff and get out of here."

✂- - - ✂- - - ✂

They almost made a clean getaway.

Harriet left her aunt and Mavis under the covered walkway in front of the gym while she dashed across the parking lot through the rain to get her car. Detective Morse was talking to them when she pulled up.

"Hey," she said through the open car window.

Detective Morse pulled the car door open and climbed into the front seat, out of the rain.

"I talked to Darcy at the fire station. She said several of the folks from the homeless camp have moved to the shelter. Is that true?"

"Yeah, one older man who has some sort of heart condition and that couple who live in a semi with the broken heater. They got stuck on this side of the slide."

"Anything I need to know about them?"

"What I just told you is pretty much all I know. One is sick, and the other two are stuck here."

"Thanks," Morse said. "I guess I'll see you at the house later."

"Do you need a ride home?"

"No, I picked up a set of wheels at the temporary fire station." She pointed to a red Jeep in the parking lot.

"Lucky you," Harriet said with a smile.

Morse got out and trotted to the door as Aunt Beth and Mavis got in.

"Anyone want to go anywhere else while we're out?" Harriet asked her passengers.

"Are any of the stores open?" Mavis asked. "We could use another bag of flour if they are."

"Let's go find out."

She drove a circuitous route that bypassed the flooded downtown area, eventually pulling into the lot at Vince's Supermarket.

The lights were dim, but a handwritten sign proclaimed they were open and a single door was propped open with a wooden box. They could hear the hum of a generator in the background, but the dim lights meant it probably wasn't big enough to power the whole store.

"Welcome," Vince called from the lone open cash register. "Can I make you a deal on some soon to be thawed hamburgers? I'll throw in some fries," he added and wiggled his thick dark eyebrows up and down.

"We're hoping to get some flour," Mavis said with a smile.

"We've got that, too, but I'd be happy to give you some premade burger patties. My generator can't power both rows of freezers. I moved all the fresh meat into the one unit, and I had to prioritize stuff. I've got some bags of frozen burgers that are going to go to waste. You can have them if you want some for dinner. My son just took off with a carload to take to the church. You'd be doing me a favor."

"If they're going to go to waste, sure, we'll take some." Aunt Beth said.

Vince gave Harriet a bag and told her where the meat was in the back of the store and to go help herself. Mavis and Beth went to get the flour.

"Help yourself to a package of buns to go with them," Vince called as Harriet headed to the back. "Aisle five on the right, halfway down."

Harriet's route took her past the powered freezer with its thick yellow cord leading outside to the gas generator. The head of the extension cord could receive three plugs, but only the single freezer line was plugged into it.

She fingered the charger cord in her pocket. Before she had time to worry about whether the addition of the charger would blow the circuit, she'd plugged Duane's phone into the outlet. She left it lying on the floor charging while she went into the back room, located the tubes of thawing hamburgers and loaded several into the shopping bag Vince had given her.

She went back up aisle five and picked up enough buns to sheath the meat she'd taken before she went back and unplugged Duane's phone, pocketing it and its charger before going to the front of the store.

"We appreciate the meat, Vince," Aunt Beth said. "We'd like to pay for it, though."

"No, I'll write it off as a loss. It will be fine. I'm just glad it won't go to waste."

✂ - - - ✂ - - - ✂

Tom's pickup was in the driveway beside Jorge's when Harriet drove into the garage.

"Where have you been?" Lauren asked when she came into the kitchen.

"At the church and the grocery store," Harriet replied. "What difference does it make?"

"If you had been here, maybe you could have stopped them."

"Stopped who?" Aunt Beth asked as she joined them.

"Jorge and Tom are unclogging the rain gutter…on the attic roof."

"What?" Aunt Beth and Harriet said at the same time.

"I tried to talk them out of it," Lauren said. She pulled Carter out of her sweatshirt and set him on the kitchen floor in front of his water dish. "A burst of rain hit while they were having a cup of coffee, and they saw the overflow gushing past the window where the downspout is plugged. When the rain slowed again, they went into the garage and dug around for a while. They came out with an armload of ropes and boards and a broken fireplace poker and headed upstairs to the attic."

"Please tell me they didn't go out the attic window," Harriet said.

"They rigged some sort of harness and anchored it to the exposed beam where the roofline slopes down to the eave."

"I can't stand it," Harriet said. "We've already lost two men since this storm began. Do we have to lose two more?" She headed for the stairs. "I'm going to lie down for a few minutes."

175

Fred jumped from his perch on top of the hallway bookcase and followed her up.

"Come on, Fred," she said when she reached her room. "Your doctor is being a real jerk, and I'm tired of thinking about it." She patted her hand on the bed, inviting him up onto the down comforter. She unzipped her hoodie and as she took it off, Duane's phone slid out of the pocket.

"Ahh, Duane. Let's see if you've left me anything useful here." She gently pressed the on button. The phone hesitated for a heart-stopping few seconds, and then the screen glowed green as it went through its wake-up cycle.

Harriet grabbed a tablet and pen from her desk and prepared to scribble notes. She wasn't sure how long the phone would last, given a five-minute charge. She hit the contacts button first, but Duane had an extensive network. There was no way she could write it all down before the phone died again. She saw the notes icon and pressed it. The first note seemed to be a list of some sort. It was all numbers—what could be phone numbers followed by another number that varied between five and six digits. She frantically wrote the numbers down.

She selected the second note and opened it. It was also numbers, but they didn't follow a regular pattern. She wrote them down.

The third and last note was an ICE notification—In Case of Emergency—followed by a name, address, phone number and e-mail address.

"Well, that's something, anyway," Harriet said to Fred as the green light faded and the phone again went dead. "Arghh," she yelled and threw the phone down on her bed. "I want my power back."

Fred looked at her as if trying to decide whether he needed to dash for cover, but her tantrum was short-lived so he settled down on the bed and closed his eyes.

"Well, we can worry about what it all means after our nap."

Chapter 21

"Hi, honey," Aunt Beth said when Harriet came into the kitchen. "Did you have a good rest?"

"I do feel a little better. I don't have any idea what to do about Aiden, but my nap did me good."

"Why don't you grab a cup of tea and join us in the living room? Tom brought brownies from the Renfros'. Jane is back, too."

Harriet came into the living room a few minutes later, mug in hand.

"Where are the brownies?" she asked.

Jorge lifted the embroidered dishtowel that was draped over them, keeping them warm.

"Oh, my gosh," she said as she bit into the warm, chewy, chocolaty goodness.

"Guess who's coming to dinner," Lauren announced.

"Besides Tom?"

"Hey, I earned my dinner," he protested. "I was the one dangling out the window, unclogging the downspout."

"And I appreciate that," Jane Morse said. "Although I think a freight train could go through my room tonight, and I could sleep through it. We had to double up at the motel where the task force was meeting when the slide happened and we had to stay longer. The only other female detective was a very nice woman from Bremerton who unfortunately snored like a chainsaw."

"So, honey," Aunt Beth said. "Mavis and I were thinking we should invite Pat and Lisa to dinner."

"Why?" Harriet asked.

"You know why," Mavis said. "You know Marjory would expect nothing less. She has her differences with her sister, but she would be the first one to console her at the loss of her husband. And since she's not here, we need to step up in her place."

"But Pat's the reason Marjory *isn't* here to do it herself. Don't you think she'll feel like we're betraying her?"

"Pat is her sister," Aunt Beth said. "She'd be there for her, no matter what she's done. Besides, we don't know if Pat had anything to do with the scheme to try to take Marjory's money. That could have been all Richard."

"Maybe we should ask her, if we have to have her here." Harriet finished her brownie and took another one.

"I wouldn't mind asking her a few questions myself," Jane Morse said.

"Let's see what shape she's in before we start planning any ambushes," Mavis said.

"Would you like me to go pick them up?" Jorge asked.

"Thanks, but if Harriet doesn't mind, I think it would be better she drives Beth or I over to invite them," Mavis said. "Besides, don't you have cooking to do?"

"I don't like you ladies driving around by yourselves in this storm," he protested.

"The worst of the storm has passed. We'll be fine." Aunt Beth assured him.

"Jorge is worried about us going out alone after dark with a murderer on the loose," Lauren said.

"I'm available," Tom volunteered.

"If it's the killer you're worried about, I'll go," Detective Morse said. "It would make my job easier if the bad guy found us—I could arrest him or her, and we could pick up Pat and her daughter all in one trip."

"Enough, everyone," Aunt Beth said. "Harriet and I will go, we'll stay on well-traveled roads and go straight to the church and back."

"Seems like all you need to do is stay away from Fogg Park and you should be good." Tom said.

"I'll be in the car waiting," Harriet said. "The sooner we go get them, the sooner we can bring them back."

"Good point," Lauren said.

✂- - - ✂- - - ✂

"Are you sure this isn't a recipe for disaster?" Harriet asked as they made their way through the still, dark streets.

"We're not going to let it become a disaster. The woman just lost her husband. No matter how bad the relationship is between her and Marjory, she's grieving her loss, and we need to respect that."

Pat and Lisa simply said yes when Aunt Beth asked them to come to dinner. Beth led them back to the car, where they got in then rode in silence until Harriet guided the car back into her garage.

Once inside, Harriet took their coats and hung them in the kitchen coat closet, and Beth guided them into the living room, offering them chairs in front of the fire.

"Have you met Jane Morse?" she asked.

"Nice try," Pat snapped. "We were grilled by the detective earlier today at the church. My husband is dead, and she's treating Lisa and me like criminals."

"I'm very sorry for your loss," Jane said. "My job is to find out who killed your husband and bring him or her to justice. Sometimes that means I have to ask questions that make people uncomfortable. I mean no offense."

"I'm sure no offense is taken," Aunt Beth said. "Pat, Detective Morse is staying here with us until the water recedes. She's not here as a police officer tonight."

"May I fix you something to drink?" Jorge asked. "We have coffee, tea and hot chocolate as well as sodas and water."

He took drink orders and went back to the kitchen accompanied by Tom.

"Will you be holding a memorial service?" Harriet asked Pat.

179

"I haven't thought about that yet." Tears started coursing down her cheeks. "I wish Marjory was here," she said. "She'd know what to do."

"Should of thought about that before she sold her sister down the river," Lauren whispered to Harriet.

"Is there anything we can do for you?" Mavis asked. "Can we call anyone for you? We have access to a satellite phone."

"There isn't anyone to call," Pat sobbed. "Richard and Lisa are all I have, and now Marjory won't talk to us, either."

"That's on you, Mother," Lisa said, speaking for the first time since she'd arrived. "I told you and Daddy you should have told Aunt Marjory the truth and thrown yourself on her mercy, but no, you had to try to be all tricky and cheat her out of Gramma's money."

An awkward silence followed.

"I'm so sorry," Pat said finally, looking at Lisa. "I didn't know what to do."

"Would you like to talk about it?" Aunt Beth said softly.

"I can't," Pat said, looking at each of them in turn. She started crying again. Her normally pink cheeks were turning a purple-red. Harriet was thankful Jorge and Tom were lingering in the kitchen and Jane had chosen to join them there.

"Mom," Lisa said, raising her voice. "These people might be able to help us fix things with Aunt Marjory. Come on—it's our only chance."

"It might help," Mavis coaxed.

Pat continued crying. Harriet held out a box of tissues, and she took several, blowing her nose noisily. She shuddered and took a deep breath.

"Richard was about to go to jail," she said finally.

Harriet looked at her aunt, but Beth was waiting patiently for Pat to continue. Lauren made the circular motion with her forefinger that meant "get on with it." She kept her hand beside her leg so only Harriet could see it.

"If we could come up with more money, Richard could buy back time," Pat finally continued.

"What?" Lauren sounded confused.

"It's because of the kind of crime," Lisa explained in a matter-of-fact tone. "Dad took other people's money. He pled guilty to avoid a trial, and the feds said if he could pay any of it back, they would reduce his time."

"So if I rob a bank, but they get the money back, I do less time?" Lauren asked.

Harriet swatted at her and put a finger to her lips, motioning for her to hush.

"Was he trying to get other people to give him money?" she asked Pat.

"No! He wanted to get my inheritance from Marjory, and then we were going to leave."

"Mom," Lisa said. "Tell the truth."

Pat went through her sighing and sagging and crying and nose-blowing again.

"Richard was trying to get my inheritance, but Lisa and I were going to tell Marjory what he was doing and beg for her mercy. We were planning on sending Richard to the store, and then while he was gone, I was going to ask Marjory if Lisa and I could live with her. Richard sold the house, our house, to buy time. He had it sold before he even talked to me about it."

"How could he do that?" Harriet asked. "He didn't forge your signature, did he?"

"No, it turns out I was never on the title."

Mavis gave a little gasp.

"When he started making money," Pat continued, "he bought a bigger house in a nicer neighborhood for me and Lisa, as a surprise. He said he was going to have my name put on the title after he gave it to me, but we got busy moving and then somehow never got around to it. He already had it sold before he told me about going to jail. He'd been hoping he could raise enough money that he wouldn't have to do any time, but that was foolishness. He could have sold ten houses, and he still couldn't have paid all the money back."

"Was he embezzling from his company?" Harriet asked.

"Worse," Lisa said.

"What could be worse than that?" Lauren asked.

"It was investment fraud," Pat said.

"Like a Ponzi scheme?" Mavis asked.

"Exactly like that," Pat said. "This is so embarrassing." She put her hands over her face.

Mavis went over and put her arms around the sobbing woman.

"You'll get through this," she soothed. "You don't have to solve it all right now. Let's let it rest for tonight. We'll eat a nice dinner, and then everyone can get a good night's sleep, and you can start making a plan tomorrow."

"I'll show you where the bathroom is. You two can freshen up," Aunt Beth said and led them past the half-bath and on upstairs to the main bathroom.

"I call Harriet," Lauren stated when Aunt Beth came back down alone.

"What?" Harriet said.

"I call you—as a roommate. Someone has to give up their room when your aunt invites those two to stay here. It's probably going to be me, so I choose you to double up with. Don't worry—there are two more air mattresses upstairs. You have the biggest room, the chimney passes through your bedroom wall, so your room is the warmest and you have your own bathroom so I don't have to share with those two."

Harriet looked at Aunt Beth.

"We can't make her go back to the shelter given the shape she's in," her aunt said.

"She could be the murderer," Harriet protested. "For all we know, she just bought herself a big insurance pay-out."

Aunt Beth's shoulders sagged.

"Didn't think of that, did you?"

"She had no reason to kill the other guy," Mavis said.

"She might be a copycat killer," argued Lauren. "Someone else killed Duane, and Pat decided to go for the insurance money by killing Richard and making it look like the first guy did it."

"Sounds a little far-fetched," Mavis said.

"I hope so," Harriet said.

"Everyone ready for dinner?" Jorge asked as he came into the living room. "We've got burgers and fries ready in the kitchen. Everyone can come fill their plates."

Pat and Lisa came back downstairs and joined everyone in the kitchen. Jorge was a master of presentation. He had cut tree-shaped slices of cheddar cheese using one of Harriet's cookie cutters and placed them on the burgers. Detective Morse had cooked the semi-frozen French fries in two large iron skillets. Tom had put together a plate of sliced tomato, lettuce, and pickles and set out ketchup and mustard.

"Oh, this looks lovely," Pat said as she assembled her burger on her plate.

"We haven't had a normal meal in days," Lisa said.

"Eat your fill, chiquita," Jorge said. "We have plenty."

Pat and Lisa filled their plates first, followed by Mavis and Beth. When they were safely in the dining room, Harriet filled the detective in on what had been revealed.

"I'd be surprised if it turns out Pat killed her husband, but you never know," Morse said. "I wish we knew more about the first vic."

"I might have something," Harriet said, and explained about Duane's cell phone.

"Given the circumstances, I'm going to overlook the fact that you tampered with evidence, including removing it from the scene. Next time a murder happens anywhere in this county, stay away from it. Can you promise me that?"

Harriet retrieved the phone and handed it to Morse.

"I promise, never again," she said.

"I believe you mean that—at the moment, anyway. I can't believe I'm saying this, but you're probably right about the other campers destroying evidence. If you hadn't taken the phone when you spotted it, who knows where it would be now."

"The young alcoholic at the camp had taken Duane's quilt at some point," Harriet said. "And someone else had taken one of the spare quilts we'd given Joyce and covered Duane's body with it. When Tom and I were there, right after they found Duane, they all claimed they either hadn't been in the men's room or they had only taken a quick look, but clearly someone covered Duane. I can't imagine him taking a spare quilt when he had his own new one in his usual sleeping space."

"We better join the group before they come looking for us," Lauren suggested. Harriet, Tom and Jane followed her to the dining room.

Dinner was a strained affair. Harriet racked her brain for a topic that didn't relate to the house Pat no longer had, the money that had evaporated or Pat's murdered husband.

"Pat, do you quilt like your sister?" she finally asked.

"No, that was always Marjory's thing. I tried when we were young, but my efforts were never as good as hers. My points weren't sharp enough, my stitches weren't small enough, my color combinations weren't as pleasing..." She sighed.

Pat sighed a lot, Harriet noticed. She really had the long-suffering routine down.

"Mom knits really well, though," Lisa said when the silence had stretched to the breaking point.

"What sort of things do you knit?" Mavis asked.

It turned out Lisa was telling the truth. A lively discussion of knitting ensued, with Pat pulling an intricate green lace scarf from her purse as a show-and-tell.

Tom and Jorge took the dogs out for a walk while Jane Morse and Harriet cleared the table and began washing the dishes.

"What do you know about the trucker couple?" Morse asked. "I interviewed them at the church today, but they didn't have much to say. I was a little surprised."

"Why?"

"They seem pretty sharp, and yet, they ate and slept with the homeless folk for several days without seeing or hearing anything? I find that hard to believe. It makes me wonder what they're hiding."

"I can answer that," Harriet said. "They may have other secrets as well, but the big one is that they are homeless themselves. Kate was embarrassed and didn't want anyone to know. They lost all their money, their business and their house in a Ponzi scheme, which considering this evening's revelation might move them to the top of the suspect list in Richard's death."

"Did they say who their fund manager was?"

"I certainly would have told you if she'd said anything like that. I figured it was a coincidence that both Kate and Pat had lost all their money. Kate said they lived in Sequim when they had their business."

"I'm definitely going to be talking to them again tomorrow," Morse said.

"Kate was with Lauren, Tom and I in the parking lot when Richard was killed. Owen was working on their truck. I suppose he could have circled around the camp and approached from the back side. And that still leaves Duane. Isn't it more likely the same person killed both of them?"

"Maybe there's a connection between Duane and Richard we haven't discovered yet," Morse said.

"But Pat said they were coming to Foggy Point to try to get Marjory's money. She and Lisa didn't say anything about meeting a homeless man or anyone else."

"Sounds like Richard kept a lot of secrets from those two. He may have seen an opportunity to take care of business with Duane and collect money from Marjory at the same time."

"They made such a mess of trying to get Marjory's money it's hard to believe he could have carried off Duane's killing without leaving a shred of evidence behind."

"And yet he defrauded how many people out of how much money?" Morse asked.

"Point taken."

Tom came into the kitchen from the garage, a wet Curly held in one hand, her leash in the other.

"I was starting to think you were trying to avoid me," he said.

Detective Morse excused herself with a wink at Harriet and went into the bathroom, giving them a little privacy.

"Jane and I were just washing the dishes and cleaning up the kitchen. Besides, it was getting a little crowded in there."

"I know what you mean. It's a struggle to come up with things to talk about that don't set Pat off on a crying jag." He took Harriet's hand and pulled her toward him as he spoke.

"I appreciate the fact that you're here."

"I wish we could be alone, but I'll take what I can get, even if I have to dangle off your roof to get it."

"Thank you for fixing my gutter," Harriet could feel the heat in her face. "How can I ever repay you?"

"I'm sure we'll think of something." He leaned in for a quick kiss. "But not while you have a house full of people, and anyway, I need to go back to the Renfros to check on them. By the way, I didn't get a chance to tell you earlier, but I heard on the truck radio when I was driving over here that they expect the Muckleshoot to go down below bridge level overnight. You want to go for a ride in the morning and check it out?"

"What time?"

"Eight?" he suggested and kissed her again.

"I'd love to go," she said with a smile.

Tom took his jacket from the kitchen closet and left through the studio.

"I came to see if you two had drowned in the soapy water," Lauren said.

Jane came back into the kitchen as if on cue.

"And I'm supposed to make a pot of decaf coffee," Lauren added.

She handed the empty coffee pot to Jane to fill with water while she filled the percolator basket with coffee grounds.

"Good thing your aunt saved this old relic," she said as she put the assembled percolator on the stove burner and turned the gas on, lighting it with a match. "Before you ask, your aunt did, indeed, ask Pat and Lisa to join our slumber party, and Jorge is leaving after coffee to take Pat to fetch their car from the church parking lot."

"I don't know about you two, but I've had enough group drama for one day." Harriet said. "Let's deliver the coffee then get Lauren's bed set up in the dormitory formerly known as my bedroom. My aunt and Mavis can get Pat and Lisa settled."

Chapter 22

Harriet had both coffee and hot water ready when Tom arrived the next morning.

"I wasn't sure if you wanted coffee or tea," she said.

"You didn't have to do that," he said and handed her a warm foil-wrapped package.

"You didn't, either." She smiled.

"I think we both know I didn't. Mrs. Renfro sent this coffee cake over for you and your guests."

"We wouldn't want to offend Mrs. Renfro."

She unwrapped one end of the package and sliced two pieces from the loaf then rewrapped it before putting the cake on paper napkins. Tom poured himself a cup of coffee from the percolator and sat down at the kitchen table while Harriet prepared her tea.

"Where are your aunt and Mavis? I can't believe either one of them sleeps in," he said.

"They left just before you got here. Jorge also heard about the bridge and is anxious to get to his restaurant."

"Where does he live, anyway?"

"He has property somewhere that he's been building a house on for years, but he lives in an apartment over the restaurant. Aunt Beth and Mavis are going to help him clean out his refrigerators."

"They probably were happy for the opportunity to get out of here," Tom said. "Not that you aren't a gracious hostess or anything."

"I'm sure they were, for a lot of reasons. They're being very supportive of Pat and Lisa, but I know it's taking a toll on them. Plus, this whole storm thing is hard on everyone. And all of us are used to living by ourselves. We spend a lot of time together, but that's not the same as living together twenty-four-seven." Harriet sipped her tea.

"On the other hand, I, for one, feel a little better knowing none of you are living alone right now with a murderer running loose in the community."

"I'm hoping the return of Detective Morse will take care of that. She's out detecting as we speak."

"Has she had a breakthrough in the case?"

"If she has, she didn't tell me about it. It would help if we knew what the connection was between Duane and Richard. Assuming there is one."

"Have you asked Joyce or Ronald or Brandy?"

"Now that you mention it, no. When Duane died, we were focused on making sure Ronald wasn't having a heart attack."

"And then when Richard died, Brandy was hysterical, so again we didn't talk about the deaths, I never talked to any of the homeless people about it, did you?"

"Let's go check out Marjory's shop and, assuming we're going to have to clean the basement out, we can go get Joyce and Ronald to help us. It would be natural to talk about what happened, don't you think?"

"Do you have the key?" Tom asked.

"No, we'll have to go by Aiden's and get the key from Carla. She might even want to come help us. Let me go call her."

Carla answered on the first ring, and Harriet explained her plan. Carla jumped at the chance and volunteered to bring the key and meet them at the shop in half an hour.

"Mr. R. has a ham radio set in his basement," Tom said as they made the short drive to town. Harriet had suggested taking her car, which held eight people and had four-wheel drive. "He's been

188

communicating with the outside world. He said the governor has arranged for emergency supplies to be brought in by helicopter this afternoon. I guess they're bringing cases of bottled water and canned food. And he said they're working on a patch to reconnect the power at the slide."

"That would be so nice. We haven't had it as bad as some people, but still, I miss my power."

"Is that Carla's vehicle?" Tom asked as he parked at the curb in front of Pins and Needles and handed Harriet her keys. He indicated an older Bronco. It was the car Aiden usually drove. A carseat was visible in the back.

"Yes, but I don't see Carla." She went to the store window and peered inside. It looked pretty much as they'd left it.

"Hey, Harriet." Carla came down the sidewalk carrying a white paper bag in one hand and Wendy on her hip. "I was just picking up some day-old doughnuts from Annie's They had them in the freezer but they're starting to thaw so…anyway, it doesn't matter, let's go inside and see how the shop survived."

A thorough inspection revealed a layer of mud in the basement but not much else. The water had come in through the street-level basement windows, bypassing the main floor. A few more inches, and things would have been very different.

"We're going to go see if the people at the homeless camp want to help with cleanup," Harriet told Carla.

"Wendy and I are going to drive back to Aiden's and get a couple shovels and some buckets and stuff from the garden shed, then I'm going to drop her off at Robin's."

Harriet and Tom went to Fogg Park and explained their plan to Joyce. She agreed to come, but only if Brandy would come, too.

"This could be interesting," Harriet said to Tom while Joyce was attempting to roust Brandy, but to everyone's surprise, Brandy walked under her own power into the common area. She was holding a bottle of water in one hand and had a tattered-looking hobo-style purse slung over the opposite shoulder.

"This is as ready as I'm getting," she said, her slur less obvious but still there.

"Let's go, then," Tom said. "We need to go by the church and check on Ronald. We can see if he's recovered enough to be of any use, and we can also see if Kate and Owen are available to help."

"Kate might, since it doesn't involve being at the camp."

Joyce and Brandy got into the second row of seats as Harriet again handed the keys to Tom.

"The trail repair you all did yesterday really helped," Joyce said when they had their seatbelts buckled and were underway.

"I'm glad," Harriet said. "I'm sure that mud is a real problem."

"We're used to it," Joyce said. "It's like this every winter."

"I'll have to find out what the park has to say about it," Tom said, "but if they don't object, I'll come back when it dries out a little and see what can be done about putting a proper drain under that first section."

"That sounds wonderful," Joyce said.

"Duane could pay to have a paved highway put in," Brandy said.

"Duane is dead, dear," Joyce reminded her in a soothing tone and patted her hand.

"His money isn't dead," Brandy slurred and pulled her hand away. "It's sure buried, though. I just need to find out where."

"What are you talking about?" Harriet asked.

"I need a drink," Brandy slurred, "that's what I'm talking about."

✄ - - - ✄ - - - ✄

The women stayed in the car while Tom went into the church to check on Ronald. He was apparently feeling better—his color was improved and Harriet thought she detected a spring in his step as he followed Tom back to the car.

"You're looking well," she said when he was settled.

"I hate to seem like a wimp, but living indoors does seem to agree with me," he said with a smile.

Carla was waiting in the store when they arrived. As promised, she'd brought shovels, buckets, rubber gloves, two mops and a new package of sponges.

"As I see it, there are two main tasks," Harriet said. "First, scooping up mud and carrying it out, and then washing all the surfaces the first group removes mud from."

She and Tom said they'd haul buckets, Ronald and Joyce took the shovels and Carla said she would wash floors. When Brandy didn't volunteer for anything, Carla got in her face.

"Come on, Brandy," she said, "look at me. You're helping my daughter and me. Take a mop."

To Harriet's surprise, Brandy followed Carla's orders without comment.

✂ - - - ✂ - - - ✂

"I brought some bottled water," Carla said nearly two hours later. "Anyone need a break?"

She didn't have to ask twice. They hiked upstairs to the kitchen, and she brought out her bag of doughnuts. Harriet and Tom pulled chairs down from the tables in the classroom and, after a moment, were joined by Ronald. The older man took off his foul weather jacket and set it on the back of his chair. He wiped his brow.

"Whew, it's hot working down there."

"Are you feeling okay?" Harriet asked, searching his face for signs of illness.

"I'm fine," he said, "just a little out of shape."

"Are you sure? I don't want you making yourself sick helping us."

"No, no, don't worry, I know my limits and..." He patted his shirt pocket. "I have my medicine at hand if I need it. I never go anywhere without it."

Tom had brought a plastic container of Mrs. R's cookies with him. He opened it and set it on the table.

"I heard we may have power back today," Ronald said as he sat down. "Have you two heard anything about when the slide might be cleared?"

"No," Harriet answered. "All I heard about was the power. Why? Are you planning on leaving?"

He took a bite of cookie, chewing slowly.

"I'm afraid I am," he said finally. "I'd hoped to live close enough to my daughter to be able to visit and maintain some sort of relationship, but I'm afraid my constitution isn't up to outdoor living conditions. The young people who were here when I arrived encouraged me to join them in southern California. They said there's a camp there that's an easy walk to a soup kitchen, and the weather is mild year-round."

"I'm sorry you don't have better options here," Harriet said.

"I had hopes it would have worked out differently. I put an application in to be a greeter at Wal-Mart, but it seems even they don't want me."

"Did you know Duane very well?" Harriet asked him.

"Not really. It was natural, us both being men of a certain age, that we would spend time together talking, but he wasn't very forthcoming about his past. I could understand that. I didn't want to relive my failures. Why would he?"

When Joyce didn't come upstairs, Harriet excused herself and went down to see if everything was okay. She was halfway to the basement when she heard voices.

"Tell me the truth," Joyce said. "Did you see Duane with money?"

"He had lots of money," Brandy said, slurring the S.

"Why was he living with us in the camp if he had money?" Joyce persisted in a gentle tone. "That makes no sense. Remember what I told you about telling the truth?"

"He gave me money, but now he's gone and I need more brandy. If I could just find the bag…"

Harriet went a few steps farther down, until she could see Brandy sitting on the floor, her knees drawn up to her chest and her head resting on them.

"Don't you go to sleep on me, Brandy," Joyce commanded. She pinched her until the younger woman looked up, pulling her arm free in the process.

"Leave me alone."

"I will when you tell me about Duane's money."

"Duane gave me money," Brandy said. "Now he's dead. Leave me alone."

"Is everything okay here?" Harriet asked as she came down the last few steps.

"It's fine," Joyce said. "I was just trying to coax Brandy into coming upstairs to have some water."

"I don't want to go upstairs," Brandy complained. "Just leave me alone."

"Could you please bring some water bottles down here?"

Harriet went up and got two bottles of water, wrapped a half-dozen cookies in a napkin and brought it all downstairs. Neither Joyce nor Brandy was speaking, and neither thanked her when she delivered the snack.

"That was weird," she said when she was at the classroom table again.

"What?" Tom asked.

"When I was going down the stairs, I heard Brandy and Joyce arguing about Duane's money."

"Duane didn't have any money," Ronald said. "Why on earth would he be sleeping in the forest during a storm if he had the resources to be somewhere safer?"

"I don't know," Harriet said. "But that's what they were arguing about."

"Come on," Tom said. "Let's get this finished."

✂— - - ✂— - - ✂

"Would you like us to take you anywhere else while we're in town?" Harriet asked Joyce as everyone helped load the tools back into Carla's vehicle.

The group had removed the mud from the basement and washed the floor and walls with bleach. They decided to wait for Marjory's input before bringing the inventory down from the attic.

"If it's not too much trouble, could we stop by the post office?" Joyce asked.

"Sure," Harriet said. "Anyone else?"

"The liquor store?" Brandy said, slurring the S on *store*.

"Got any money?" Ronald asked her.

She didn't respond.

"Just the post office, then," Ronald said. "I'll go to the church shelter to get my things, but then I'll be moving back to the park. If the power comes on, they'll be closing the shelter in any case."

"When the power comes back on, I'd like to have you all over for dinner at my house to thank you for all the work you've done," Harriet said.

"That would be real nice," Joyce said.

"I'm never one to turn down a meal," Ronald agreed. "I'm sure Brandy would be happy to come, too."

"I'll come back for you in…let's say…two hours after the power comes back on."

"Our schedules are pretty flexible," Joyce joked as Tom pulled away from the curb.

Chapter 23

"You want to go back by Jorge's on the way home?" Tom asked when they had dropped their passengers at the church and the homeless camp.

"No, let's let them have their space. What I'd really like to do is go see Scooter."

Tom was silent for a few minutes.

"I take it Aiden will be there, too," he said.

"It's his place of work," Harriet said. "But that's not why I'm going there."

"Are you trying to convince me or yourself? And be honest."

"My relationship with Aiden is not at a good place," Harriet began. "And it has nothing to do with my relationship with you. His sister is trying to con him out of his money."

"And it's up to you to solve that problem?" Tom asked.

"I'm his friend."

"I suspect he and his sister have been dancing to this particular tune for a lot longer than the less than a year that you've known him."

"But he's more vulnerable since his mother died. His sister is playing on his grief."

"So you're going to take his mother's place?" Tom asked.

"We're through talking about my relationship with Aiden," Harriet said, her face turning red with anger.

They made the rest of the drive back to Harriet's in silence.

He parked in her driveway next to his car.

"I guess I'll see you around, then," he said and started to get out.

"Wait, Please."

He sat back.

"I know I'm not explaining this right, but Aiden is in trouble. He's angry with me, and I'm not the kind of person who can walk away mad. I need to have some sort of resolution. You knew I was in a relationship with him when you came back to town. I never kept that a secret."

She started to go on, but he put a finger to her lips.

"You're right, I'm pushing you, and I said I wouldn't do that. I just hate to see you so torn up over Aiden—again. Can't you see? Love doesn't have to be hard. And I'm not trying to scare you with the L-word, and I'm not saying we're there now or ever will be, but I like you and I think you like me, and I'd like to see where things might go. No stress, no drama." When he finished talking, he moved his finger from her lips and kissed her gently.

"Go see your dog and his doctor. Resolve what you need to, and if the offer is still open, I'll come back here for dinner when the power comes back on."

With that, he got out of her car and into his own.

Harriet pounded her fist on the dashboard once he was out of sight.

"I do *not* need this," she said to no one.

Unwilling to face Lauren, who had stayed home to keep an eye on things, much less Pat and Lisa, she got into the driver's seat and headed down the driveway and on to the veterinary clinic. The hum of the generator greeted her as she got out.

No one was in evidence in either the waiting room or the adjoining office area.

"Anyone here?" she called. She let herself into the interior hallway and headed toward the socialization room. "Aiden?" she called out again, this time louder.

"Be there in a minute," he called back.

Harriet went in and turned the heater on. True to his word, Aiden appeared with Scooter and his furry pad a few minutes later.

Aiden looked tired.

He sat down across the small room from her and held his hands out, warming them at the heater.

"Can I talk to you for a minute?" she asked when she could no longer stand the strained silence. "I want to talk without you saying anything until I'm finished. If you don't like what I'm saying, when I'm done, you can get up and leave."

He held his head in his hands then raked his fingers through his silky black hair.

"Go ahead," he said finally.

"I know I shouldn't be sticking my nose in your business, and I'm sorry for that. I just want to say that before I begin. I asked my aunt and Mavis about your mother and her past."

Aiden stood up, and she could see he was about to argue. She held her hand up to silence him.

"Let me finish before you react," she repeated quietly. "I asked my aunt and Mavis what had happened in your mother's past that your sister could be using to try to manipulate you. They told me that she had killed a girl in France."

Aiden's face reddened, but he kept quiet.

"She killed a girl in an *accident*—a tragic, unavoidable accident. The young woman was trying to escape an abusive boyfriend and ran into the street in front of her. There was nothing she could have done. The visibility was poor, and the girl darted out.

"There were witnesses who supported your mother's innocence, but that didn't stop the family from dragging your mom through the French equivalent of a civil trial. It was *officially* declared a terrible, tragic accident.

"Your mother was devastated. Your parents decided to move to America to start over. They had you, and life went on. Your mom never forgot what had happened. That's why she spent so much money and effort working with women's charities."

Harriet paused for a moment to let him absorb what she'd said.

"Carla told me your sister was working on some sort of cut-and-paste craft project in the nursery a few days ago. I'm wondering if she faked some kind of proof to convince you your mother was a murderer—but she wasn't. Your uncle Bertie is a murderer—there's no denying that fact—but your mother was *not* a killer. She was the victim of a tragic accident, just as surely as the girl who died was."

Aiden sat in silence for a few minutes then left the room.

"I thought that went well," Harriet said to the little dog in her lap. "He didn't yell or grab my arm or cry, even. Well, okay, I didn't really expect that last, but you never know. He's going to go think about things, and when he's calmed down, he'll realize his sister is crazy and he shouldn't listen to a word she says."

She held Scooter for the rest of her allotted time, which was up when a vet tech she didn't know came to tell her the generator was about to go off again. She handed him the little dog after assuring Scooter he'd be coming home soon.

A familiar semi was parked in her driveway when she pulled into her garage, and she watched Kate and Owen approach in her rearview mirror.

"I hope you don't mind us coming to visit," Kate said.

"We won't be long," Owen added.

"Come on in," Harriet said.

"I'd rather talk out here," Kate said. "It looked like there were other people home, and what I have to say is for your ears only."

"We don't want to run into Richard Reigert's wife or daughter. If I'm not mistaken, that's their car in your driveway," Owen explained.

"I have to say I noticed some animosity between you and Richard the other day."

"That's putting it mildly."

The door to the kitchen opened, and Lauren leaned out.

"Anyone want to come in for coffee?" she asked.

Harriet, Owen and Kate all glared at her.

"Sorry I asked," she said and shut the door again.

"Look, we have enough problems to last a lifetime," Owen said. "We don't need any more, and it seems like Foggy Point has more than its share right now. We heard the electricity is about to be turned back on."

"And they expect to get one lane of the highway open within the week," Kate said.

"We're going to leave as soon as we can get out," Owen continued.

"That makes sense," Harriet said.

"Look," Kate told her, "when we talked at the church, I didn't tell you the whole story, and I feel like I need to come clean before we leave town."

"If you know something that relates to either of the murders, shouldn't you be telling Detective Morse?"

"You have to promise you won't tell *anyone* until we're out of town," Kate pleaded.

"Neither of us killed Duane or Richard," Owen asserted. "But we do *know* Richard."

"Richard Reigert was the man who convinced us to invest our money in the Ponzi scheme." Kate said.

"You definitely need to tell the detective."

"If we do that, she'll take us in for questioning. She may even hold us for a few days, insuring that we'll miss our next load, and then we'll have to get our lawyer involved, which will cost us even more of the money we no longer have," Kate argued. "Please."

"We just want someone to know that Richard has a lot of enemies besides us and to point the police in the right direction," Owen said.

"I'm really not comfortable with this," Harriet admitted.

"But you won't tell anyone until we're out of town, will you?" Kate's tone was pleading.

"I can't make any promises."

"I guess we'll just have to trust you to do the right thing." Owen took his wife's hand and led her back to the truck.

Harriet reached into her car to get her purse and noticed Ronald had left his coat when they'd dropped him at the church shelter. She picked it up and brought it into the house, laying it over the back of a kitchen chair.

"So, what was that all about?" Lauren asked.

"You wouldn't believe it if I told you."

"Try me."

Harriet was trying to decide how much, if any, of what Kate and Owen had told her to share when the kitchen lights blazed to life and the clocks on the stove, microwave, and electric coffee-maker all began blinking.

"Oh, Thank you God," Lauren said.

Harriet could hear the television blaring upstairs and the clock radio in her room beeping rhythmically.

"Help me reset stuff," she said to Lauren.

"I'll start at the top." Lauren headed for the stairs.

Harriet flipped light switches and set the clocks in the kitchen before moving to the dining and living rooms. The dishwasher started filling with water. She reached over and twisted the dial to the off position.

"I gave an open invitation to everyone who helped clean things up at the quilt store to come for dinner two hours after the power came back on," she called.

"Have fun with that," Lauren called back.

"Oh, come on, roomie. You're not going to bail on me now, are you?"

"I've got to go check out my place. I think I turned everything off, but I want to make sure the heat comes back on."

"What if I go with you, and we stop by Jorge's to talk to Aunt Beth and Mavis about dinner then go to the store if we need to."

Lauren rolled her eyes as she came back downstairs.

"Okay, fine, but you owe me." She picked up Carter and tucked him into her sweatshirt.

✂- - -✂- - -✂

Mavis, Aunt Beth and Jorge were sitting at one of the tables in Tico's Tacos when Lauren and Harriet came arrived.

"How did *your* clean-up project go?" Harriet asked.

"Jorge's fresh produce was pretty ugly, but otherwise, his refrigerators weren't too bad," Aunt Beth reported. "We're fortunate, I guess, that our storms come during the coldest part of the year."

"It was about forty-five degrees in here until the power came on," Mavis said. "The refrigerators have to be about the same."

"So, how do we all feel about a party?" Harriet asked.

200

"Oh, honey," Aunt Beth said. "I'm ready to take Curly and go back to my little house."

"Too late," Lauren said.

"What do you mean?"

"Harriet invited everyone over to her house for dinner two hours after the power came back on, which by my calculations was twenty minutes ago." She smirked at Harriet.

"Everyone who?" Mavis asked.

"Just Joyce and Brandy and Ronald," Harriet said.

"And Tom and Pat and Lisa," Lauren added. "And I assume Detective Morse, since she's got to come back to get her stuff anyway."

"Well, if you're going to do that then we should call Robin and Connie and Carla to see if they want to come over, too."

"What do you want to cook?" Jorge asked.

"I've got some frozen chicken breasts I'm sure need to be used," Mavis offered.

"Me, too," Aunt Beth said. "We hit the same sale last week at the supermarket."

"I've got plenty of potatoes," Jorge said. "We could do mashed potatoes and gravy and fried chicken."

"I've got green beans in my freezer," Harriet said.

"And we can make some baking powder biscuits," Mavis said thoughtfully. "I think I've got some canned cherries at my place, too. We could throw together a couple of pies."

"We better get moving if we're going to do all that in an hour and a half," Lauren advised.

"We can call the others from here," Jorge said. "I tried my cell phone, but they aren't working yet. I suppose they'll have to reset circuits or something."

"Lauren and I are going to her house, and then we can go by the homeless camp to pick up Joyce and Brandy," Harriet said. "We won't be able to get Ronald, because we're in Lauren's car."

"We can go pick him up," Jorge volunteered.

✂ - - - ✂ - - - ✂

Joyce was waiting in the common area at the camp. She had her arm looped through Brandy's, and the younger woman was struggling to get free.

"Let me go," she said, still sounding inebriated. "I need Duane's money. We need to buy some brandy."

"Duane didn't have any money, and we are certainly not going to buy you any brandy in any case," Joyce said.

"Come on," Harriet said and went to her other side, putting her arm through Brandy's and hauling her to her feet. We've got hot food, bright lights and a fully functioning furnace. And if you two want, you're welcome to use the showers at my place."

"Do you have bubble bath?" Brandy asked as Joyce turned her around and pushed her toward the parking lot. Brandy dragged her feet.

"Yes, I have bubble bath," Harriet said.

Brandy straightened her jacket and pulled her arms free.

"Okay," she said. "I'll go anywhere for a bubble bath."

Jorge arrived with Mavis, Aunt Beth and Ronald just as Harriet pulled into the garage with her guests.

"Come on," she said to Brandy. "I'll show you where the bathtub is." She led her up the stairs and opened the door to the bathroom. "Let me get you some towels. If you want, I can run your clothes through the washer and dryer while you soak."

Brandy gave her the first genuine smile she'd seen on the girl.

"Let me get you a bathrobe," Harriet offered.

She opened the bathroom closet and pulled out a white velour robe with the name of an expensive hotel embroidered on the chest. "Here's the shampoo and bubble bath, and there's a hair dryer under the sink."

Brandy stared at the robe, almost as if she were afraid to touch it.

"Here, take it, it won't bite."

"I've seen people on TV wearing these kinds of robes, but I didn't think they were real."

"What can I say, I've traveled a lot. Set your clothes outside the door, and I'll pick them up in a few minutes and put them in the wash."

She went into her room and waited until Brandy had slid her bundle out into the hall and she heard the splash of water filling the tub.

Jane Morse had joined the group while Harriet was upstairs.

"I came to pick up my overnight things."

"You have to stay for dinner," Harriet said. "We're having a power's-back celebration."

Morse scanned the room, her eyes resting briefly on Joyce and then Ronald and Pat and Lisa in turn.

"Sure, I'd love to," she said.

"I called Carla," Aunt Beth told them. "She and Wendy will be over as soon as she lays out the dinner she prepared for Michelle and Aiden. She said they weren't home."

"Aiden's probably at the clinic, but it's hard to imagine where Michelle went," Harriet said.

"I heard there was a party going on," Tom said as he entered the crowded kitchen.

"You came to the right place," Jorge told him. "Now I'm going to put you to work. There are some folding chairs along the wall in the garage. Can you bring them into the dining room?"

"Harriet, can you bring one of your folding tables from the studio and set it up in the dining room?" Aunt Beth asked. "Move the main table toward the window and you'll have space."

"Sure, I'd be happy to help." Lauren raised her eyebrows and grinned. "You know you were going to ask me anyway."

Ronald and Joyce were sitting in the dining room when Harriet backed in carrying her end of the table.

"What's this I hear about Duane giving Brandy money?" Ronald asked in a hushed tone.

Harriet cleared her throat loudly. He jumped up,

"Here, let me help you with that." He took her end of the table. "We really appreciate you inviting us to your home," he added as he unfolded the table legs and locked them into position.

More people arrived, and Harriet and Aunt Beth directed the setup while Jorge and Mavis cooked.

"I think we're ready to eat," Jorge said finally, and Harriet carried the announcement to the living room, studio and front entry, encouraging people to assemble in the dining room.

"Where's Brandy?" Joyce asked, her brow furrowed.

"Surely, she's not still in the bathtub," Connie said.

"I'll go check," Harriet said and went to the garage to get Brandy's clothes from the dryer. She headed upstairs but found the bathroom door open and the light off. The used towels were neatly folded on the edge of the tub.

A quick door-to-door check turned up Brandy—asleep on Harriet's bed. Her hair was splayed on the pillow, the robe demurely covering all but her hands and feet. She looked so innocent and peaceful, Harriet decided to let her be. She set the clean clothes on the end of the bed.

"Brandy decided to take a nap in lieu of dinner," she reported when she rejoined the group.

"Is she okay?" Joyce asked.

"She looks fine," Harriet said. "She's just sleeping."

"This is delicious," Tom said. "My compliments to the chef."

Everyone raised their glass and clinked it with whomever they could reach. People ate and drank and made idle conversation until the main dinner was through.

"The pies aren't quite cool enough," Mavis announced. "Perhaps we can have coffee and tea, and I'll put them in the garage to cool."

Harriet lingered in the kitchen, loading the dishwasher and putting food in the refrigerator. Lauren and Tom drifted in to help.

"I'm sorry," Lauren said as she set Carter on the floor next to the heater vent. "I couldn't stomach Pat playing the grieving widow any longer."

"I'm sure she *is* grieving," Harriet said. "Just because she was awful to her sister doesn't mean she didn't love her jerk of a husband."

"Whoa, when did you decide Richard was a jerk?" Lauren asked. "He *was* a jerk, but you're usually the last one to call a spade a spade."

"When Kate and Owen told me they were actually homeless. The truck they're driving belongs to a relative. They lost everything in a Ponzi scheme, and Richard was the guy who sucked them into it."

"Don't you think that's something I need to know about," Detective Morse said. No one had heard her come into the kitchen.

"I haven't had a chance to say anything about it to anyone until now." Harriet said. "And might I point out that our cell phones still don't work? In point of fact, I was asked not to share that information, and I told Owen and Kate I couldn't promise that."

"Where are they, anyway?" Lauren asked.

"They said they just wanted to get out of town. I suppose they're parked somewhere near the slide. They swore they had nothing to do with Richard's death. And they didn't really want to cross paths with Pat and Lisa."

"At least they're telling the same story," Tom said. "They all agree Richard was a con man."

"That doesn't help us figure out if Owen killed Richard," Detective Morse said. "It just corroborates the fact they had good reason to kill him."

"You're welcome to spend the night again, if you want," Harriet told her.

"I may take you up on that," Jane said. "Let's see how long everyone else stays. I better go mingle some more, see what else someone might have forgotten to tell me."

She turned and left the kitchen.

"Hey," Lauren said, "I've got three bars of power on my phone."

"I'm going to go check on Brandy," Harriet said when she had the dishwasher as full as possible.

✂ - - - ✂ - - - ✂

Brandy was no longer on Harriet's bed. The robe was puddled on the floor, and her fingerless gloves lay on the rumpled bed. Harriet noticed the list of numbers she'd copied from Duane's phone sitting on her nightstand. She picked it up along with the phone charger and took them downstairs.

"I guess she got up," Harriet said. "She must have come down when we were in the dining room."

"That's weird," Lauren said. "How could she have gotten past us?"

"There are fifteen or twenty people here," Tom said. "And cleaned up she probably doesn't look the same."

"Whatever," Lauren said.

"I'll go back out and find her in a minute," Harriet said. "But now that we have phone service again, I want to try some of these numbers I copied off of Duane's phone. They looked like phone numbers, let's see if they are."

She plugged her cell phone into the outlet by the kitchen table then dialed the first set of numbers. An answering machine picked up, but it only identified that she'd reached the number she'd dialed.

"It's a telephone number, anyway," she said and began dialing the next one. She pressed the speaker button on her phone.

"You have some nerve calling here," shouted a man's voice when the signal connected. "If I find you before the police do, you're a dead man."

Harriet tried to interrupt, but the connection went dead.

"You need to tell Detective Morse," Tom said.

"I gave her the phone almost as soon as I found it. They've probably already called all these numbers and his contacts with their sat-phone."

"Try the next one," Lauren said. "Someone semi-normal is bound to answer one of these."

The next number had a "no longer in service" message.

"Okay, one more, and then I'm going to go look for Brandy."

She dialed, and the sound of the ring was echoed from somewhere in the kitchen. She flipped off the speakerphone, and there was no doubt—a phone was ringing in the kitchen.

Tom and Lauren went for Ronald's coat at the same time. Lauren got there first, pulling a ringing cell phone from the side pocket. She looked at the screen and confirmed that, indeed, it was Harriet's phone that was calling Ronald.

"So much for Ronald's claim that he'd never met Duane before." Harriet said. "I don't know what this list is, but Ronald's on it, which has to mean they knew each other before they started living in the homeless camp."

"Or maybe they charged their phones when they went to town and exchanged contact information," Lauren said.

"I'm with Harriet," Tom said. "Why would they pay a cell phone bill if they couldn't afford a roof over their head?"

"Yeah, I always thought that whole fancy-tent routine was a little suspicious, too." Lauren said.

"Let's go find Ronald and ask him," Harriet suggested.

She got up and went into the dining room, followed by Tom and Lauren. Ronald was nowhere in evidence. Tom checked the living room while Lauren went to the studio.

"I didn't see him anywhere," Lauren said. "And ditto for Brandy."

Tom approached them and spoke quietly.

"Neither one of them is in the living room, but Connie's husband said he heard Ronald asking Joyce about Brandy's insistence that Duane had money hidden in the forest. He said Ronald left the room shortly after that."

"You don't suppose Ronald took Brandy to look for the money, do you?" Harriet asked.

"Considering how long a walk it would be, I'd say that's a no," Lauren said.

"We need to tell Morse," Harriet said.

"Tell me what?" Morse said. "Do you have more information you've failed to report?"

"No, we just noticed that Brandy and Ronald are both missing," Harriet told her.

"Yeah, right after someone heard Ronald asking Joyce about the hidden money Brandy keeps saying Duane had," Lauren added.

"Hidden money? What hidden money?"

"We don't know if there *is* any hidden money, but Brandy insisted Duane gave her money from a stash he had hidden," Harriet explained. "And Joyce did say Brandy tends to wander in the woods."

"They don't have a car," Tom said.

"But they are both missing," Harriet countered.

"I can go check in the park, but it's a big place," Morse said and pulled out her phone. "I'll see if any other officers can help."

She dialed, spoke briefly then dialed another number, repeating the story.

"The patrol officers are dealing with an injury accident downtown," she said.

"Do you want us to go with you?" Harriet asked.

"No, you stay here with your guests. If Brandy and Ronald are on foot, I should catch up to them pretty quickly."

"Okay," Harriet said. "You have my number, and our cell phones are working again, so let us know when you find out anything."

Detective Morse put on her all-weather coat, grabbed her purse and went out into the night. She came storming back in, moments later. She was talking on her cell phone as she entered the kitchen.

"They took my car!" she shouted. "My lousy fire station Jeep. Gone." She threw her purse onto a kitchen chair, punched a button on her phone and shoved it into her pants pocket.

"I could drive you," Harriet offered.

Morse raked her fingers through her hair as she paced across the kitchen. She stopped and stared at the ceiling, taking a deep breath then letting it out in a rush.

"Okay, but you don't get out of the car," she ordered. "This complicates things," she said, more to herself than to Harriet. "They'll make it to the park ahead of us. After that, it's anyone's guess where they go."

"I got the impression Brandy usually went farther down the trail from the homeless camp." Harriet said.

"Do you have any idea how many hundreds of acres of forest that park has?" Morse shot back.

"I guess not." Harriet got her purse and keys and put on her jacket.

"I call shotgun," Lauren said.

Morse rolled her eyes.

"I suppose you're coming along, too," she said and looked at Tom.

"Only if you want me to," he replied.

"Good, you're staying here," Morse said. "Let's go."

Lauren grabbed her jacket and wallet.

"Take care of Carter," she yelled back to Tom as she went into the garage.

"I might be able to narrow down our search area," Harriet said as she backed out. She handed her phone to Lauren. "Call Aiden."

Lauren keyed her way to Harriet's favorites list and touched Aiden's name on the screen. She handed the phone back.

"I need your help," Harriet said when he answered. "You said you ran on every trail in Foggy Point when you were on the cross-country team in high school...Can you think of a particular trail in Fogg Park, near the homeless camp, that would lend itself to hiding cash?...I realize it's not much to go on...Okay, we'll see you there."

"Please tell me he's not joining us," Detective Morse said.

"He said there's a place that isn't too far beyond the homeless camp. There was a student-run drug operation when he was in high school. They hid their inventory in a small cave off one of the trails. He said the group was broken up and the kids sent off to jail. He said it was easier to show us then to try to describe it."

"Oh, great." Morse sank lower into her seat.

"There's the jeep," Harriet said as she turned her car into Fogg Park. Aiden guided his vintage Bronco in right behind her.

"That was quick," Lauren said.

"You two stay here," Detective Morse said as Harriet and Lauren got out of the car.

"What's going on?" Aiden said.

"Two of the homeless people disappeared, and we think the guy was forcing the girl to lead him to a stash of money that may or may not exist and was or wasn't stashed in the woods by the homeless man who was killed during the storm," Harriet said in a rush.

"What?"

"Let's just go look for the people," Detective Morse said.

Aiden started down the trail at a ground-eating pace; Morse struggled to keep up. Harriet and Lauren went to the common area of the camp.

"Do you think Ronald killed Duane?" Lauren asked her.

"I don't know. It could just be that he wants Duane's money—if there is money."

"But they had some sort of connection," Lauren argued.

"You'd think if they knew each other, Ronald would have known about the money."

"I suppose Brandy could be messed up enough to have imagined it all," Lauren mused.

"Let's go check out Brandy's space again," Harriet said and pulled a small flashlight from her purse. "Who knows what else she has hidden in there."

She led the way down the trail.

"What was that?" Lauren asked as they reached Brandy's space.

"What was what?" Harriet asked.

"Shhh," Lauren said.

The two women stopped, and Harriet strained to hear what Lauren was talking about.

"If I had a drink, I know I could find it," Brandy said in her customary slur.

The sound of a slap echoed through the woods.

"I'll give you a drink, alright," Ronald boomed. "You show me where Duane hid his money, and you can drown in it, for all I care."

"It's hard to see in the dark," Brandy whimpered.

Harriet shone her light around the young woman's campsite, stopping at one place where the branches that formed the back-drop of her sleeping area were broken in a regular pattern.

"Look," she said to Lauren. "It looks like there might be a trail through here."

They pushed their way through the brush, following the direction of the broken branches, and soon found themselves on a cleared trail that was above and parallel to a wider trail.

"That must be a branch of the main trail," Lauren whispered.

They heard the unmistakable sound of flesh slapping flesh.

"Come on," Harriet said then stopped suddenly and pointed.

They were directly above Ronald and Brandy—and Ronald's gun. He poked the young woman in the ribs with the barrel.

"Okay, okay," Brandy cried. "It's ahead. You have to move that log to the side."

"Oh, young lady, you don't think I'm going to fall for such a simple ruse, do you? As soon as I bend over to move the log, you either hit me in the head or take off down the trail."

"No, I wouldn't lie to you, really. I promise," Brandy whined.

"Let her go," Detective Morse said. She and Aiden had appeared from a side trail. Morse was holding a nasty-looking black gun in her hand.

"It seems we have a standoff," Ronald said. "Take another step closer, and I shoot the girl. Walking in the woods is not a crime, so you see, you really have no business here."

"If you're not doing anything wrong, let the girl go." Morse said in a level voice.

"I think we both know I can't do that." He pointed the gun at Brandy's head. "Now, step back and put your gun down, or this ends very badly for my young friend."

Morse backed up and slowly set her gun on the trail in front of her.

Ronald had his back to Harriet and Lauren. Detective Morse was focused on Ronald. Aiden looked up and caught Harriet's eye. He remained motionless, giving no indication that he'd seen anything.

Harriet backed up slightly, pushing Lauren backward until they were out of sight of either group below.

"What are you doing?" Lauren whispered.

"Morse doesn't have any backup coming," Harriet whispered back. "Even if we left here undetected—where would we go? Who would we call?"

"So, what's the plan, Ace?"

Harriet looked around.

"We could hit him with rocks," she suggested.

"And he could shoot Brandy as a result."

"He's likely to do that anyway. He's got nothing to lose. And Aiden spotted us. He can distract Ronald, and we can hit him with a rock."

"Are you nuts?"

"Maybe," Harriet whispered. "But if we use a big enough rock, we don't have to be very accurate."

"We both know you have no backup," Ronald said to Detective Morse. "And I'm thinking the fact you showed up at this exact location means you have some reason to believe this is, in fact, where Duane hid his money. I've been patient with you, but frankly I'm getting cold. So, what's it going to be? Will I shoot you all? Or will you move this log for me and fetch the money?"

Morse looked at Aiden.

"We better move the log," she said.

Harriet gestured at a large rock that was at the side of the trail. It took both of them to pick it up. They shuffled into position directly above Ronald.

Harriet looked at Aiden; he gave the slightest of nods.

On three, she mouthed.

They swung their rock back, forward, back again then launched it over the bank and onto Ronald.

Aiden sprang forward as the rock crashed into Ronald's back, forcing him to his knees. The gun fell from his hand, and Aiden kicked it toward Detective Morse as he attempted to haul Ronald to his feet. Ronald's face had gone white.

"His heart medicine is in his pocket," Harriet said.

Aiden fished in Ronald's pockets until he found the pills. He opened the tube with one hand and tipped one out. He pushed it between Ronald's lips, but Ronald promptly spat it out. Aiden pulled out another one then pinched Ronald's nose closed before pushing the second one between his lips.

Ronald gasped, and the pill disappeared.

"You're not taking the easy way out," Aiden said and pulled him to his feet.

Detective Morse took a pair of handcuffs from her belt and secured them around Ronald's wrists.

Harriet and Lauren backtracked through Brandy's sleeping space then down the trail into the woods, making several turns based on where they now knew the rest were.

"That was a risky move," Morse said after she had finished reciting the Miranda warning to Ronald. "You're very lucky it worked out."

"I think *you're* the lucky one," Aiden told her.

Harriet felt the weight on her heart lift a little.

"This guy could have shot us all."

"And would have," Ronald said, puffing his chest out.

"Did I mention…" Morse asked, looking at Ronald, "…you have the right to remain silent? I suggest you exercise that right."

"You want me to move the log?" Aiden asked.

Morse sighed a world-weary sigh.

"Given the resources I have at the moment, there's little chance I can secure this crime scene, so yes, go ahead and move the log and see what's behind it."

"I can help," Brandy offered.

"I think you've helped enough for one night," Detective Morse said.

"I need a drink," Brandy mumbled.

Aiden swung the log toward the clearing and pulled out several large dried fir boughs; his torso disappeared into the hillside. He backed out a moment later, a bulky leather messenger bag in his hands.

"Jackpot," he said and handed the bag to Morse.

Jane Morse opened the bag's flap. The bag was stuffed with stacks of bills. Harriet couldn't see what the denomination was, but there was a lot of money in the bag, in any case.

"Harriet, could you drop us at the jail, please?" Detective Morse asked. "I want Darcy to process my vehicle as part of the crime scene."

"Sure, but what about Brandy?"

"She's home, isn't she?"

"Oooh, that's cold," Lauren said.

"How about I take you and this guy," Aiden said, "and Harriet can take Brandy and Lauren back to wherever they were before this all started."

"That works," Morse said.

Harriet and Lauren told their story to the group gathered in Harriet's dining room at least four times before Aunt Beth finally said, "Enough."

"I think it's time to have that pie now," Mavis said.

"I'll get the dishes," Harriet said.

"You'll do no such thing, chiquita." Jorge followed Mavis into the kitchen.

"Here, take this little rat," Tom said and plopped the freshly walked Carter into Lauren's lap. "He whined the whole time you were gone."

"That's a fact," Connie said.

"Well, I'm back, and as soon as we have our pie, we're going back to our house. We've had enough excitement for one day."

Mavis and Jorge served cherry pie to everyone then helped themselves to pieces. Then, one by one, the dinner guests left, with Tom giving Brandy and Joyce a ride back to the homeless camp before heading back to the Renfros'.

Chapter 24

 wo days later, Robin called with the news everyone had been waiting for. The highway out of Foggy Point was open again—only one lane, and there were frequent delays to allow the dump trucks that were hauling the tons of soil and rock to get through, but open.

With weekends and power outages, Marjory's seventy-two-hour hold had turned into one hundred and twenty-eight hours, not including the two extra days she spent in a motel because of the slide, but at long last she was coming home. Aunt Beth called the Loose Threads to convey the message she had secured Marjory's permission to bring the fabric down from the attic. All the Threads who were in town agreed to meet at nine o'clock to start working.

"It'll take Robin two hours to get there, and then two hours back plus a little if they stop for coffee," Aunt Beth said as she and Harriet got out of her silver Beetle. "We should be able to get a real good start before she gets back."

"Hey," Carla said when they came through the shop door. Wendy was perched on her hip.

"Rod will be here in a few minutes," Connie said. Rod was the official grandfather to every small child he knew, and Wendy was not immune to his charm. "He plans on wheeling her around to look at storm damage downtown. You did bring the stroller, didn't you?"

"Oh, yes," Carla said. "Wendy's looking forward to it."

"Did you ever have a chance to check on Sarah?" Harriet asked Connie.

"We went to the house where she's staying, but she only cracked the door open. I couldn't see her very well, and she insisted she was fine, but she didn't sound fine."

"I wonder what that means."

"I'm not sure what else to do. I asked her if she needed any- thing, but she said no." Connie was clearly worried.

Harriet couldn't think of anything short of an all-out interven- tion, and she wasn't ready to suggest that option.

The rest of the group arrived and divided up the tasks involved in reversing the process they'd done a few short days before.

"Harriet and I will take the stairs," Lauren said.

"I can do the cart again," Carla said.

Aunt Beth, Mavis and Connie set the fabric back on the shelves, neatly tucking the raw edges under before sliding the bolts side-by- side into the metal uprights that kept them from tipping over.

"Have you talked to Aiden since the Ronald takedown?" Lauren asked Harriet.

"No, but then, I didn't expect to."

"Really?"

"Okay, so maybe I thought he'd call, but he didn't."

"Carla!" Lauren yelled down the stairs when she saw the cart through the opening in the attic floor. "Have you heard any more conversations between Aiden and his sister?"

"She took off the other night. She was gone when I got back from the power's-on party."

"Wow," Harriet said. "Did you hear anything before that?"

"They had a fight, but all I heard was Aiden saying he didn't know who to trust anymore. She started using language that wasn't appropriate for Wendy's little ears, so I had to turn the intercom down, and by the time I got Wendy doing something in the other room and came back, their fight was over, or they had moved out of range."

"He'll settle down once he's had a few days without her," Aunt Beth said from down below. She'd come up beside Carla. "If I know that boy, he'll do his own research. He'll find out the truth. He's an emotional one at first—that's what makes him such a good veterinarian—but he's also very analytical. He won't do anything without checking his facts, and then Michelle will be out on her ear."

"I hope so," Harriet said.

"Why don't you gals come on down for a break? Mavis went down the street to pick up doughnuts." She looked at her watch. "Marjory should be getting here pretty soon, anyway."

"How's it looking down there?" Lauren asked.

"Come see for yourself. There's still work to be done, but it's taking shape."

The Threads assembled in the larger classroom, each with their favorite hot beverage in front of them.

"Can anyone join this party?" Jane Morse said as she came into the room. "I ran into Mavis at the bakery, and she invited me to stop by for doughnuts. The shop's looking better."

"Marjory's lucky the water stayed in the basement," Connie said.

"She's lucky to have a group of friends like you."

Mavis came in with the doughnuts, which cut off all thought of conversation while everyone made their selections and took their first sugary bites.

Finally, Morse sat back in her chair.

"I hate to admit this, but given our extreme conditions and our unusual situation, I couldn't have taken Ronald into custody without your help. Thank you."

"That was all Harriet and Lauren," Connie said.

"I know, but as usual, you all played a role along the way."

"Cut to the chase," Lauren prompted. "We've got more fabric to put away."

Morse smiled. "I was going to give you a lecture on how you shouldn't involve yourselves in police business, but I suppose it won't do any good, and in any case, as I said, you did play a role, so I suppose you deserve to know what happened."

"Ronald is the campground killer, right," Lauren said.

"It does appear that way. Of course, he needs to be tried by a jury of his peers," Morse reminded her.

"The question is why," Mavis said.

"You know part of it," Morse continued. "Pat Reigert told you her husband Richard was in trouble, headed for jail."

"She said something about trying to buy back time," Harriet said.

"He was one of three men involved in a Ponzi scheme. Ronald was one partner, and Duane was the third."

"Duane?" Aunt Beth sounded shocked. "He seemed like such a nice man."

"In the end, he was the only one with a shred of conscience. He wanted out, and the other two said no. They, of course, were living on the money people were investing in good faith, all the while mailing their victims monthly statements showing amazing gains."

"Don't those investors ever stop and wonder why their fund is doing so much better than everyone else's?" Harriet asked.

"There are two kinds of people who fall for Ponzi schemes—the very greedy and the very naive." Morse said.

"So, how did Duane end up in a homeless camp?" Harriet asked.

"All evidence points to the fact that Duane wanted out and he was trying to give back as much money as he could. That list on his phone was the people he was sending money to. It's going to take months to sort out all the details, but we think he tricked the tricksters."

"He was stealing their money?" Harriet clarified.

"That's what it looks like. We think he slowly bled Richard and Ronald's accounts down during his set-up phase, creating false bank statements for them—they all had accounts that appeared to be growing as a result of their investment skills. When things got to the point where checks were going to start bouncing, he cleaned out their accounts and got out of Dodge."

"That's bold." Mavis said.

"Moving to a homeless camp was an inspired move," Morse said. "He was there for months before Ronald caught up to him.

218

Ronald and Richard had hired a private eye and eventually found him.

"We think Ronald had set up an offshore rainy-day fund Duane couldn't access. Ronald summoned Richard with tales of Duane having money they could take back. It appears Ronald's plan was to get rid of his two partners and leave the country. He got stuck here, and then he realized it was possible Duane might still have some of the money, so he tried to get the information out of Brandy. You know the rest."

"Wow," Carla said.

"What was that story about buying back time?" Harriet asked.

"In this sort of prosecution, there's a relationship between how much money is recovered and length of sentence. So, that was true. If they had given all the money back, they would have had minimum prison sentences. That never happens, but depending on how greedy the players, they sometimes have enough money stashed around to soften the blow on their investors, and the government likes to give them some incentive to hand it over."

"So, what about Richard and Pat trying to get Marjory's inheritance?" Aunt Beth asked.

"Richard was sort of a junior partner in the scam. He was the salesman, if you will. His job was to talk up his gains to people and direct them to Roland and Duane. He wasn't in on exactly how corrupt the business was. He knew it was too good to be true, but Ronald assured him the money would keep coming in if he kept his mouth shut.

"He only got as much money as they told all their customers *they* were getting. Ronald and Duane were getting much more. In the eyes of the feds, however, it didn't matter if he was a junior partner or not—he was liable for the whole amount. He needed to get his hands on all the money he could."

"There you have it," Mavis said. "Crime doesn't pay."

"That's for darn sure," Marjory said as she joined the group. "And I didn't even commit a crime. I just said I was going to kill my sister, but apparently, that's not allowed in this state."

Aunt Beth and then Mavis hugged her, and the rest of the group stood up and crowded around her. Harriet went to refill her mug

219

and noticed a familiar silhouette in the window. She went into the store and saw Aiden peering in, a small dog in one hand, a thin leash in the other.

"Scooter's going for his first walk outside, and I thought you'd want to be there for it," he said. A stray lock of hair fell over his forehead, and without thinking, Harriet reached up and swept it back so she could look into his ice-blue eyes.

"You better go get your camera," he said. "You're going to want pictures of this for his baby book."

Harriet pulled her cell phone with its on-board camera from her pocket and clicked off a quick picture of Aiden's tentative smile.

"Don't tug too hard," he instructed as he set the little dog down on the sidewalk and handed Harriet the cord that connected to his little collar. "He's not used to being tied down."

"No, he isn't," she said and took the leash. "He definitely is not."

End

ABOUT THE AUTHOR

ARLENE SACHITANO started life as a military brat. Her dad retired and moved the family to the Pacific Northwest where she still lives. She started knitting, writing and sewing at a young age and still does all three. A thirty year diversion into the high tech industry, along with marriage and children, prevented her from taking action on her desire to write novels inspired by her love of Agatha Christie until recently.

Arlene spends her days writing her novels, babysitting her grandchildren, quilting, knitting and promoting her books. She is active in the Harriet Vane Chapter of Sisters in Crime in Portland, Oregon.

ABOUT THE ARTIST

APRIL MARTINEZ was born in the Philippines and raised in San Diego, California, daughter to a US Navy chef and a US postal worker, sibling to one younger sister. For years, she went from job to job, dissatisfied that she couldn't make use of her creative tendencies, until she started working as an imaging specialist for a big book and magazine publishing house in Irvine and began learning the trade of graphic design. From that point on, she worked as a graphic designer and webmaster at subsequent day jobs while doing freelance art and illustration at night. April lives with her cat in Orange County, California, as a full-time freelance artist/illustrator and graphic designer.

CPSIA information can be obtained at www.ICGtesting.com
Printed in the USA
BVOW030606260213

314166BV00002B/8/P